A ROSE *for the*
ANZAC BOYS

Praise for *A Rose for the Anzac Boys*

'. . . rousing stuff, and it hasn't been watered down.
French doesn't shy away from the nightmarish
conditions of trench warfare. Highly readable,
scrupulous in its history . . . an ideal text for schools.'
Sydney Morning Herald

'A book of many voices. Poignant, graphic and
compulsive fiction about women who
volunteered during WWI.'
Sunday Age

'An important story. The use of a sixteen year old
protagonist will make the story more real and more
confronting for teen readers.'
Aussie Reviews

'A well-researched story about the invaluable
support women provided during the war.
Recommended for secondary school-aged children.'
Australian Bookseller and Publisher

A ROSE *for the* ANZAC BOYS

Jackie French

Angus&Robertson
An imprint of HarperCollins*Publishers*

Angus&Robertson
an imprint of HarperCollins*Publishers*, Australia

First published in Australia in 2008
by HarperCollins*Publishers* Australia Pty Limited
ABN 36 009 913 517
www.harpercollins.com.au

HarperCollins*Publishers*
25 Ryde Road, Pymble, Sydney NSW 2073, Australia
31 View Road, Glenfield, Auckland 10, New Zealand
1–A, Hamilton House, Connaught Place, New Delhi – 110 001, India
77–85 Fulham Palace Road, London W6 8JB, United Kingdom
2 Bloor Street East, 20th floor, Toronto, Ontario M4W 1A8, Canada
10 East 53rd Street, New York, NY 10022, USA

National Library of Australia Cataloguing-in-Publication data:

French, Jackie.
  A rose for the Anzac boys.
  For secondary school age.
  ISBN 978 0 7322 8540 1 (pbk.).
  1. World War, 1914–1918 – Fiction. I. Title.
A823.3

Cover design by Natalie Winter
Cover images: girl and line of soldiers courtesy of Getty Images
(# ca20950/#53373806); rose decoration courtesy of Shutterstock
Typeset in 11/16pt Sabon by Helen Beard, ECJ Australia Pty Limited
Printed and bound in Australia by Griffin Press
60gsm Bulky Paperback used by HarperCollins*Publishers* is a natural, recyclable product
made from wood grown in a combination of sustainable plantation and regrowth
forests. The manufacturing processes conform to the environmental regulations in
Tasmania, the place of manufacture.

8 7 6   09 10 11

To Private John 'Jack' Sullivan, who faced and
survived it all; to (Colonel) Dr A.T. Edwards, who
did his best to help; to 'the boys' of today, and their
girls too; and most of all to those indomitable
women, the 'forgotten army' of World War I,
with love, respect and admiration.

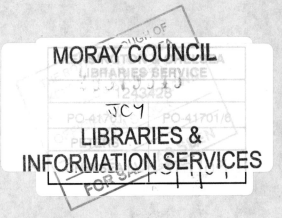

The Route of the first Anzac Troops to WWI

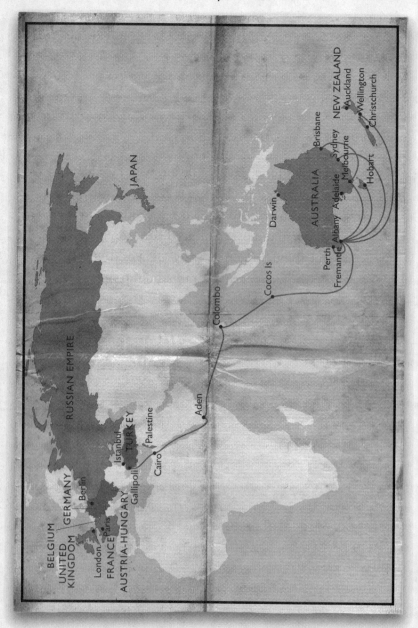

Western Front, France, 1916

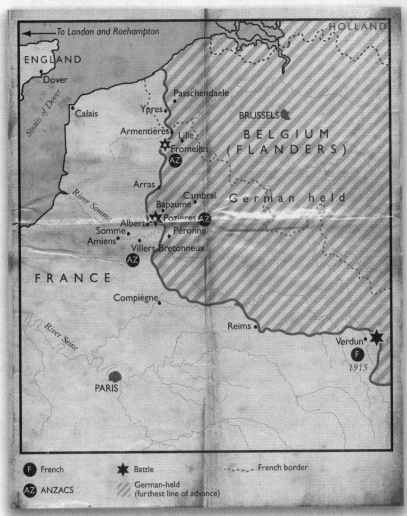

To London and Roehampton

ENGLAND
Dover
Calais
Straits of Dover

HOLLAND

Passchendaele
Ypres
Armentières
Lille
Fromelles
AZ

BRUSSELS

BELGIUM
(FLANDERS)

German held

Arras

River Somme

Cambrai
Bapaume
Albert Pozières AZ
Somme Péronne
Amiens
Villers-Bretonneux
AZ

FRANCE

Compiègne

Reims
Verdun
F
1915

River Seine

PARIS

F French
AZ ANZACS

Battle
German-held
(furthest line of advance)

French border

The Middle East during WWI

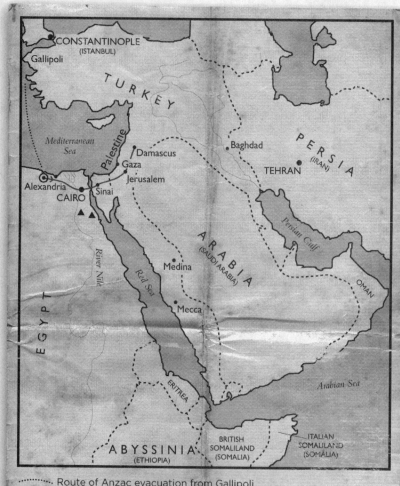

Map showing the Middle East during WWI, including:

CONSTANTINOPLE (ISTANBUL)
Gallipoli
TURKEY
Mediterranean Sea
Palestine
Damascus
Gaza
Jerusalem
Baghdad
PERSIA (IRAN)
TEHRAN
Alexandria
CAIRO
Sinai
EGYPT
River Nile
Red Sea
Medina
ARABIA (SAUDI ARABIA)
Mecca
Persian Gulf
OMAN
Arabian Sea
ERITREA
ABYSSINIA (ETHIOPIA)
BRITISH SOMALILAND (SOMALIA)
ITALIAN SOMALILAND (SOMALIA)

.... Route of Anzac evacuation from Gallipoli.

⊙ Anzacs landed in Alexandria after the Gallipoli evacuation of December 1915.

▲▲ Anzac camp at Giza.

〜 Route of Anzac trek to Palestine.

Gallipoli, 1915

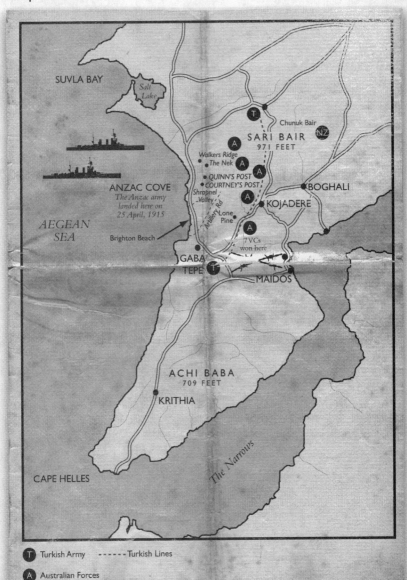

SUVLA BAY

Salt Lake

ANZAC COVE
*The Anzac army
landed here on
25 April, 1915*

Brighton Beach

*AEGEAN
SEA*

Walkers Ridge
The Nek
QUINN'S POST
COURTNEY'S POST
Shrapnel
Valley

T

A

SARI BAIR
971 FEET

Chunuk Bair

NZ

A

A

BOGHALI

A

KOJADERE

Artillery Rd

Lone
Pine

A

7 VCs
won here

GABA
TEPE

T

MAIDOS

ACHI BABA
709 FEET

KRITHIA

The Narrows

CAPE HELLES

T Turkish Army   - - - - - Turkish Lines

A Australian Forces

NZ New Zealanders

Lachlan

BISCUIT CREEK, ANZAC DAY, 1975

At 10 a.m. the street was empty.

The shops showed blank faces to the footpath. Even the Royal Café was shut, though the scent of yesterday's hamburgers lingered. A kelpie lifted its leg against the butcher's, then wandered up into the park. It was so quiet you could hear baaing in the distance. Someone must be rounding up sheep on the hill, thought Lachie, as Pa's ute drew up outside R & G Motors. Dad had been crutching too yesterday. It had been a wet summer. The fly strike was bad.

Lachie slid across the ute's cracked leather seat and walked round to help Pa out from the driver's side. You had to tug the driver's door open, too, and Pa couldn't manage it alone. Pa refused to buy a new ute. He wouldn't even drive Dad's. 'This one will last me out,' he'd said, when Dad tried to argue with him. 'We've grown old together.'

Last year Pa had marched in the Anzac Day parade by himself. That was before he'd fallen down the steps at the doctor's and broken his hip. Pa could hobble again now. But not up the hill to the war memorial. This year Pa had insisted Lachie push him in a wheelchair. 'He's the youngest,' was all Pa had said. 'It's important he remembers.' As though that explained anything.

It was going to be embarrassing walking up the street in front of everybody, pushing his great-grandfather in a wheelchair. Why couldn't Grandad do the pushing? Grandad had even been in a war, though he never actually fought because they'd had to take his appendix out, and by the time he was better the war was over. He never marched on Anzac Day.

What if Lachie ran out of puff halfway up the hill? If he had to stop and get his breath back with everybody staring?

Pa looked at his watch. 'Should be getting here now.' Pa's voice was always too loud. It came of being deaf, Dad said.

Lachie handed Pa his walking stick and then lifted the rose out of its jam jar of water. It wasn't much of a rose. It was pink, with a smudge of white, and its stem was short and floppy, not like the roses from the florist that stood tall and straight. Pa had picked the rose from the tangle that grew along the fence outside the kitchen, and Lachie had held the jar all the way into town, trying not to let the water spill.

Now he handed Pa the rose. 'The paper said everyone was to meet at ten-thirty.'

Pa ignored the comment. He never argued. He just ignored what people said till they did what he wanted. He peered down the street, the rose drooping in his hand, just as Mum and Dad drove up with the wheelchair they'd borrowed from the hospital.

Lachie ran to help them get it out of the back of the car, mostly so he didn't have to stay and talk to Pa. He loved Pa, but talking to him was hard now. Pa could only hear these days if you yelled and moved your mouth clearly. Both were embarrassing in public.

Dad pushed the wheelchair up to the ute. Some people looked helpless in wheelchairs, but Pa looked like he was royalty, about to be carried off by his slaves.

That's me, thought Lachie.

'Are you sure about this, Pa? It's a long way for a kid to push,' Dad said, moving his lips so Pa could lip-read. 'Bluey would be glad to help out.'

Bluey Monroe was the butcher. He'd served at Tobruk, which was in World War II, the war that Grandad had almost been in, which was different from World War I, where Pa had fought, though the Germans had been the bad guys in both of them.

It was hard to keep the wars straight sometimes, especially with all the other wars since.

Pa ignored Dad, turning away. Pa used his deafness like a weapon. As far as he was concerned, it was settled.

3

Pa never spoke much at any time. Dad said that came of being deaf too. The war — the *First* World War — had taken Pa's hearing, though Lachie wasn't quite sure how. When Pa did speak, he either said no more than was necessary or else he spoke lots, like he'd been saving it up in the cupboard of his mind.

Another car drew up, and another. People appeared in the street now, strolling round corners or heading in from out of town, all making for the war memorial by the park, the men in suits and the women in their not quite Sunday best. The wind whispered up the street, an early breath of winter. Lachie shivered. He wished he'd brought a jumper.

Other ex-soldiers began to gather outside R & G. Three men in uniform, with medals on their chests. A couple of old friends of Pa's, in suits but with medals pinned to them. A woman in a naval uniform.

Jim Harman slid out of his ute. It was a new blue one with a shiny bull bar. Jim had been in the Vietnam War, which wasn't long ago, but he didn't wear his uniform. Other men from Biscuit Creek had gone to Vietnam, but Jim was the only one here today. Jim hadn't marched before. Pa lifted a hand to him. 'Glad you made it, son,' he said.

There was something in Pa's voice that puzzled Lachie. 'Glad you made it' — was he just welcoming Jim to the march, or did he mean something more?

The men lined up. There were fifty-six marchers now. Lachie had counted them. Pa was in the front row, which was extra embarrassing because what if Lachie couldn't keep up with the others as he pushed the wheelchair? It was all uphill to the memorial. He wished he'd rehearsed it with Pa, tried pushing him uphill last week. But he hadn't thought of it till now.

Pa held the rose in his hand. It looked even floppier than it had at home.

Mr Hogan from the school began to beat the drum.

Boom. Boom. Boom.

The men began to march, and Lachie pushed.

It wasn't as bad as he'd thought it would be, at least not at first. Up the main street with dozens of onlookers staring, the men with their hats off, the kids with their bicycles all standing still for these few minutes of respect. Even the dogs stared at the marchers curiously.

Lachie's arms began to ache.

Boom, boom, boom.

The men's shoes clumped on the bitumen. Even with the drum and the beat of feet, Lachie had never heard the town so quiet. No one was talking. No one at all.

Boom. Boom. Boom.

Past the post office, the stock and station agency. He was going to make it! It felt good too, with everybody watching. He glanced at the men on either side. Mr Heffernan's face was expressionless. But Lachie was shocked to see tears in Mr Byrne's eyes. Mr Byrne had lost three brothers in the war after Pa's, he remembered. It was funny to think of people missing their brothers even when they were old.

Pa wasn't crying, was he? Lachie looked down at him in his chair.

Pa's face, what he could see of it, was . . . strange. He wasn't looking at the people in the street. He wasn't even looking at the others beside him in the parade. It was as though he was watching something far away.

Battles, thought Lachie. He'd seen battles on TV. Was that what Pa was watching? His friends blown to bits, maybe? Did they have guns back in World War I when Pa was young? Or was it swords and bayonet things? Nah, there must have been guns. Pa had a hole in his back from stuff he called shrapnel. He let Lachie put his finger in the scar sometimes.

And then Pa smiled. Lachie saw his cheeks move and bent his head around to see more. It was a soft smile. A smile of love and happiness.

No, thought Lachie, wherever Pa had been it wasn't in a battle. It was some place good.

They were at the war memorial statue now, the bronze soldier in his uniform with his rifle by his side, and the names of the men who had served and those who had died underneath. Miss Long at school said that the soldier's uniform was Italian rather than Australian, which was why the Biscuit Creek Committee, who had raised the money, had got the statue cheap. But the soldier looked good at the top of the street, as though guarding the preschool and the dogs sniffing the trees in the park next door.

The procession stopped. The speeches began. Lachie didn't listen. He was good at not listening. Sometimes he could go through the entire school assembly not hearing a word.

Pa wasn't listening either, Lachie realised. Of course Pa couldn't listen, being mostly deaf, but Lachie had a feeling that it made no difference. Pa was staring across the town.

'I used to dream about those hills,' he said suddenly to Lachie in his normal voice, which was half gruff and half yell.

People stared. Lachie felt the blush prickle down his body. But no one looked cross. They just looked . . . tolerant. Even pleased. As though Pa was like the copy of Ned Kelly's armour down at the museum, thought Lachie suddenly. Pa was their war memorial, even more than the Italian soldier.

Suddenly the speeches were over. The wreaths were laid, six of them, all rosemary and bay leaves and florist's flowers. Pa stood as the Last Post began to play, although Lachie didn't see how he could have known. Pa saluted.

The crowd began to move over to the rotunda for more speeches by the mayor and the president of the local RSL. Later the servicemen would head over to lunch at the Rissole, which was what Dad and Uncle Ben called the RSL club by the golf course. Their wives would have tea and scones or the roast chicken special at the Royal Café, while the kids headed for the park.

Lachie waited. He knew what came next, though he'd never been so close before.

Pa was still standing. Now he took a step — shaky, but upright — over to the memorial. He bent down. When he stood again, the single rose lay among the wreaths. It looked small and faded against the yellows, reds and greens.

Pa saluted again. For a moment he didn't look like an old man. His movements were as crisp as lettuce.

'A rose for the Anzac boys,' said Pa, a bit too loudly. 'Rest in peace, my Rose.'

And then it was over. Pa shuffled back and sat in his wheelchair, his trousers baggy on his skinny legs. Lachie took hold of the chair's handles and pushed it over to the footpath where Dad was waiting to take Pa down to the Rissole.

He glanced back. The rose was still there, now strangely bright among the plastic-looking florist's wreaths.

The rose for the Anzac boys.

Chapter 1

Miss Hollington's School
for Young Ladies
Surrey
England
5 June 1915

Dear Miss Davies,

Thank you for the talcum powder and the handkachiefs. (I still can't spell that!) It was good to get a birthday present from home, even though you're not at Glen Donal any more. It's hard to imagine you being a governess somewhere else. I hope the Mackenzie children are nice, but that you don't think they're quite as nice as me and Tim!

Aunt Harriet and Uncle Thomas sent me a silver-backed hairbrush and mirror set. It was lovely but not the same as getting

9

a present from someone you really know. I hoped I'd hear from Tim or Doug, but I don't suppose Doug can just leave the war and gallop down to a post office in Flanders, or that Tim has time to write letters at that Gallipalli place (can't spell that either) that's in the papers so much. Aunt Lallie sent me a wonderful Egyptian bracelet, but I opened that weeks ago so it doesn't count either.

I'm liking school a bit better, though I still miss Glen Donal DREADFULLY. I still don't see why Dougie had to dump me here when he decided to enlist in England. I could perfectly well have stayed at home with you and Mrs Campbell. After all, I was almost sixteen, not five years old!

It's not as though I'm learning anything useful here, just 'how to be a lady', which means walking with my tummy held in and learning embroidery. (I am never going to embroider another tea cloth in my life once I leave here!) Oh, and French irregular verbs, which are a fat lot of use as I can't even holiday in France now, with the war, and I'll never need them when I come home. Maybe I can say 'Parley Vous Francais' to the sheep and see what they say. Probably 'Baa' which is what I'd like to say to Mademoiselle some days.

Sometimes I wake up hoping that when I open my eyes I'll see the river and the willows out the window. I even try listening for the sheep and maybe a kea's cry. Then Miss Jenkins plods into the dormitory bleating 'Girls! Girls! Rally! Rally!', which she does to wake us up every single morning. Miss Jenkins sounds a bit like a sheep and her hair is woolly too. But I don't think you'd get much of a price for a bale of teacher hair.

At least I have a couple of good friends now. Anne is the daughter of an earl, which makes her an Honourable and impresses all the teachers frightfully, though they try not to show it. Her mother is called Lady George, which makes me giggle every time I say it even though it's the right thing to call an earl's wife. If his name is George, anyhow.

Ethel's mother is dead like mine, and her father is a wholesale grocer and has pots of money. Of course it's dreadfully rude to talk about how much money someone has, but somehow everyone at school knows Ethel's dad has more money than — who was that ancient rich chap? Crokus? Him, anyway. Ethel's family live in Yorkshire, which means Ethel has a broader accent than I do. But Anne says my New Zealand accent isn't too bad, and that Ethel just clings to hers because she's too stubborn to give it up.

Ethel's dad sent her here to make her ladylike. But Ethel isn't interested in being ladylike. Or in French verbs or anything much. But she's a good friend. She and Anne were wonderful to me when I first got here and was so lonely.

There isn't much news from Dougie, except what I read in the papers. He wrote to me last month but didn't say much. I think he has forgiven Tim for enlisting under another name. It just wasn't fair to expect Tim to wait another four years till he was 'old enough' to enlist when Dougie and I were gone. I am so glad Dougie didn't report Tim to the authorities. Of course Tim wants to do his bit for England, just like Doug!

Tim writes whenever he can, but maybe that's because twins are closer than just brother and sister. He and I have great plans for after the war when we are both home again, so there is a lot to discuss.

I am so very proud of having two brothers in uniform, and a cousin too, as well as an aunt who is a nurse. One of the girls in my class has three brothers in the army, but there are only six of us who have two. It's hard to be a girl sometimes, stuck at school when there is such a great cause to fight for. We do first aid training here every Saturday and Wednesday, and bandage-rolling Tuesdays, and making baby clothes for refugees on Friday afternoons. But it isn't like DOING something; it isn't glory or adventure.

I'm sorry this has been such a long letter. Writing to you makes it almost seem like I'm home. If you get a chance and if it isn't too much trouble, would you mind putting flowers on Mummy's and Daddy's graves? Daddy always put flowers on Mummy's grave for her birthday (it's 19 July). It would be horrible to think that no one did this year, just because I'm at school in England and Tim and Doug are away at the war.

Your loving ex-pupil,
Midge Macpherson

~❦~

ENGLAND, 14 JUNE 1915

It began with letters.

Letters were delivered twice a day to Miss Hollington's School for Young Ladies, but girls could only collect their mail after classes were over, from the table in the big hall that smelled of furniture polish. Pupils at Miss Hollington's weren't allowed to run, except on the lacrosse field, so Midge forced her feet to walk sedately across the courtyard's too neat grass, her skirts swishing around her ankles.

Would there be a letter today?

Not that Tim's letters said a lot since he'd joined up. The censor blacked out his words if he wrote much more than 'Hello there, Sis old girl, don't worry I'm well'. But he'd managed to tell her about a sandstorm before they left Egypt, the sand so deep it covered the barbed wire; and about marching through the desert, all of them so thirsty that men licked the dry taps, desperate for a stray drop of water.

Please let there be a letter, Midge prayed. Tim was her only link to the future now — that blessed time when they would both be twenty-one. Tim would inherit half of Glen Donal and Midge would inherit the money her parents had thought more suitable for a girl than land. When that day came, when the war was over, when they finally sailed home, Tim would farm their land between the mountains and they'd use her money to build a house there, on the far bank of the river at Glen Donal.

Glen Donal. Home. It was an ache and absence in the heart. The scent of rough grass and the sharp tinny smell of snow from the mountains, the dangling arms of the willow trees, the neat lines of Mummy's rose garden, the flowers more flamboyant than any Midge had seen in England. Even grass smelled different here, not as strong and sweet as home. At least school was in the country, away from the yellow smoke that buried the sky at Aunt Harriet's. But everything was so small, she thought, as she hurried up the hall steps. The land divided into its tiny fields and smaller lanes. Even the people looked like they'd shrunk in the rain. A land of sparrows when she wanted to soar.

Her shoes tapped on the polished wood floor. She glanced at the table. Yes! There were two letters under 'M'. One on cheap thin paper from Tim; plus a blue envelope with a water stain on one corner and precise nursing sister's writing on the front. A letter from Aunt Lallie — the second-best letter she could get.

Letters were too precious to read here, where anyone could interrupt. But there was a willow down by the pond, almost like the ones back home, with a curtain of green branches.

Midge ran out the door (school rules could go hang), holding her skirt high and trying to look as unavailable for rounders or lacrosse games as she could. She ducked her head under the willow's branches and settled on the damp leaves that covered the ground.

She'd open Aunt Lallie's letter first and keep Tim's to savour last. Even having his letter in her lap made him seem close.

She tore open Aunt Lallie's envelope. Her aunt's last letter had been from Alexandria where she had ridden a camel with an upper lip just like Uncle Thomas's. It had spat at Aunt Lallie's friend Sister Atkins.

Midge's eyes skimmed the letter. Then she stopped in shock. This wasn't like any letter her aunt had sent before.

My dear niece,

I hope this finds you as it leaves me, for I am well, though tired. Tired perhaps is not the right word. I think by now we have gone past tiredness, into another world.

I do not know if you received my last letter from Alexandria. Since then I have been on the [here the word was blacked out by the censor], *a transport ship from* [another crossing out, but not enough, so that by lifting the letter to the light Midge could still see the impression of the word *Gallipoli*]. *Initially it had been intended that the transport ships take the wounded to* [crossed out] *where I was posted, little more than an hour's sail away. But there have been so many casualties that the ships were forced to sail two more days to the hospitals at Alexandria, which is how I have come to be transferred here. Now even our hospitals are full and the ships full of wounded boys have to sail on to Malta instead.*

My dear, I cannot describe [here the words were crossed out by Lallie's hand].

They call ships like ours the 'black ships' and, my dear, they deserve the name. We kept the men with gangrenous or suppurating wounds on deck, in the fresh air. The fever and dysentery cases were carried below, into a hold that had not been cleaned since the horses they had carried earlier were unloaded. The heat was worse than anything I have ever known; the air so thick you felt it needed a soldier's strength to fight through it, but a stronger soldier than our poor boys.

My dear, I am so glad that you are too young to be a nurse in this war, as you told me in your last letter you would like to be if you were old enough. Those ships were not nursing as any of us have known it or imagined. No pillows, no blankets, one bedpan to forty men, dehydration, the living next to the dead, the flies, the smell — it is a memory only death, I think, can erase.

Conditions here at the hospital are little better. I am on one of the dysentery wards. Sister Atkins and myself are in charge of 230 men. We can give them little; we try to keep them clean and give them emetine by hypodermic injection. But it is not enough. Nothing is enough. They waste away so that strong young men look like they are eighty, their faces shrunk to wrinkles, their hands too weak even to hold a cup to drink.

I cannot remember the last time that I slept — there is never a moment when it does not seem cruel to take a nap, knowing the agony that you must leave untended.

I have just written another letter. It was for an Australian soldier, as are many here. He asked me to write a letter to his mother. He said, 'Tell her I am too weak to write.' And then he died. I sat there, looking at the blank space on the paper, not knowing if it was crueller to send it or to crumple it away. In the end I sent it to his commanding officer, who will do as he thinks best with it.

It fills me so with rage to think [a half-page blacked out here, and even by following the indentations of the pen with her fingers Midge couldn't make out the words. And then, almost as though it were another letter:] I hope your studies are going well, my dear, and that your holiday with your aunt and uncle was satisfactory. I wish more than I could tell you that I could have offered you a home myself when your dear father died. But one day this madness

will be over. One day you and Tim and Dougie will be home.
Perhaps I will join you there, in the quiet fields of Glen Donal.
   I remain as always, my dear Margery, your most loving aunt,
                                          Eulalie Jean Macpherson

Midge put the letter into the pocket of her tunic and stared out through the branches. What had Aunt Lallie been through to write like that? How could things be so bad? The war Lallie described was no glorious adventure. It sounded so different from the victories and heroism in *The Times*.

Why hadn't Tim or Doug or one of Anne's cousins said how bad things were?

Maybe, she thought hopefully, it's not as bad where they're fighting. Maybe it's just that the hospitals can't cope . . .

She felt almost reluctant to open Tim's letter now, afraid of what she might read. Aunt Lallie was — well, old. Experienced. Suddenly she couldn't stand the thought of Tim in pain, like the young soldiers in Lallie's letter.

Tim's letter was written in pencil. The writing was tiny and scrawled across the page. Even with the summer air around her, she grew cold as she deciphered it.

                                                24 May, Gallipoli

Dear Sis,
   Well, here we are. You wouldn't believe how much it stinks, or how many flies could land on one person. Am writing this during a truce with the Turks. There have been thousands of Turkish bodies

17

in front of our trenches. Some have been there for three weeks. Which is why it stinks so much. I thought old sheep guts smelled bad. But dead men smell worse.

Felt something squelch under my boot this morning. I looked down and it was a man's head, all green and black. It moved suddenly and for a moment I thought it was alive. Then I saw it was just the maggots that were moving. Couldn't tell if he was ours or theirs. Remember old Campbell burying rabbit and sheep heads under Mum's rose garden, and the time you and I dug one up when we were three? Well, think of that.

Anyhow, it rained this morning, and thank God for it, as it broke the smell a bit. We went up onto the plateau and through these gullies all covered in thyme, and there were about 4000 Turkish bodies. The Turkish Red Crescent blokes were giving out wool drenched in disinfectant to hold over our noses. Johnny Turk's a good chap but I can't say the same for Fritz. The blighters accused us of digging trenches while we pretended to dig graves. Lieutenant-Colonel Fenwick — he's our medical officer, a good man — speaks a bit of their lingo. He told them in no uncertain terms that the corpses were so rotten we couldn't lift them and we had to dig pits right there to put the awful things into.

When we'd finished we shook hands with the Turks and said, 'Good luck'. One of them spoke English and said, 'Smiling may you go, and smiling come again.' I like that.

By the way, there's a good story going around the ranks. Seems the Turkish and British generals were in the British HQ tent discussing the details of the truce when this New Zealand batman puts his head in the tent and yells out, 'Hey! Have any of you muckers pinched my kettle?'

Don't blame him either. The one thing that makes life worthwhile here is a good cup of tea and bleak is the night when you can't get it. You just have to hope no maggots drip into it but, like old Campbell would say, a bit of muck is just a bit more tucker. Wonder if he'd say that about lice. We've got some big ones here. Tried washing my clothes in sea water the other day to get rid of them but it just made the blighters hungrier!

Don't know if you've got any of my other scrawls. I'm sending this to the first aid post with one of the boys so hopefully it will get away. Look after yourself, Sis, and don't worry about me. None of our lot have caught it yet. I've made some good mates here. I reckon we're too tough to die.

'Smiling may you go, and smiling come again.'

Your loving brother,
Tim

'Midge? Midge, are you there?'

The high, clear voice was unmistakable. Midge looked up as the pale and spotty face of the Honourable Anne peered through the curtain of branches.

Anne was always pale, apart from her spots. 'Mummy believes red cheeks are ill bred,' she'd said once, as though Lady George had sent the midwife a polite note requesting exactly the correct details in a daughter: the straight blonde hair (so much easier to put up than curls), the long pale hands. Only Anne's spots and her big feet failed to be aristocratic. 'My dear, the feet come from great-grandmama's gardener,' she said. Midge never knew if she was serious or not. Anne was more concerned about her spots than her feet.

Midge stared. Her . . . yellow . . . spots.

'Anne, what on earth —' she began.

Anne touched her face automatically. 'Miss Scatchley's latest idea,' she said. Miss Scatchley was the science mistress. She wore a white lab coat and had even studied science for two years at Oxford, though of course had not been allowed to sit the exams. 'Flowers of sulphur dusted on each lunchtime.'

'Does sulphur get rid of spots?'

Anne shrugged. 'One suspects I'm her latest scientific experiment. Item: one spotty aristocrat. Item: one pot of flowers of sulphur. Process: combine the two. Result:—'

'Did you find her?' Ethel's big square face appeared beside Anne's, tendrils of red hair escaping from her plaits. 'I *said* she'd be under the willow tree.'

'It must be a colonial thing,' said Anne. 'Trees and whatnot.'

'It's nothing to do with being a New Zealander,' Midge protested.

Anne grinned. 'Of course not. *Everybody* prefers a tree to a sitting room these days. Darling, the Hollow Beast wants to see you. Urgently. In her study. Now.'

The Hollow Beast was Miss Hollington.

'Cripes, lass, what has tha doon?' said Ethel in her best exaggerated Yorkshire accent. She held out a hand to help Midge up. Ethel's hand was large and square like her face.

'Nothing. At least I hope it's nothing.' Midge brushed the leaves from her tunic.

'You've got mud on your stocking,' said Ethel helpfully.

'Have I? Blow.' Midge rubbed at the patch of dirt.

Anne's grin grew wider. 'Pull the dirty bit round to the back. That way the Beast won't see it till you're going out.'

'Yes, and maybe you can walk out backwards, like she's the Queen and you can't show her your bum,' added Ethel.

A year ago, Midge had wondered what the daughter of an earl was doing making friends with the orphaned daughter of a New Zealand sheep farmer and the daughter of a Yorkshire wholesale grocer and Quaker. Anne's company was cultivated even by the sixth formers. 'All hoping,' said Anne once, with a small grimace, 'for invitations to one of Mummy's little parties. Just dripping with dukes and viscounts, you know, in case one of them decides to marry her youngest daughter.'

Which was, Midge realised, one answer to the question. She longed for Glen Donal, not an English fiancé. And as soon as she turned twenty-one and inherited her money, she'd be back there with Tim no matter what Uncle Thomas said. And Ethel . . . well, the daughter of a wholesale grocer, five feet ten inches tall and with shoulders like a rugby player and a face like a pony, would never be accepted into society, even if befriended by the daughter of an earl, no matter how much deportment Miss Hollington tried to drum into her, or how wealthy her father was.

Or maybe it was simply that Anne liked them.

'What were you doing under there anyway?' demanded Ethel.

Midge held up her letters. 'From Aunt Lallie and Tim.'

Anne nodded sympathetically.

The three walked slowly back towards the school.

'How are they?' Ethel kicked one of the stones on the drive with her shoe.

Midge bit her lip. 'I don't know,' she said. 'Tim's all right so far. He says none of his lot have been hurt yet.'

Anne stared. 'Are you sure? The casualty lists are enormous.'

'Well, that's what he wrote,' Midge said uncertainly. 'But that Gallipoli place sounds like a nightmare. And Aunt Lallie's letter was strange. She's never written anything like that before. She's in charge of a dysentery ward in Egypt. But it all sounds — I don't know. Chaotic. Like nothing's organised at all.'

Ethel screwed up her nose. 'Dysentery is where you get the trots, isn't it?'

Midge nodded. 'Really badly. And they don't stop. Oh, it sounded awful! Just two nurses for two hundred and thirty men. I should be out there too. Helping!'

'We're doing what we can,' said Anne gently. 'I'm sure the army will get things under control soon.'

'Will they? All we're doing is bandage-rolling! Making baby clothes for refugees! It's not enough!' Not when Tim was facing guns, she thought, and Dougie too, and Aunt Lallie with all those dying men.

Suddenly, it was all too much. When you were young, you were helpless, Midge thought. She'd been helpless when her mother had died, leaving her a tiny baby; helpless when diphtheria took her father, not even allowed to visit him in case she was infected; helpless when her older brother brought her across the world to an aunt and uncle she'd never met. And helpless when her twin brother followed everyone else to the war. Tim and Dougie were doing something. And she was just a problem to be shoved away at school.

She bit her lip, unwilling to say anything that might hurt her friends. Three of Anne's cousins were in France as well. And Ethel's brother had decided his future lay in wholesale groceries, not in uniform, which was an even touchier subject these days when everyone was expected to do their bit.

Anne looked at her curiously. 'Darling, be sensible. Even if they let you leave school, you couldn't be a nurse or even a VAD overseas till you're twenty-three.'

'Eight years away! The war will be over by Christmas,' Midge said.

Anne nodded. 'My uncle in the War Office says that the French and English could drive the Germans back now if they wished. They're just waiting for the New Armies to come out to make the victory a decided one. Midge, my sweet, you just have to accept it. Even the Duchess isn't taking on girls our age.'

The Duchess was Millicent, Dowager Duchess of Sutherland. As soon as war had been declared she'd sailed for France and established the Millicent Sutherland Ambulance. Other women, like Mrs St Clair Stobart, had followed, organising private cars, nurses, doctors, medical supplies, whatever they could gather to help the official medical services that were overwhelmed by the numbers of wounded and dying.

Midge turned to Anne eagerly. 'You know the Duchess? I can drive, you know. I could drive an ambulance. '

'Mummy knows her, of course. But, darling, she wants professionals. We haven't even passed our first aid certificates yet. Or at least women with . . . with experience.'

'Older, you mean,' said Midge bitterly.

'Well, yes.'

'There has to be something we can do!' She clenched her fists in frustration. It was illogical, she knew. But it seemed like the war *must* be over sooner if only she could *do* something.

'Comforts for soldiers,' suggested Ethel.

'Packages of toffee and writing pads! They don't even have enough food over there sometimes! Dougie said the last time they were sent anywhere, they were two days without any food at all. One lot of men went three weeks without rations!'

'Ah, lass, they be needing Carryman's Cocoa.' Ethel deliberately spoke in the broad accent that Miss Hollington was working so hard to get rid of.

'What good is your dad's cocoa when it's over here?' Midge said. 'They need it there!'

'Cocoa makes you spotty,' said Anne.

A bell chimed in the distance.

'Prep,' Anne said. 'Come on, Eth. The war is far away, darlings, but Miss Jenkins and her posture classes are all too near. And you, Midge, still need to see the Hollow Beast.'

24

Chapter 2

Miss Hollington's office looked like a parlour with a desk shoved in the middle. It had blue damask curtains, a pink and blue chintz sofa, and polished wood floors with a blue and red Turkish carpet.

Why do we demand that German butcher's shops close down yet still keep Turkish carpets, wondered Midge, as she shut the office door behind her.

Miss Hollington looked up from her desk. 'Ah, Margery. I'm afraid . . . well, I'm not sure . . .'

Midge stared. She had never seen Miss Hollington uncertain before.

'You have received a letter,' Miss Hollington said, starting again.

Midge nodded. 'I got two this afternoon.'

'I mean another one.' Miss Hollington picked up a plain buff envelope from her desk. It had 'OHMS' printed on it. She cleared her throat. 'As I am in the position of your temporary guardian here, I thought it my duty to open it.'

And you wanted to stickybeak, thought Midge.

'I have to say its contents surprised me. But perhaps you can explain.'

Miss Hollington pulled out what looked like a form and handed it across the desk.

'B104-83,' read Midge. 'It is my painful duty to inform you that a report has been received from the War Office to the effect that Private Timothy Smith was posted missing on 22 May . . .'

It was like the breath had been sucked out of her body. Tim dead? No! The words wriggled like worms in the sand. Missing. Missing, not dead. Of course he wasn't dead. Tim couldn't be dead. Death had taken Mum and Dad. It was impossible that Tim could go as well. She'd know if Tim was dead! Twins . . . felt things, didn't they? Not that she ever had before, but surely if Tim were . . . hurt . . . she'd know . . .

Dimly, Midge was aware that Miss Hollington was still talking.

'These letters are sent to the man's next of kin. But when your uncle enrolled you he did not mention any relative called Smith.'

'Timothy Smith is my brother.' Was that her voice? It sounded small and far away.

'Your brother?' Miss Hollington cleared her throat.

'According to your enrolment form, your brother's name is Douglas Macpherson.'

Midge shook her head to clear it. 'Tim's my twin brother. He was too young to enlist. So he enlisted as a private under another name.'

'Ah.' The suspicion melted into sympathy. 'My dear Margery, I am so dreadfully sorry. How wonderfully brave of him. You must be so proud . . .' She broke off. 'Of course that explains it. I assumed your brother would have to be an officer, and officers' next of kin receive telegrams, not letters . . .' She seemed to realise Midge wasn't listening. 'Margery? You will have to tell your aunt and uncle of course.'

'Yes . . .'

Miss Hollington patted her hand. 'Would you like me to inform them for you, my dear?'

'What? Yes. Oh . . . yes.'

There was something wrong. Tim *couldn't* be dead. She'd know if he were dead. There'd be an ache . . . an absence . . .

Something *was* wrong! Midge looked at the date on the form again: 22 May. She grabbed the letter from her pocket and scanned the date: 24 May.

'Miss Hollington! That letter's wrong!'

Miss Hollington stared. 'My dear girl, what do you mean?'

'Tim wrote me a letter two days after it says he went missing! It's all a mistake. There have to be lots of soldiers called Smith,' she added eagerly. 'Someone else has died —'

'My dear,' said Miss Hollington gently, 'I think it is more likely that your poor brother got the date wrong.'

'But he can't have! It was just after the truce! Tim was *there*! I read about the truce in the paper. It *has* to be a mistake.'

Miss Hollington looked troubled. 'My dear, I would hate for you to keep hoping. I am very much afraid your brother is dead.'

'He's not dead!'

'Of course he isn't,' declared Anne.

Ethel looked uncertain. 'No, but what if it's this officer who's made a mistake with the date? What if he meant to write the 26th?'

They were in Miss Hollington's private parlour, with its stuffed owl and tasselled curtains. A gesture, Midge thought, to the grief she refused to feel. Miss Hollington had even called Anne and Ethel from prep to be with her; had told the maid to bring them cups of tea and seed cake. Ethel had eaten the cake, while Anne made Midge sip the tea. But Midge couldn't cry. She couldn't mourn. Tim *wasn't* dead!

'If he's alive he'll write to you,' said Ethel practically.

'But what if he's been taken prisoner or injured? That would be why they think he's dead, because he's not there! There's lots of reasons why men go missing.' Midge put down her teacup and began to pace around the Turkish carpet. 'I need to talk to the men who were with him.'

'Well, you can't,' said Ethel, picking up the last of the cake crumbs with her finger.

'I hate being young!' Midge cried passionately. 'And I hate being a girl too!'

Anne and Ethel exchanged glances.

'Darling, I wish we could help,' Anne said.

Ethel hugged her, which was a bit like being hugged by a friendly gorilla but comforting. 'We'll keep hoping for you, lass. Keep hoping the poor lad is safe in some nice Turkish prison with his own harem.'

'I don't think Turkish prisoners get harems.'

'Then we'll have to send him one in a food parcel. There, now you're smiling.'

'Of course I'm smiling, it's all a mistake!' But inside Midge felt cold, as though the snows on Big Jim mountain had seeped into her heart.

She smiled through dinner too: Irish stew and spotted dick, with the lumpy custard the girls called 'mouldy blanket'. Her smile had worn out, though, by the time they were sent up to bed. But she still refused to feel sorrow. She just felt empty, as though not feeling sad had used up all of her emotion.

Midge had thought that the pupils at an exclusive English girls school would be pampered, with rooms of their own, a maid to help them dress perhaps. She had discovered that the more exclusive the school, it seemed, the hardier they tried to force their girls to be. The fifth formers at Miss Hollington's slept on the verandah, with just a thin wall and an open window between them and the

English damp. At least, thanks to Miss Hollington's respect for Anne — or for her title — the three had beds together.

Midge sat on her narrow bed to pull off her stockings. Bother, a ladder. She must have got it under the willow tree. Was it only this afternoon that she'd read Tim's letter? But she couldn't, wouldn't, think of Tim. She had to think of ordinary things. The stain on the ceiling shaped like a sheep. The French exam tomorrow . . .

Anne lifted her candle and peered into the tiny mirror that was all Miss Hollington allowed her boarders. 'Fourteen spots,' she said gloomily. 'Yes, that's a new one by my nose. And that one on my chin — it's not a spot, it's a volcano.'

Midge shoved her stockings into the darning bag. She'd have to mend the ladder before she put them into the wash or it'd run even further. (Tim, she thought. Tim. And shoved the thought away.)

'How many were there this morning?' asked Ethel.

'Twelve and a half.'

'You can't have half a spot!'

'It was only a red blotch this morning. Now it looks like Mount Vesuvius.'

'I think they'd go away if you stopped worrying about them,' said Midge wearily, pulling her nightdress over her head.

'Easy for you to say. You've only had four spots since the beginning of term. And Ethel's only had one. A teeny one too. Which is simply not fair. She's been *raised* on cocoa.'

'You counted my spots?'

'My life is ruled by spots,' said Anne, pulling back the bedclothes and getting into bed. 'You just don't understand! They're the first thing Mummy looks at when I come home each term. How can she present a daughter with spots? Four daughters successfully married off and now the last one has to get spots. I think she'd rather I ran off with a footman.'

The springs creaked as Ethel plonked herself down on her own bed. 'But you don't want to be presented.'

'My dear, what else can one do?' Anne tried to fluff a little life into the hard flat pillow. 'One's job is to look so totally ravishing that the marriage settlements are signed and sealed by the end of one's first season so Mummy doesn't have the expense of a second. Which means no spots.' She glanced at Midge's face. 'Darling, forgive me. Here I am blithering on about my spots when you're torn up about your brother.'

'It's all right,' said Midge. She tried to smile. 'I like the blithering. It takes my mind off Tim.'

Tim laughing that year he brought a jack-in-the-box back from school and she screamed when it leapt out at her. Tim's face as he waved goodbye as the train carried her away on the first leg of her journey to England . . .

'Lights out, girls.' Miss Jenkins' shoes clattered over the wooden floor. The shadows from her lantern swung back and forth across the walls.

Midge blew out her candle; listened to the puffs as the others blew out theirs too. Darkness descended as Miss Jenkins and her lamplight retreated down the corridor.

Night was the hardest time. Impossible not to think of home. Impossible not to think of Tim. Was he really in a shallow grave in that strangely named place, Gallipoli? No. Impossible. But impossible to lie here doing nothing too, when Tim . . .

'Are you all right, darling?' It was Anne's whisper.

'Yes.'

Tim had to be alive! What would she do without him? All their plans . . . Glen Donal was her world! Other girls dreamed of marriage and children, or even of going up to Oxford when they left school, even if girls couldn't be awarded a degree. But all she wanted was Glen Donal. The mountains with their caps of snow, the air so sharp you could brush your teeth with it, the lambs' tails dancing . . .

Even Anne and Ethel couldn't understand.

She turned her face into her pillow to muffle her tears. It wasn't fair! She was locked up here, knitting socks and studying verbs.

'Midge?' It was Ethel's voice, a whisper in the chilly darkness.

'What's up?' Anne sounded half asleep.

'I just got an idea.' Ethel was a grey bulk now, sitting up in bed.

'Can't it wait till morning?' Anne said.

'Maybe I'll have forgotten it by morning.'

Anne rolled over and pulled her pillow over her ears. 'Unless it's a way to get rid of spots I'm not interested. Not till after breakfast anyway.'

'Listen, clever clogs, I'm serious. It's about the war. About us doing something. Something real.'

'What?' Midge wiped her eyes and peered across at Ethel in the dimness.

'Just an idea, mind, so don't go jumping at me like fleas on a blanket. But I wondered . . .'

'Come on!' urged Midge. Ethel had never had an idea in all the time she'd known her.

'Well, I know you were joking about Carryman's Cocoa, but I was just lying here and suddenly I thought, maybe that's it. We take them cocoa.'

'That's your idea?' said Midge blankly. 'Cocoa?'

'Listen up, will you? There are thousands of soldiers going through the railway stations over in France every day, and wounded coming back. And what is there for them to eat or drink? Nowt.'

'She's right,' said Anne. She sat up and pulled her pillow onto her lap. 'Those little stations only have a tiny café, if that. Nothing that can cope with thousands of soldiers.'

'And if the trains are like the ones here, they'll be waiting a precious long time for them. So this is the plan. We organise a — what's it called? A buffet.'

'Bu-*ffay*,' said Anne.

'Bu*ffay* then. A canteen. Over in France. Calais, maybe. And we give them a good thick buttie each —'

'A sandwich,' Anne translated for Midge. 'Ethel, do try to speak the King's English.'

'And cocoa — something good and hot to line their stomachs. My da will pay for the lot of it and make sure we get supplies as well.'

For the first time since Midge had known her, Ethel's voice had a note of eagerness and passion.

'But why should he? Surely he'd never let you —' began Midge.

Ethel snorted. 'I could go sail one of those submarines for all my da cares. It's our George he cares about, keeping him safe to run Carryman's Cocoa in the future. And this'll keep the newspapers off George's back, and Da's too. If anyone starts muttering, they can point to me over in France and the grand job Carryman's Cocoa is doing for "our boys".'

Midge was silent. Serving cocoa — it was a long way from nursing, like Aunt Lallie. No romantically holding a mug of water to a dying soldier's lips, or striding onto the battlefield to bring back the wounded, or driving an ambulance through a hail of bullets. But Ethel was right. No one would let them go and nurse in France, not for years and years. But they might just let them do this. And maybe she'd meet soldiers over there who'd fought with Tim, or who knew someone who had. And even if no one knew anything about Tim at all — well, she'd be fighting in the same war as him and Doug. She'd be *doing* something. Something grander and braver than studying irregular verbs. Something for King and country!

'Well?'

Midge lifted her chin. 'You're on.'

'Anne?'

Anne hesitated, her pillow in her arms.

'Come on, lass!' Ethel said. 'I'm offering thee a chance to get free of this place forever! Do you want to come or not?'

'Of course one would like to. In another year, perhaps, when we leave school . . .'

'Garn,' said Ethel rudely.

'The war will be over in another year,' urged Midge. 'And we'll just have been stuck here learning how to walk with books on our head.'

'They'll never let us! It will never work,' said Anne.

'Then we'll have to make it work.' Ethel's eyes glinted in the darkness, as though she could see it all.

Chapter 3

The Firs
Sussex
6 August

Dear Aunt Lallie,

Thank you for your letter about Tim. But I am sure that he is all right, that he has just been taken prisoner. It's all a mistake! He sent me a letter dated AFTER he was supposed to be 'missing', you see. So I am sure we will hear from him soon. Uncle Thomas has also put an advertisement in The Times and The Guardian asking for anyone who may know anything to write to us.

I hope things are better at the hospital now. I wish I could help. In fact, I hope I will be helping the troops soon, just a little bit. My friends, Anne and Ethel, and I want to open a canteen *for soldiers in France — NOT near the battle lines, just where we can give them a hot drink and something to eat at the railway station.*

I know Uncle Thomas is my guardian now Doug is away, not you. But if he asks you, PLEASE will you tell him it's a good idea? I am sure we can make it work — especially Ethel. It's funny, Ethel never did anything much at school — everything bored her, even games. But she has been dashing all over the country with her father's car and chauffeur these holidays, seeing how people run their canteens.

We really, really want to do our bit and make this work.

Your loving niece,
Margery

~❦○

'It will never work!' said Uncle Thomas.

He was sitting at his desk in what was supposed to be his study. But because it got the best morning light of any room in the house, his wife used it as well. A silken knitting bag sat on one end of the sofa and a bag of dog hair at the other. The dog hair was one of Aunt Harriet's projects. All over the country, women were combing reluctant dogs for their hair so it could be woven into light pyjamas for wounded soldiers who could bear no other weight on their shattered limbs.

Midge faced her uncle with determination. 'But it will work! Mr Carryman — Ethel's father — says he'll arrange all the supplies we need. Please, Uncle. Anne is allowed to go.'

Privately Midge wondered if Lady George saw the canteen as a way of keeping her youngest daughter out of society till she was spot free. But she wasn't going to mention that to Uncle Thomas. And perhaps, she thought, she was doing Lady George an injustice. Two wings of Anne's home were being turned into a convalescent hospital and two of her daughters had brought their families home so that they could help run it. And Lady George had set up a committee to scrape linen for bandages and another to collect peach seeds for gas masks.

'Anne's parents say if she feels it's her duty then of course she must go,' Midge added.

'That's all very well . . .' Uncle Thomas clearly felt that the world would be far more protective of an Honourable Anne than an unknown Midge Macpherson. He hesitated. 'My dear, I know Tim's death has been a terrible blow.'

'He's not dead! Just missing in action.'

'Well, yes.' He bit his lip. 'Margery, my dear, you just have to accept —'

'Missing just means . . . well, missing! There was even that bit in the paper about the army making a mistake over a boy who was killed. You know — the Private Richards they said was killed in the 15th Battalion Tank Corps but it was really Private Jenkins in the 25th. And Smith is such a common name.'

'Why he had to go and —' began Uncle Thomas, then broke off as he saw the expression on Midge's face. 'Of course, one has to admire him. An example to us all. But —'

'Uncle, please, please, let me go. There's so much that needs to be done over there, and so few people to do it. And if anything should happen to me . . . well, there's no one still here to miss me, is there?'

Uncle Thomas had the grace to blush. 'We would miss you,' he said.

But not like I was one of your own children, thought Midge.

'It's not as though it'll be dangerous,' she urged. 'Nothing can happen to us at the railway station in Calais. We'll be miles away from any fighting. And Anne and Ethel are taking their maids, so they'll look after us. It's only a short sail and a train ride away.'

Uncle Thomas was shaking his head.

She said desperately, 'Uncle Thomas, they need help over there.'

He held up his hand. 'I know they do. I . . . I had a letter from Michael yesterday.'

He picked up a piece of paper from his desk. Midge recognised Cousin Michael's writing, the round letters of the schoolboy he had been till six months ago. She'd only met him once, but he still wrote to her, just like she was one of his sisters. Uncle Thomas looked down at the letter in silence for a moment, then he said abruptly, 'Very well.'

'You mean I can go?'

'You may go. I will see if one of the housemaids will go with you. Gladys, perhaps. She's steady. If the other girls have maids then you must too.'

'And an allowance —' began Midge.

He shook his head. 'I won't let you touch your capital. I owe it to your father to keep that intact till you're twenty-one or married. But the interest — you'll find that quite enough for your needs, I think. You're a wealthy young lady, you know. Or will be. Perhaps if I called on Mr Carryman . . . Yes, I think that's what I need to do.' He hesitated again. 'Will you be giving them fruit cake?'

Midge stared. 'I don't know. Cocoa and bread and canned meat, we thought.'

'Perhaps that is best.' Her uncle looked vaguely down at his son's letter, as though surprised to find it still in his hand.

'Uncle, may I read Michael's letter? Please?'

He hesitated again, then said, 'Of course, my dear. Excuse me, will you? I must go and break this to your aunt.' He smiled faintly. 'You will probably hear her protests from down here.'

'But you'll convince her, Uncle?'

'Yes,' said Uncle Thomas. 'I think I can convince her.'

The heavy door closed behind him. Midge picked up the letter.

27 July 1915

Dear Pater,

I am writing this on the edge of a bunk in the dugout I'm sharing with an officer of the [removed by censor]. *Our trench is only 70 yards away from the Germans. Two bullets have just skimmed along the roof but as it's well protected by* sandbags there is no danger. Outside our guns are shelling a farmhouse behind the German lines. You hear the boom as the shell leaves the gun, then a scream as it passes overhead, then the crash as it bursts. Of course you cannot look over the edge of the trench or a sniper would pot you, but the men have rigged up periscopes. But the worst danger is being hit with fragments blown back from our own shells.

Sorry, this letter is being written in pieces. Every three hours I need to go around the men and make sure they are in their right places, even at night. It takes me an hour or more if one of the boys has caught it, so I don't get much sleep. We can't take our clothes off here, so I just scrape as much mud off my boots as I can with my bayonet, tie a bag over them and get into my sleeping bag boots and all. Don't tell the Mater but washing is not something we give much mind to here!

You get used to the tiredness though, just like you get used to the noise and the . . .

Later

One of the boys started screaming just as I was finishing your letter. Some silly ass put his hand up over the trench and the Jerries blew it off. That wasn't what the screaming was though. After they took him away, some other blighter found his hand buried in the mud, still moving.

Just at the end of our trench are thirty graves, all men of the last regiment who served here, and three German graves with no names, just a piece of board with RIP on it in German. But thankfully only four of us have caught it so far.

The wind has changed. We can hear the Germans now. Their voices sound very young, like the boys at school.

41

Give my love to Mater and the girls and tell them not to worry about me and that I am very well off for socks! I could do with some chocolate or other food though, if you can manage it. The grub here is pretty rough, and sometimes when they move us we can go for days without rations. It's silly but the one thing I long for is a big slice of fruit cake, the one the Mater makes for every birthday. It is strange how fancies like that take over. It's harder than we thought, Pater. Much harder. But we will beat them. I feel sorry for any Englishman who isn't here.

Your loving son,
Michael Macpherson

Chapter 4

Dear Aunt Lallie,

I hope you are well.

Well, we are finally here and all set up. I don't know if I told you that there was already a canteen at Calais? So we have come here, instead, a bit further north and inland. It's only a small town — a big village rather. The fields start right opposite the railway station so I can watch the cows (French cows and pigs are sort of sleepy) and think of home. It is slightly closer to the battle front here but absolutely in no danger, and a good place to be as this is the nearest railway station in these parts to the front lines. The

43

men get off here and are collected in cattle trucks, or else march if there are no trucks or carts available.

Most of the soldiers are French so far. I never thought those irregular verbs would be useful! Though to be honest, I haven't used one yet. I mostly stick to 'Bonjour' or 'Bonne chance, monsieur'. The hospital trains also go through here to take men to the hospitals in Calais or Paris or over to England, but they don't stop at our station so we don't get any wounded men here either, just the troops heading off to the front lines.

Ethel dragged us to every canteen she could find in London. (If you could meet Ethel you'd see that when she decides to drag you there's no stopping her.) Her father will send us a shipment of bully beef, flour, cocoa and powdered milk twice a week. We can store it in what used to be the railway waiting room till Ethel persuaded the station master to let us use it. Ethel doesn't speak much French yet, despite the best efforts of Mademoiselle at school, and Monsieur the Station Master doesn't speak English. I think he gave up arguing with her out of sheer exhaustion.

We need to store as much as we can as the troops and the wounded have priority on the railway and we can't rely on supplies arriving regularly. We have the bread made here, but Ethel had to battle to get the bakers to take us seriously and give us what we ordered.

The hotel is small and very plain, but it is right across from the railway station. I thought my feet were going to drop off the first couple of days, they were so sore, so it is good the hotel is close by. Madame is kind to what she calls 'les jeunes femmes anglaises'. Monsieur is a prisoner somewhere in Germany, but her father helps and so do her two daughters and her grandson — when he is not minding his geese!

Anne, Ethel and I share a tiny room. It's got a little coal fire that's never lit and hard narrow beds so it is just like school, and our maids are all in one other room, even more crowded than ours. We are still trying to convince Anne's maid, Beryl, that Anne doesn't need help to dress and wash and things. The poor woman is trying to serve cocoa for twelve hours at a time and still do all the regular maid work too! She even carried up hot water for Anne's bath the other day! (We all used it after Anne.) But things have been sorted out now, I think. We work two shifts with three on each shift, one of us serving and the other two making the sandwiches or stirring the cocoa.

Well, I had better go as we are rather busy. We served nearly 1 000 men yesterday. We give each of them a pannikin of cocoa, a bully beef sandwich and two cigarettes. Some of the men look younger even than we are. They are all eager to fight the Hun and it is good to think that we are finally doing our bit too.

I had a letter from Dougie yesterday. He is well and in good spirits.

Your loving niece,
Midge

The railway platform was long and narrow with a line of buildings on one side: the ticket office, the waiting room (now the storeroom) and the station master's office. There was no spare room for the canteen, which was a nuisance when it rained. But after the first two days of drizzle, Ethel had found a man to rig up an open canvas tent to cover their four trestle tables, two coppers for boiling up the cocoa and two coke braziers. This made up the canteen.

Now in the dawn's grey light French soldiers tumbled out of the trains bleary-eyed from travel. They lined up along the platform for their cocoa, then took the pannikins and their bread and beef out to the station courtyard and sat propped against their kitbags or the walls. They were cheery for the most part — or at least put on a good show for the canteen girls.

At times like this, the war seemed very near, thought Midge, as she lugged yet another box of cocoa along the platform and tried to ignore her cold fingers. But at other times, the rumble of the guns could have been simply thunder. And on the other side of the railway lines stretched farmland: neat fields still untouched by war; cattle that gazed curiously at the commotion at the station; and geese that grazed the grass along the line, herded by small boys with bare feet and ragged pants.

The dawn was brighter than the gaslights as Midge dropped the box by the two big coppers Ethel had scrounged to heat the cocoa on the two small braziers of coke or coal.

'Thanks, lass.' Ethel began to tear open the box. 'I'm fair clemmed this morning. It was hard work last night.'

Midge nodded. It would be good to hand over to the others in an hour or so and get some sleep. She glanced at Ethel. Ethel didn't look 'clemmed'. Ever since they'd left school, it was as though she'd found a new source of energy. She was like a steam engine, Midge thought with a private grin, as another train clattered into the station.

It thundered through without stopping. Hospital train, she thought. Six of them went through the station each day. Ethel had discovered that each carried four hundred sick and wounded men, with two or three medical officers, four nursing sisters and about forty orderlies to tend them.

Midge yawned and trudged over to the pump to fill a bucket of water to pour onto the powdered milk in the copper. Add half a bucket of cocoa, she thought as she pumped the handle up and down and watched the water splash into the wooden bucket, ten more buckets of water, stir for an hour, and there'd be cocoa for the next troop train later that morning.

The noise of a different sort of engine floated over the morning sounds of roosters and the cows plodding off to be milked by Monsieur Brabant, the dairy farmer down the road. Midge looked up. A van was pulling into the courtyard. It looked like one of the new motorised grocer's delivery trucks — there had been great excitement at school when one rumbled up the drive instead of the usual horse and cart. But this one was painted white, with a wobbly-looking red cross on the side.

The driver leapt out, followed by a large spotted dog. His boots clicked on the cobbles as he dodged through the few civilian passengers waiting for the train, then strode up to Midge, the dog's ears flapping at his heels.

'Down, Dolores! Hello there! Any chance of a couple of quick cups of tea?'

Midge stared. The driver was a girl.

Midge had learned to drive Dad's car back home. But she'd never seen another female drive before. The girl was a few years older than Midge, and tall in men's trousers, boots and jacket. She grinned and held out a hand. Midge shook it, stunned. It was the first time she had ever shaken hands with another woman, too.

'I'm Slogger Jackson. That's Jumbo.' She gestured to another girl leaning in to do something in the back of the van. 'And this is Dolores, and that's Boadicea. Down, Dolores!'

Midge pushed Dolores's nose out of the bucket of water. 'Boadicea?' she asked.

'Our truck. Beautiful, isn't she?' said Slogger proudly. 'Dolores, no! The nice soldier doesn't want you sniffing him there. Boadicea used to be a butcher's van. Jumbo and I gave her a coat of paint before we brought her over — well, you can't have wounded men riding in a butcher's van, can you? Might give them all sorts of ideas. Dolores, *don't* kiss the poor man either! He doesn't like it. *Pardon, monsieur.*' She grabbed the big dog's collar firmly and turned back to Midge. 'Any chance of that tea?'

'I'm sorry, only cocoa.'

'As long as it's hot and wet. Any grub going? I'm starving. We've been on the go since dawn yesterday. There's another big push on.'

'A push?'

Slogger nodded. 'Poor blighters are ordered out of their nice muddy trenches to try to take another few yards of mud. Mostly they're just forced back — what's left of them

48

— but it makes a lot of work for us.' She looked around the quiet station. 'No one told you you're for it today?'

'For it?' Midge felt as though she'd stumbled upon yet another foreign language.

'We've been ordered to start bringing the wounded here for the hospital trains. The stations down the line can't cope. You're going to have hundreds of wounded men here soon. Maybe thousands.'

'Thousands?' said Midge faintly. She pulled herself together. 'I'll tell the others.' She hurried down the platform, her heels clicking on the damp concrete.

Slogger strode beside her, Dolores bouncing at their side. 'Don't forget that cocoa.'

'Ethel!' Midge called.

Ethel turned from slicing bread. 'What is it, lass?'

'They're going to bring the wounded men here. Thousands of them! What are we going to do?' she asked desperately. 'There's no way we can cope with that many! We haven't got enough milk or bread.'

'Then we'll have to find it. Settle down, lass. I'll see what we have in the storeroom.' She hurried away down the platform.

Midge turned back to the waiting Slogger. 'Here's the cocoa. Sorry the fresh stuff isn't ready yet. You'd better take a couple of sandwiches too. I didn't know they had women driving ambulances,' she added curiously.

'Could you make it three sandwiches? Just to keep Dolores happy. My dear girl, anyone and anything are drafted into service these days. As long as you've got hands or wheels. Or paws. *Down*, Dolores! No, you can't have that poor man's sandwich. We're with the Duchess's mob.'

'The Duchess of Sutherland? I thought she was in Flanders.'

'No, ours is the Duchess of Westminster. She's wonderful — as soon as war was declared, she rounded up trucks, drivers, supplies and just came over. Dolores is hers. Her ladyship says she needs the fresh air.'

'She brought her *dog* over?'

Slogger bent down and rubbed Dolores's ears. 'A dalmation, two wolfhounds and a Pekingese, plus three trunks of evening dresses. Am I glad I wasn't given Peke duty. It's a horror.'

'Bites?'

'Wees. Her ladyship says having us in evening dress each night and the dogs around is good for the men's morale. But I say it's bad enough being wounded without being weed on by a Peke too. I'd better dash. Have to get our poor chaps onto the platform then get going again. We've got three more runs at least tonight — they're really piling up. Those bloody generals ought to be shot.'

Midge stared. She'd never heard a woman say 'bloody' before. 'You mean the German generals?'

'No, ours. Silly asses. They give the orders and we pick up the results. Thanks for these. Dolores, that is very, very rude! Be seeing you!'

She strode off across the platform. Dolores gave one of the men dozing by the storeroom a final loving sniff, gulped the crust of bread from his hand, then loped after her.

More ambulance trucks had arrived while they'd been talking. There were horse-drawn ambulances too, the horses thin and tired-looking, and even a few carts, the wounded lying on the straw. As Midge watched, orderlies unloaded stretchers and laid the men out along the platform, then hurried back for more. Most of the orderlies were women, in trousers and boots like Slogger's or dresses with big white aprons like the canteen girls wore. Already a third of the station was covered. The tiny courtyard was full of vehicles, and others lined the street waiting to get in. How could this peaceful station change so fast, thought Midge dazedly. Midge had read Aunt Lallie's letters and the newspaper reports. But nothing had prepared her for this.

The stretchers seemed endless, laid on the cold ground. The men lay without blankets to cover them, much less pillows or sheets. Their uniforms — muddy, stained and torn — were French. Some of them had roughly bandaged wounds; others had been left with their wounds open when the bandages ran short. There were men with grey faces, white faces, faces cut by shrapnel. Men with closed eyes who might be dead or just blessedly unconscious. Men with strange hooped cradles where their arms or legs had been. They looked so still. So quiet. There were some groans and cries, but strangely few. These were men who had seen hell. And now they waited for what help a distant hospital might bring.

Only the orderlies and drivers in their skirts or trousers were still whole. Even as Midge watched, the carpet of bodies grew. Whatever she had expected, she thought, it wasn't this.

Ethel strode back along the platform, her arms full of loaves of bread. 'No point standing there staring. Reckon we'd better get cracking, lass.'

'What if we run out of cocoa?'

'Just keep adding water. So long as it's hot and wet.'

Midge followed, half running to keep up. Impossible to expect these wounded and shocked men to line up like the soldiers they'd been serving, she thought. 'We'll have to take the pannikins to them, help the men to drink,' she said.

'Yes. I sent the goose boy to ask Madame for help. We need more hands.' Ethel was already cutting bread as she spoke.

Midge tried to think. She could carry four pannikins at once, but she'd have to put them down to help each man to drink . . . Impossible. There must be two thousand men here already, more than they had ever served before. And this was just the start, Slogger had said. They couldn't serve a tenth this many. Her knees felt weak with the smell of blood.

Suddenly, she thought of her grandmother fording a river flooded with snow melt on horseback to get to her new home. Her mother facing what she must have known was her death in the isolated highlands, rather than leave her home and family for less pain and a hospital. Lallie working herself into exhaustion for the boys from Gallipoli, and Tim and Dougie out there somewhere, fighting for all of them . . .

Impossible not to try.

'*Pardon, monsieur*? Cocoa?'

The man smiled with bloody lips. His hands reached for the cocoa. Thank goodness he could hold it.

'*Pardon, monsieur*? Cocoa?' This time she had to hold the pannikin while the boy sipped. One of his hands was bleeding, the other a stump strapped to his chest. His eyes were vague, but at least he drank.

'Cocoa, *monsieur*?' No answer. Sleeping? Unconcious? Dead? No time to check, nor was it her job. '*Monsieur, un peu* cocoa?'

She glanced out at the courtyard. More ambulances ... and more. The road was jammed with vehicles: carts, cars, trucks. How many more, she thought frantically, then bent to her job again. Anne and Beryl hurried between the stretchers up the platform to help Doris with the mixing and bread-slicing. For a time, Midge and Ethel simply handed the pannikins to the hands capable of reaching for them. Ethel strode away to get more powdered milk and Midge looked at the men reaching desperately for something, anything, to drink. Please, she prayed silently. Help us, please.

'*Cacao, mon brave*?'

It was a stranger's voice. Midge looked up. All along the platform, she saw young women in grey skirts with handkerchiefs about their heads, old women in black lace, girls with aprons over neat print dresses. The village women had come to help. Now at least it was possible to also give drinks to everyone.

A hospital train arrived, steaming and snorting as it stopped. Orderlies climbed out — all men, this time, and in uniform — lifted stretchers from the platform and carried them one by one on board. Inside the train Midge could see nurses, their veils a brilliant white even through the window glass. But as soon as one stretcher was taken from the platform, another took its place.

Midge glanced out into the courtyard again. It was still crowded with stretchers, the road still lined with vehicles waiting to unload. There were no more motor ambulances. Now the wounded came in farm trucks, delivery trucks, carts that a year ago had carried cows or sheep and still smelled of hay or manure. Others came in private cars with leather seats and empty silver vases for the nosegays there was no time to pick, the men stretched out on the back seat or propped awkwardly with linen pillows.

Midge returned to her task. '*Pardon, monsieur*? Cocoa?'

Mopping blood from a soldier's face so it didn't drip into the cocoa. Replacing a bandage pad that had slipped off a wound. More trucks, more cars, and then the ambulances again, returning from hell, carrying a second load.

'*Pardon, monsieur*? Cocoa?'

The shadows grew shorter, then long. Dusk thickened the air as the first of the walking wounded limped down the cobbled street and lay panting against the walls of the station master's office or stretched out on any patch of platform or in the station courtyard.

The station master lit the gaslights. They hissed above sounds of pain.

'*Pardon, monsieur*? Cocoa?'

And still the wounded came staggering along the village street, on foot now as well as in the carts, an endless procession, desperate to reach the station and a hospital train, a doctor's hands. One man helped another; two carried a comrade between them; men with bandaged eyes pushed bath chairs, their passengers giving them directions.

Villagers rushed into the street to lend a shoulder; some brought wheelbarrows to help those who collapsed along the road. School children lugged buckets of water, while women held cups to the dry cracked lips of bleeding men who rested on steps or leaned against walls on their way to the station.

The gaslights flared on the platform, turning the pale faces yellow. Here and there buckets of smouldering coke provided a little heat, and a thin transparent smoke that choked you if you went too close.

Cocoa and more cocoa. Loaf after loaf to be sliced. And still the ambulances came and left. And the wounded staggered in.

Dimly Midge was aware of Slogger and Boadicea coming back a third time; unloading more stretchers. Slogger swayed up to grab more cocoa, Dolores at her heels. Even the big dog seemed weary now.

'Smile,' Slogger whispered, her eyes red with tiredness.

'What?' Midge stared at her, not understanding.

'It's all we can do for the poor chaps sometimes — smile at them. Comfort them. Give them a pennyworth of hope. And if they're dying . . . well, let their last thought be of home, of comfort.'

How could you smile in this, thought Midge desperately. But Slogger was right. They had so little to give. She forced her lips to move, her face to relax from grimness to what she hoped was comfort.

'Pardon, *monsieur*? Cocoa?' Smile. Lift and fill and smile . . .

More powdered milk to be mixed. More bread to slice. Midge stared at the loaf in front of her. How many hours had she been working? The knife seemed to blur back and forth whether her hands moved or not. She blinked hard, but the world still swam.

'Darling, go and sleep.' It was Anne.

'I can't.' The world was pain and hungry men, stretchers, the rumble of engines and the snort of tired horses. Sleep was a demon that tried to lure you away. But she couldn't sleep. Not with so much to do, so many men, the blood and desperation.

'You have to. Darling, you've been on your feet for a day and a night.'

'Take her into the storeroom.' That was Ethel's voice. 'Bring more powdered milk while you're there. You! Station master! I need to send a telegram to England. *Angleterre*! "Need more supplies. Urgent." No, you silly man, I know you don't send telegrams. Take it to post office. *La poste*!'

Anne's hand on her arm, leading her, guiding her. Stumbling over something, a stretcher. Anne keeping her upright . . .

The sacks were hard and lumpy, but just to close her eyes was an indescribable luxury. The world vanished.

A scream outside woke her.

'*Non, non, non* . . .'

Midge sat up and shook her head to clear it. How long had she slept? Her head ached, her body — or was it her feet? The scream had faded, but now she could hear voices, groans, a strange hoarse laugh and then the rumble of a train.

Was it night or day? She peered at the window. Night: the light outside was still yellow gaslight, the moths flickering about the flames. She must have slept two hours, or three. She stretched and tried to straighten her dress, then went outside.

'Your turn,' she said to Anne. 'Go and sleep.'

Anne didn't argue. Her spots stood out bright red against her paleness. She trod drearily over to the storeroom and shut the door.

'Eat,' said Ethel, handing Midge a roll. It was thick with butter, ham and cheese, the best thing she had ever eaten. 'Madame sent it over from the hotel. Everyone is doing what they can . . .' Ethel's voice broke for a moment, then steadied. 'You slept for three hours. Are you all right to carry on?'

Midge nodded.

'Maybe you'd best help slice the bread then, and do the cocoa. Your hands will be steadier than mine. I'll serve. I got a telegram back from Da,' she added. 'There'll be more supplies in tomorrow.'

'That was quick.'

'He was waiting by the phone, I think. All England's waiting.' She shrugged. 'A few yards taken. More lives lost. Daft, daft, the lot of them.'

'Ethel!'

'Well, they are. That Sir John French is a fool.'

'Are you sorry you came?'

Ethel looked at her strangely. 'Sorry? No. We're needed. I've never been needed before.' She shook her head. 'Don't mind me, lass.' Then turned to a young soldier who was asking if they had any writing paper. '*Non, Monsieur, je suis,* um, *desolée. Mais je peux faire le cacao pour vous.*'[*]

'*Donnez-moi un sourire alors!*'[**] the boy said cheekily.

Ethel obliged with a giant grin as she poured him some cocoa. A day and a night, thought Midge dazedly, and Ethel could still grin.

Loaf after loaf of bread, can after can of bully beef. Ethel was thinning out the cocoa with water. The powdered milk must be finished. What had Slogger said, Midge thought. 'As long as it's hot and wet.'

The smell of milk and cocoa mingled with the smell of blood; the sharp odour of antiseptic mixed with the smell of bully beef. Midge saw VADs moving among the wounded now. They must have arrived on one of the hospital trains while she was asleep. They looked like crows, she thought, with their long black cloaks, their braid-edged shoulder capes, thick black stockings under the drab dress, and the tiny black straw bonnet trimmed with black bows and held on by white strings. A mob of crows preying on the wounded. Then she saw the concern on every face, the tired smiles that attempted to give

---

[*] 'No, sir, I am sorry. But I can make cocoa for you.'

[**] 'Give me a smile then!'

comfort where there was none to give as they tried to sort the most urgent cases to go on the next train.

The sky grew grey with dawn. A man with a bandaged face stared at Midge with strange blank eyes. '*Avance à l'aube,*' he whispered. '*Suivez-moi, mes amis. Avance à l'aube.*'*

Another man took his arm, his hand black with blood from a wound on his shoulder. '*Ne vous inquiétez pas par lui, mademoiselle,*' he said. '*Venez, Marcel, prenez votre cacao.*'** And he led his comrade off to find a place to sit.

Another train arrived, this one carrying new troops heading into battle. Clean, fresh faces startled into fear as the men jumped from the carriages and saw what they were heading into: a world of horror populated by wounded men, dying men, men who staggered blindly, men who wept.

Another hospital train, a brief space as the stretchers were carried aboard, then the platform grew its carpet of bodies once more.

Midge slept again, no longer sure how long she had been working or even what day it was. She woke as a new train crept into the station, bringing sacks and boxes for them from England; Ethel's father performing miracles, or her brother perhaps, out of who knew what sense of guilt or conscience.

Another night. Another dawn. And suddenly it was over. The platform was strangely empty. Only the memories of pain and death remained.

* 'Advance with the daybreak. Follow me, my friends. Advance with the daybreak!'
** 'Do not worry about him, Miss. Come, Marcel, take your cocoa.'

Midge watched the last hospital train pull out. If those men were lucky, they would be unloaded at Boulogne. If the hospitals there were full, they might go to Le Touquet or Rouen, Le Havre or Paris, or be sent on another nightmare journey, crammed into ships bound for England.

She turned back to the canteen, trying not to stagger. Her apron was more cocoa brown than white, splattered with bloodstains. She wondered, briefly, what her hair looked like. Their counter was filthy, splashed with cocoa and crusted with crumbs. A few ambulance drivers still slouched on the platform; most were men, she thought, but it was hard to tell the women from the men. Sometime during the night Dolores had crept into the storeroom. She was stretched out on the case of bully beef, her lips stained with cocoa froth, snoring softly. Slogger and her friend Jumbo stood nearby, waving their mugs of cocoa as they sang.

Could you get drunk on cocoa and tiredness, wondered Midge.

No, she thought, she couldn't write to Aunt Lallie about all that had happened. Lallie would understand, if anybody could. But Aunt Lallie might tell Aunt Harriet, who would worry and call her back to England. It was all so different from the girls' romantic idea of war. But there was no way they could desert their canteen now. This was work, not adventure.

Chapter 5

MARTEL, FRANCE

17 September 1915

Dear Dougie,

I hope this finds you as well as you were when you wrote your last letter. I'm sorry I can't send you any soap. I've asked Aunt Harriet to send you some, and some to me as well. I'm sorry you are not happy about my coming here. But I am 'behaving myself' as you put it. I'm nearly two years older than when you saw me last, remember. I'm not a baby any more. We really are needed here, and I can't go back to England just to get you soap and knit you socks.

Sorry to be a grouch. I know that is the last thing you need. I am so proud of you and all our men. Some Tommies passed through here last week and when they heard I was from New Zealand they said the Anzacs were the bravest, stubbornest troops around. Well, one Tommy spoke of someone 'swearing like an

Anzac' too, but I promise he did it with great admiration. But you see, that is why I have to 'do my bit' too. I can't just sit back in England and knit socks, and I promise you I am not 'being a nuisance' to everyone!

I am sure that if you saw our canteen you would realise that we really are doing our bit for the war. We served ten thousand men last night — Ethel keeps count so we know what supplies we need to order. I know you would like Anne and Ethel too, and they would love to meet you. I think you and Anne would really hit it off.

I had better go now. We are expecting a shipment of bully beef and if we don't count every box some of them always go missing!

Your loving sister,

Margery

P.S. Do let me know if you hear any word at all about Tim.

The Firs

Sussex

14 November 1915

My dear Margery,

I hope you are well. We are all well here and the news from Michael in Flanders has been good. I hear Dougie has his promotion. We are so glad and proud, and you must be too. I have sent him the soap you asked for, and six pairs of socks. I hope they fit. There is nothing worse than badly fitting socks.

We have had two convalescent soldiers billeted with us this last week. They are both young Scotsmen and very sweet. They come from crofts in the Highlands and I think living in our house must be as strange to them as they sometimes are to us. Cook found them one morning brewing tea in a dustbin in her kitchen; they had thrown the refuse out onto the lawn! They had never seen a dustbin, it seems, or gaslights either. They have worked out how to turn the lights on now, but turning them off seems beyond them! But they are both good lads and we will miss them when they go. They both knit as well as I do and, I confess, turn the heels of socks much better.

Your uncle is excited over the news of the new War Cabinet. You must be shocked too about the news of conditions at Gallipoli, but I am sure that all the problems will be sorted out now and we will have victory soon.

We often think of you over there in France and are so very proud of you.

Your loving aunt,
Harriet Macpherson.

─ ❧ ─

Dear Midge,

Just a short note. Sorry I went on at you in my last letter. It's a bit of a shock hearing that your baby sister has upped and gone to France, you know. But Uncle says you are with a grand group of girls and being well looked after. Aunt sent me the soap, and socks too. Just what I need — more socks! But the other men are grateful for them, so don't tell her I have enough. My feet are warm at least!

Sam, my batman, just brought me a cup of tea. If I'd had any sugar to put in it, the spoon would have dissolved too, it was *stewed so strong. Do you remember the shearers' tea, how Dad always said it tanned your insides?*

We are in a lot of wet tents on wet ground under wet bivouac sheets but I've got the men singing lustily. Never underestimate an Anzac's ability to organise a singsong.

We have just received an order that all men must wash their feet in hot water. I don't know what the British command think we will wash in — the dixies we make our tea in, I suppose, or maybe the canteens we use to eat and drink from. Never underestimate the lack of imagination of the British officer behind the lines either!

We are a long way from the front line ourselves at the moment, and I think it will be a while before we are sent back again. I didn't tell you in my last letter but Captain Andrews commanding BN Company was killed by a sniper while we were on exercises last week, poor chap. I think you met him at the tennis party at the Baxters'. He joined up at the same time as me. His parents are both dead but you might write to his sister. Not that there is much you can say at times like this, but I think she would be glad to hear from you.

There is no real news of Tim, I'm afraid. It seems he was in a spot called Mule Valley, where the fighting was pretty fierce. I wrote to his commanding officer but the poor chap was killed the day after Tim went missing, and the NCOs as well. I think that is probably why the date of his disappearance was wrong — there just wasn't anyone to do the blessed paperwork for a while. We just have to keep our fingers crossed, old girl, and hope the Turks have him and that we hear from him soon.

Let the folks in England know I am well — I haven't had time to write to them this week — and thank Aunt for the socks. She sent a big package of rock cakes too. Though as they took nearly three weeks to reach me they were rock cakes indeed, but there is no need to tell her that.

Your loving brother,
Dougie.

꩜

14 January 1916

Dear Dougie,

I hope you got the Christmas pudding. I made it myself in Madame's kitchen. Anne says if you don't want to eat it you can lob it at the enemy. I didn't think it was THAT bad, but after all it is the first one I have made! We all had a stir of it for luck, and all our love and best wishes went into it.

Everyone here is still trying to come to terms with the retreat from Gallipoli. It is hard to believe that so much was lost for nothing. There is a lot of criticism of Sir John French in the papers and Kitchener too. But the evacuation seems to have been a triumph.

We had a busy Christmas here. Aunt Harriet's Comforts Committee sent us more than 200 puddings! They even had sixpences in them. We were able to give every man a slice on Christmas Day, as well as extra cigarettes. At midnight some of the ambulance girls sang 'Silent Night'. It was very moving. For the first time we have mostly Tommies here now, so at least they understood the words! My French is improving but it is still hard to make myself understood sometimes.

If there is any chance of leave in England do let me know in time and I will find someone to take over for me here for a few

days somehow. It would be so wonderful to see you. I miss you and
Tim and home so very much. But it is easier now I am working
here, not just twiddling my thumbs at school.

I still haven't heard from Tim, but Uncle Thomas says that mail
from the Turkish prisoners of war is only just starting to get
through, so we may get a letter from him any day now.

Your loving sister,
Midge

―♨◎

1 MAY 1916

The baker's shop was small, like a cupboard. It smelled of
burnt flour, smothering the scent of spring and chestnut
trees. The wire bread racks behind the counter were empty;
the lunchtime loaves bought and sliced and eaten.

Midge tried again. '*Pourriez-vous dire Monsieur —*'

The woman narrowed her dark eyes, then broke into
another torrent of speech. The meaning was obvious.
Monsieur the Baker was not there.

'*Je comprends. Je comprends. Mais pourriez-vous lui
dire que les pains ne sont assez lourds. Non, non — je veux
dire qu'il n'y a pas assez des pains —*'*

The woman broke in with another burst of talk.

---

* 'I understand. I understand. But could you say to him that the
loaves are not sufficiently heavy. No, no — I want to say that there
is not enough bread —'

Either my French is even worse than I thought, Midge decided, or she's deliberately trying to confuse me. Probably both.

'*S'il vous plaît, madame* . . . No, madame, don't go. I mean, *ne pas aller, s'il vous plaît.*'

'Hey, Harry, she's English!'

Midge turned as two large bodies filled the shop's doorway. 'I am not.'

'Stone the flaming crows, she's a flaming Aussie!'

'Watch your language,' ordered the man called Harry. He was so tall he had to bend his head to pass under the lintel. Even in the dimness his hair shone like sunlight on winter grass. Both men were in uniform, with the peaked caps of Australian army privates.

'I'm not Australian either! I'm from New Zealand.'

'Hey, a Kiwi! Well, they're white men too. Except for the Maoris, of course.' He pronounced it 'mowrees'. 'Them Kiwis can outfight any blighter this side of Flanders. Except for us, of course,' he added.

'Can it, Fred.' Harry slapped him lightly on the shoulder, then held out his large hand to Midge. 'Harry Harrison. And this gorilla is Fred Randall. Don't mind him, miss. Some idiot's been feeding him meat.'

Midge felt the hand gently shake hers. As though he thinks I might break, she thought. 'I'm Margery Macpherson.'

'Pleased to meet you, Miss Macpherson.' Harry looked over at the shopkeeper who was standing with her arms crossed, glaring at them as though they were the invaders, not the Germans. 'You need a hand here?'

'I don't suppose either of you can speak French?' Midge asked. 'Or at least speak it better than I can?'

Fred grinned. 'Inky-pinky parley-voo, and that's about the strength of it. Hey, I saw the captain go by a minute or two ago, but. I reckon he speaks the lingo like a native.'

'Well, don't just stand there,' ordered Harry. 'The lady's waiting. Go get him.'

Fred gave an ironical salute and ducked through the door again.

'Don't mind him.' Harry's voice was suddenly serious. 'Been months since we spoke to a sheila. Reckon it's gone to his head. You're really from New Zealand? What are you doing here?'

'Some friends and I run the canteen at the railway station,' Midge explained. 'And yes, I really am from New Zealand. Glen Donal. It's up country from Christchurch on the South Island. Do you know it?'

He shook his head. 'Geography isn't my strong suit, miss. Sheep country, is it?'

'Yes.'

'Well, what do you know? We've got sheep. Merinos.'

Suddenly Glen Donal seemed so close she could smell it. 'We have merinos too! Lincolns as well, for the fat lambs, but the wool clip is —' She broke off as another man came into the shop.

'Miss Macpherson, is it? I'm Gordon Marks, Captain Marks. Private Randall here said that you needed some help.'

She looked at him gratefully, liking what she saw. Dark hair under his cap. Tall — were all these Australians tall?

68

Or maybe she'd just been seeing French and Englishmen for so long . . .

'Would you mind? You speak French?' Then, as he nodded, 'I've been trying to tell Madame here that the baker hasn't been delivering all the bread that we've ordered. I . . . we . . . run the canteen at the station. We give him a hundred kilos of flour each baking, but he's only been giving us a hundred kilos of bread.'

'Sounds fair —' began Fred.

'Thank you, Randall. I'll handle it from here.'

The young man grinned. 'Officers only, eh? Come on, Harry. We're not wanted.'

'I . . . well, thank you.' Midge was strangely sorry to see the two privates go. Was it the talk of home, of sheep — sanity in an insane world?

'Our pleasure, miss.' Harry sketched a vague salute.

Midge watched them leave, then turned to Captain Marks. 'They were kind,' she explained.

'They're good men. Now, this flour?'

'Oh, I'm sorry. A hundred kilos of flour should give us nearly two hundred kilos of bread, because the flour is mixed with water and water is heavy. I think he thinks we're fools and he can cheat us.'

'Does he now? Let's see what we can do.'

Midge watched. Two minutes of talk later the woman fetched the baker. After five minutes of argument, Captain Marks turned back to her. 'He says, one hundred and fifty kilograms.'

'*Cent quatre-vingt-dix*!'[*] said Midge

'*Cent quatre-vingts*!'[**] the baker replied.

'*D'accord*.'[***] Captain Marks, would you mind telling him that we will weigh the loaves, so there is no point trying to cheat us. And the bread must be made from first-class flour — the actual flour we give him. No potato flour or bran or acorn flour. We will check that too.'

Another exchange of French, then he smiled down at her. 'I don't think he'll try to cheat you again.'

'He'd better not,' said Midge. She began to tug her gloves on.

Captain Marks hesitated. 'Look, I know we haven't been properly introduced . . .'

'Yes, we have. Private — what was his name — Harrison introduced us very nicely. Well, almost.'

He smiled at that. 'Well then, as we've been almost introduced, I wonder if you'd care to join me for a cup of coffee? There's a café a few doors down.'

It was as though the world suddenly shifted. For months Midge had spoken to thousands of men a day. But this was different. One man and her . . . She felt a flush stain her neck. Like a schoolgirl, she thought. What would Aunt Harriet say?

She thought of her bed waiting for her in the hotel. Her lovely hard narrow bed and the glorious four hours' sleep she might get before working through the night. But coffee with Captain Marks sounded even better than sleep.

[*] 'One hundred and ninety!'
[**] 'One hundred and eighty!'
[***] 'All right.'

The chicory-flavoured coffee was hot and bitter, but at least it wasn't cocoa.

'I still can't quite believe it.' Captain Marks sat back in his chair outside the café and sipped at his coffee. The young leaves of the chestnut trees dappled the light around them. 'The three of you, running that canteen. Pardon me, but you look so young. If you don't mind my asking — exactly how old are you?'

'Sixteen.'

He blinked. 'My word.'

'Well, nearly seventeen actually,' Midge assured him. 'Sorry, I had to think if I'd had my birthday yet. We've been so short-handed lately I haven't had time to think. It started off as six of us, then eight. But Mrs Chiswick had to go home to nurse her son — he was wounded at Loos — and Ellen left to be married. So there's only six of us again at the moment. We used to work three shifts of eight hours each, but now it's twelve hours on, twelve hours off. If we're lucky.'

'I think you're wonderful. You're too young even to put your hair up. But you're here, doing all this.'

Midge flushed. 'It's nothing compared to what you men are facing. And the real work is done in England, getting the supplies to us. That's Mr Carryman and Lady George. They arrange all the donations, the transport. We just serve things out.'

'To how many?'

'About ten thousand in one night's the most so far.'

'Ten thousand!' He sipped again and made a face. 'This tastes like boiled bark.'

Midge laughed. 'I didn't want to say anything when you had been so kind as to buy it. Sometimes I feel I'd sell my last pair of shoes for a good milky cup of tea.'

'You should taste the tea my batman makes. I think he strains it through his old socks.'

'Is he also from — where did you say it was again? Goldburn?'

'Goulburn. No, he's from a farm out of Yass. Funny little chap. Boasts he could shear a sheep blindfolded.'

'Is every Australian soldier in France a sheep farmer?'

He laughed. 'Just about. Our lot anyway. I'm regular army, but most of us volunteered on the Snowy River March down to Sydney. It was a sight, they tell me — brass bands, and everyone cheering, and the young men all racing to join up as the volunteers marched into town. Even Jack, that's my older brother, joined up, and now,' he added with satisfaction, 'he's a lieutenant and I'm a captain. I tell you, it's grand to outrank your older brother.'

'I can imagine. I'd love to outrank mine. He's in Flanders now.'

'Macpherson . . . No, I don't know him. I wish him luck.'

'You . . . you didn't come across a Private Tim Smith at Gallipoli, did you?'

'Smith? Probably a dozen of 'em. Why?'

Midge flushed. 'He was my brother. *Is* my brother. My twin. He enlisted under another name because he was underage and Dougie — that's my older brother — said he had to stay at Glen Donal. That's our place on the South Island. It's a farm too.'

'Brave lad. But no, seriously, I don't think I came across him.'

Midge looked down at her coffee. 'I had a letter saying he was missing. It seems to have happened at a place called Mule Valley. But it's all a bit confused because I had a letter from him written after the time he was supposed to be missing, and, well . . .' She looked up at him. 'We're hoping, that's all.'

'It's all anyone can do, sometimes,' he said gently. 'But I'll ask around. So, tell me about this Glen Donal of yours. You know, your face lit up like a candle when you said its name.'

Midge flushed again. 'It's . . . who I am, I suppose. Margery Macpherson of Glen Donal. The mountains are behind us, with white caps — you can smell the snow all year round, even when the grass is shrivelling in the heat. My great-grandfather — my mother's grandfather — started it. Dad was English —'

'Was?'

'He died four years ago. Now it's just me and Tim and Dougie. What about you?'

'Both parents still alive and kicking, touch wood. Two boys, me and Jack, three girls. Daphne is married, June and Julie are still at school. Look, are you sure you wouldn't like anything else? Something to eat?'

She shook her head. 'It's luxury just to sit here in the sun. It's funny, isn't it, to think of it all still going on at home while we're here? All still the same. What would be happening at your place now, do you think?'

He grinned. 'They'd all be asleep.'

'No, you know what I mean.'

'Shut your eyes and dream of home? All right then. It's breakfast in the dining room. Mum is pouring tea and Dad is spooning treacle on his porridge.'

'Treacle?'

'Dad likes treacle.'

'Are you there?'

'Too right. I've got a plate of chops in gravy,' he said dreamily. 'And there's scrambled eggs and lots of butter for the toast and strawberry jam . . . and liver and bacon . . . What about you?'

'I'm on Ruby — she's the sweetest little mare — down the back of the run with old Campbell; he's our manager. We're moving the ewes up for lambing.' She smiled. 'It's funny how I think of sheep and the outdoors, and you're inside with the food. Should be the other way around.'

'Not if you saw the grub we get. It's bad enough even when we're not in the trenches. All our billet spent last Sunday afternoon dreaming of roast lamb with the fixings. You know — parsnips and roast pumpkin, roast potato and cauliflower cheese. Ah well, *fabas indulcet fames*.'

Midge frowned. 'I'm sorry?'

He smiled. 'No, I apologise. I have a habit of Latin tags. Got into it at school. It means "Hunger sweetens beans" or "Hunger makes everything taste good"!'

She grinned back. 'No need to apologise. Every time Dougie and Tim came back from school they'd throw Latin and Greek around just to show off to me. Speaking of food . . .' She glanced down at the watch on her lapel. 'Heavens, I need to get back!'

No time for a sleep now. No time even to change, except her shoes.

He stood up. 'I'd offer you a lift back, but —'

'No need. I left my car down by the baker's. Well, it belongs to Monsieur the Station Master, but he lets us use it sometimes.'

'What about your driver?'

'Don't need one. I learned to drive at home.'

'Clever girl. Admirable in every way. Look, can I write to you? You don't have to write back or anything . . .'

'Of course I'll write back.' She gave him her hand, and he held it for a moment. 'It's care of the Egremont Hotel.'

'Miss Margery Macpherson, care of the Egremont.'

She hesitated, liking the way his eyes wrinkled when he smiled. 'My friends call me Midge.'

'Midge?'

'It's a small biting insect. It was Dougie's idea, when I was two,' she added drily. 'The name sort of stuck.'

'Brothers . . .' He looked at her consideringly. 'No, the name doesn't suit at all.'

'Too late to change it now.'

'Midge it is then. And I'm Gordon. Come on. I'll walk you back to your car.'

Chapter 6

22 May 1916

Dear Gordon,

It was grand to get your letter. I loved the story about your uncle being rescued by the pig. I read it out to the other girls and it kept us laughing all morning. I could just imagine that pig sitting up on its chair in the kitchen every morning ever afterwards, waiting for its breakfast like a proper hero.

All is well with us here, though the village is still in mourning over General Gallieni's death. I wish we had more generals like him! Madame still talks about how he marshalled all the taxi cabs and other cars when the Germans were marching on Paris, as well as all the reserve troops. She is sure Paris would have been lost without him. Our hotel has black garlands over every window. Madame is in black too, but then she is in black every day so that

76

doesn't count. But to please her we put on black armbands when we are at the canteen.

The supplies are coming through, though there have been some delays lately, but that is to be expected. Ethel sent a lot of letters to friends of her father who are in the grocery trade too, and at times we now have biscuits and sometimes even chocolate to give to the men. The chocolate is greatly appreciated, as you can imagine, as the men can take it with them — as long as they do not leave it in their pocket like one poor Tommy who then sat down on it. You should have seen the mess! Poor boy. It looked as though he'd had the most embarrassing accident.

I hope you don't mind my reading your letters to the other girls. They all send their best wishes, as I do too.

Your friend,
Midge Macpherson

~❦⊙

31 May 1916

Dear Midge,

Another week has passed since I wrote to you last and by and large it has been an easy and quiet time. The men have been doing navvying on the nearby roads. I think it was Napoleon who said an army marches on its stomach. Well, ours marches in ruts big enough to bury a cart horse unless the roads are maintained pretty regularly. We can hear the shells over the hills but are pretty much out of it. It was strange today to watch the horses ploughing the fields unaware that a stray shell might plummet down, destroying them.

You'd hardly know you were in France these days. I think I've only seen six French in the past week, and those were mostly horses. It is all Tommies and Anzacs where we are.

I don't know when we are for the front again, but my big news is that I am getting leave — two whole days of it. Could you bear to spend one of them with me, or even both? I could arrive on the ten past eight train — or whatever time it chooses to get in these days. Would Madame at your hotel be able to put me up? I can fit in with any plans you have. Or to bring up another of those Latin tags: Malum consilium quod mutari non potest *— 'It's a bad plan that you can't change!'*

Do let me know if this would be an imposition. But as much as your letters mean to me, I would very much like to see you again in person.

I remain, yours sincerely,
Gordon Marks

11 June 1916

Dear Gordon,

I have only time for a short note — things have been so hectic here. Please excuse all the blots too. My pen is weeping tonight — the ink here is so old it has lumps in it, or perhaps Madame makes it out of soot. I would so like to see you. I will arrange for the others to take my shifts so I can spend the whole two days with you. Carpe diem! *(I do know that much Latin! Or is it Greek?) And* mirabile dictu *too! (I got that one from Anne.)*

Madame will have a room for you. She is so impressed that Anne has a title that she does whatever she can for us, and perhaps she is a little grateful for what we do for 'la belle France' as well. Anyway, she will give you the room of her sister's husband's nephew, who cleans the shoes and lights the fires and tends the geese in the afternoons, and he can sleep with his family and run back to the hotel for his petit-déjeuner.

I am so looking forward to seeing you.

Your affectionate friend,
Midge

—⁂—

4 JUNE 1916

'Happy birthday, old thing.'

Midge looked down at the parcel in Anne's hand. 'What is it? Chocolate! Oh, you darling. I thought we'd given out the last weeks ago. How did you get it?'

Chocolate was their one luxury, to be nibbled in the cold corners of the night, when faces blurred and it seemed the whole world was cocoa and cans of bully beef.

'It's from both of us. Ethel and I have been saving our ration for the past fortnight. Chocolate's bad for my spots, anyway.' Anne grinned from her seat on the bed. She was on the day shift too today. Her apron still held its morning crispness, freshly ironed by Beryl as though it had been a morning dress back home. 'Now, of course, your lovely captain will bring you a whole box of chocs and our effort will be put in the shade.'

'He's not "my captain". He's . . .' What was he, wondered Midge. Her friend?

Anne's grin grew wider. She put on a cockney accent. 'He's the bloke you're walkin' out with, that's what.'

'We haven't done any walking yet!'

'True. But you've written to him every second day for the last month. *And* you let him call you by your first name.'

'How do you —'

'I saw one of his letters. No, I didn't read it. You left it on your bed and I only saw the beginning. Darling, I'm not your aunt. Or your chaperone. What does he look like? A nice warrior Achilles? I always loved Achilles at school. Even Miss Torrens couldn't spoil him.'

Midge hesitated. 'He's . . . he's nice, Anne. He makes me think of . . . oh, things other than the war.'

'And undoubtedly you do the same for him,' said Anne drily. 'My dear, you grab it with both hands. Now, hadn't you better get dressed? His train will be here soon.'

'What shall I wear?'

'As though one had a choice — unless you've sent a wire to your aunt for more clothes in the last two days? Blue serge, grey serge, blue wool . . .'

Midge put down her grey serge and picked up the green one, the colour like the willow trees of home. 'Anne . . . do you think one day that you'll —'

'Fall in love? I'm immune,' Anne said lightly. 'When one knows one's marriage arrangements have been planned since the day one was born . . . well, it puts a crimp in any dreams of love. Every day we're here I bless the war. I'm probably the only person in the world who does. No debutante season till the war is over. No one to count one's spots. No feathers in one's hair and damned court dress. No smiling at every eligible in the stud book for little Anne. Not till my spots are gone and I can do Mummy proud at any rate. Now, darling, you go and enjoy yourself. Make hay while the sun shines and all the rest of it.'

Midge peered out through the limp curtains. 'It's raining. Drizzling, anyhow.'

'What does one make in drizzle then?' Anne sighed. 'Cocoa. Another thousand gallons of bloody cocoa.'

'Anne!'

Anne giggled. 'Wouldn't Mummy be shocked. Maybe I should try it when I go home. Give one another bloody sherry, Wilkins. It'd do you good to swear a bit.'

'I'll swear when you say "weekend".'

'Darling, that middle-class word! Mummy would have pink kittens.' Anne looked down at the small gold watch on her wrist. It had been a present from Lady George before they left. 'Darling, I don't want to hurry you, but what time did you say his train arrived?'

'Ten past eight. Oh . . .' Midge hesitated.

'Say it, darling. Damn. Bloody hell.' Anne sighed theatrically. 'You colonials. Always so proper.'

Midge grinned. 'Bloody hell then, I'm late. That satisfy you?' She slid the dress over her petticoat and reached behind to do up the buttons. Anne helped her.

'What do you plan to do with him?' she asked.

'You make it sound like I'm holding up a post office. I don't know really. Walk to the hotel with him, wait while he leaves his bag. He's only got the two days' leave. Maybe a walk along the river if this rain stops. I asked Madame if she could make us some sandwiches for a picnic.'

'*L'amour parmi les meules de foin.*'

'I beg your pardon?'

'Love among the haystacks, darling.' Anne stretched. 'To think we could be back in school now. You could be brushing up on your irregular verbs instead of thinking about irregular behaviour.'

Midge was blushing. 'Anne, I'm not —'

Anne laughed. 'Don't mind me. You know, for the first time in my life I feel free. In all the months we've been here, no one has known who I am . . . well, cared, anyhow. You've no idea what it's like to always be the Honourable Anne, to always have people's eyes on one. To know one has to behave impeccably, not let the side down, don't you know.' Her face grew serious. 'It's going to be terribly hard to go back to normal life after this.'

'Maybe the war will go on for ages — another year even,' Midge said and shivered. 'Horrible to think it might. Oh, bloody hell, it's nearly eight o'clock. I *am* late!'

The drizzle had cleared to dappled clouds as she left the hotel. It felt strange to go to the train station and not be working. For once the tiny platform was peaceful. The red geraniums glowed in the sunlight. The station master was feeding his pig behind his cottage. Even the seat outside the storeroom was empty, of soldiers and the few ordinary travellers. A small boy in ragged shorts wandered down the train track, looking for fallen lumps of coal.

Midge sat, and stretched out her legs.

The train must be late again, she thought. She shut her eyes for a moment. It was so good to sit down, to let the pain seep out of her feet for a while, to feel the sun on her face. For a moment even the distant thunder of the guns faded.

'Midge?'

She opened her eyes. It was Ethel.

'Sorry to disturb you, old thing. I just had a note from the brigadier's office. He says all hell's going to break loose here later.'

'He didn't!'

'Well, no, he sent his compliments to Miss Carryman and said he thought she might like to know that things could be busy today.'

'Another push,' said Midge slowly. 'I thought there was more noise than usual last night. I counted five dispatch riders' motorbikes before I went to sleep.'

'Look, I know you and your captain have only two days, and it's your birthday too, but do you think you could lend a hand tonight, just for a few hours?'

Midge smiled. 'If he wants to spend time with me, he can help serve cocoa. It'll be a good test of his mettle.'

'Thank you, old thing. Oh, here's the passenger train now.'

Midge peered down the track at the smoke in the distance, puffing grey and white above the trees. In a few seconds they could hear it, feel the tiny vibrations in the platform, and suddenly there it was: brakes screaming, the windows of its carriages looking blankly out at the station.

Midge frowned. Only two carriages. The ten past eight usually had six or eight, all crammed with men on leave going back home or to Paris.

One of the doors opened. She ran forward. But it was only an elderly woman in a black dress and black shawl. Midge helped her down to the platform. The woman patted her on the arm and thanked her in rapid French, too fast for Midge to understand.

She nodded quickly and said, '*Merci, madame,*' then looked at the other carriage. Its door was still shut, the platform empty. She ran down the train, peering in at the windows. Where was Gordon? Perhaps he had fallen asleep. He must have left really early to get the train . . . An old man with a newspaper looked at her curiously. Two children argued in a corner while their mother dozed, her basket on her lap. There were no other passengers.

Midge stepped back as the guard blew his whistle. The train grunted, then began to roll away.

'Midge.' It was Ethel again. 'Don't worry yourself, lass. He must have missed it. He'll be on the ten o'clock instead.'

'Yes, of course,' said Midge flatly. She shrugged. 'No point going back to the hotel. I couldn't sleep. I may as well give you a hand till then.'

'Better put an apron on your good dress then.' Ethel eyed her leaf green dress, with the white fur tipped on her shoulders.

They walked up the platform together. Suddenly Ethel said, 'Can you hear something?'

Midge listened. 'An engine. A truck or something.'

Ethel shook her head. 'Not just one truck . . .'

They ran to the courtyard as the first of an endless line of ambulances arrived.

There was no time to think. Stretcher after stretcher lined the platform, crammed side by side. Men slumped against the walls outside, their faces bandaged, their uniforms bloodstained. And still the trucks and ambulances kept coming.

No lining up for cocoa now. Once more the girls worked in strict order, Anne and Beryl handing cocoa and sandwiches to those who could walk, who had hands to hold the cup or bread, while the others knelt beside the stretchers, offering what they could.

The morning passed. No ten o'clock passenger train arrived, but another hospital train, with so many carriages that it was impossible to see the end. Red Cross nurses, army orderlies and ambulance drivers lifted stretcher after stretcher onto the train; the walking wounded helped one another hobble into the carriages.

And then the train was gone. The platform was empty. But not for long. More ambulances arrived, and trucks too, their trays lined with bloodstained hay. More men, with the blank faces of those whose world had narrowed into pain and waiting. Waiting for help. For home. For whatever tomorrow might bring . . .

The platform was full again. Even the courtyard was crammed, stretchers lying on the muddy gravel as the trucks unloaded their grim cargo and rumbled off again. And still they came . . .

Another train. The stretchers were loaded on. A lull.

Ethel was grim-faced. 'We're out of milk. Nearly out of cocoa too.'

Midge stared at her. 'We can't stop now.'

'And we won't if I have anything to do with it. These men deserve better than a pannikin of slop.' Ethel pulled off her apron. 'Here, take this. I'll be back in an hour, maybe more.'

'Where are you going?'

'I'm going to knock on every door of the village till I've got enough to feed our men properly.'

Midge watched her stride off down the station. Then she lost sight of her as another surge of ambulances arrived. Tired horses showed the whites of their eyes, terrified at the smell of blood. Stretchers were stacked four deep, tied together in a desperate effort to keep them stable, the blood from one man dripping onto those below.

Mix watery cocoa in the coppers, stir and serve. No more bread, or beef. Anne, next to her, ladling out the cocoa, tears running down her face. No time to ask why, or comfort her. When next she looked, Anne was smiling again, the endless practised smile of reassurance.

'Miss? That's the last tin of cocoa.' It was Anne's maid, Beryl.

'Just keep adding water,' Midge said. 'Any hot drink is better than none.'

'Yes, miss.'

A year ago, she would have thought that men in agony wouldn't want to drink. Now she knew that blood loss called for fluid; that shock needed warmth; that just a smile or a hand in theirs could help hold back the terror of pain in a strange country.

War, she thought, was the strangest land of all.

'Midge! Look!'

Midge followed Anne's gaze down the platform. A strange procession made its way towards them: Ethel in front, and behind her a line of women carrying pots, or saucepans, or bread or cake wrapped in cloths.

'Tell this lot where to put the stuff,' said Ethel shortly. 'I'm off to send telegrams to my da and anyone else who'll listen.'

More ambulances, more stretchers, but the food held out now, miraculously renewed as it grew low. A cart arrived with women from the next village, all carrying pots of soup.

'Miss, a drink, please. Miss . . .'

'Miss, my mate. He's hurt bad, miss.'

Nothing you could do but offer them a drink and some comfort, moving down the line of stretchers.

'No use giving Snowy none, miss. He died an hour ago.'

Midge looked down at the man's head she was cradling. His eyes were open, but his friend was right. She put his head back gently on the stretcher, and found something shoved into her hand. A mug of soup. She stared at it, dazed.

'Drink,' said Anne. She held out a sandwich too.

'I can't.'

'How long do you think we can go without food? Eat.'

Midge took the sandwich. Ate. Drank.

And more trucks came.

Ethel issued orders, her red hair moving amongst the other women. She had kept one of the coppers for soup and poured them all in together. The soups were all mostly some sort of vegetable, so it seemed to work all right.

Midge worked her way along the stretchers. Smile, she told herself. Smile. 'Would you like some soup? Let me help you . . .'

One man looked at her apologetically. 'I'm getting blood on your nice dress, miss.'

As though that mattered.

'Do you think you could manage some hot soup?'

All the while, she looked for his face on the stretchers, among the men struggling from the trucks or being carried by their friends. And with every man whose head she held as he sipped at the warm soup, she felt a moment's lifting of her heart that it was nobody she knew. But Gordon couldn't be there. He was on leave. And the trains were for the wounded. That was why he hadn't come. He was on leave so he was safe, and he would come when he could. There would be a letter, or a telegram, already waiting at the hotel. Yes, that was why she hadn't heard. He had sent a message to the hotel. She would get it as soon as there was time to stop, to breathe, to think . . .

'Miss Macpherson?'

A pair of boots, covered in mud, came to a stop by the side of the stretcher where she knelt. There was blood in the mud.

'Miss Macpherson, they said you were down here.'

She forced herself to smile at the man on the stretcher, a smile of apology and, perhaps, comfort for a second in a time of hell, before she stood up.

It was the private from the café, with hair like golden grass. The man who'd introduced her to Gordon. Harry Harrison. One arm was in a sling.

She knew what he was going to say before he spoke. She shook her head. But he spoke anyway.

'I . . . I'm sorry, miss.'

The world began to spin. She put out her hand, to find something to steady herself, and he took her arm with his good hand. He looked around for somewhere she could sit. But there was nowhere; the platform was crammed with the wounded.

'Can I help you back to your hotel, miss?' he said.

She shook her head. 'What happened?'

He hesitated. 'All leave was cancelled. He wasn't able to send you a telegram even. You should have heard him swearing — begging your pardon, miss. But he was that cut up. Said it was your birthday and everything. Then the colonel called for volunteers to cut the wire last night before the push at dawn.'

89

'But there was a moon last night.'

Even I know an enemy can see you cut barbed wire by moonlight, she thought. She remembered Tim and Dougie shooting rabbits by moonlight back home. A hunter's moon.

Harry's face was expressionless. 'Don't make any difference to the high-ups, I reckon. Moon or not.'

'How . . .' She found her voice didn't work.

He said very gently, 'It was sudden, miss. I reckon it got a big vein in his leg. He wouldn't have felt a thing, miss, he was out of it.'

'I . . . see.'

It was silly to feel like this, she thought. She had known Gordon for two months. Had met him only once. They'd exchanged sixteen letters . . . twenty . . . Perhaps, she thought vaguely, she was grieving for what might have been. The days they'd never have; the man she'd never really know. The man he might have been in years to come.

'Thank you,' she said to Harry. Suddenly she saw him for the first time. 'Your arm! And that's blood on your chest?'

'Not my blood, miss. Well, not much of it. Just some shrapnel. I've had worse in a scrap as a kiddie.' He bit his lip. 'I was with him, you see, miss. I carried him back. I thought he might make it. But there was so much blood. That's how I know he didn't suffer much,' he said again, as though anxious to make the point. 'He didn't know what hit him, miss. Didn't know a thing.'

The horror of what this man must have seen, have done,

washed over her. But she said nothing. There were no words.

'I'm sorry about the mess on my uniform, miss,' he said a bit helplessly. 'I should have changed. But I was that worried about you just waiting here, not knowing. I didn't think. And it's your birthday . . .'

The words trailed away, as though he realised what 'Happy Birthday' would sound like on this platform of blood and moaning.

It was as though reality pushed away the horror. Midge said gently, 'You must be hungry. They serve meals at our hotel.'

He shook his head. 'I hitched a ride on one of the trucks, miss. I'd better get back or I'll be charged.'

'Soup then.' She led him through the avenues of stretchers to the canteen. 'Beryl, soup for Mr Harr . . . I mean Private Harrison, please.'

She handed him a slice of apple cake. It was still warm from a village oven. He took it awkwardly, as though not sure whether to eat it. Finally he stuffed it in a pocket.

It seemed such a small, mean thing to give him. He mustn't even have slept, Midge realised. He had seen Gordon die, and worse, but he had still hurried here to give what comfort he could. And she had nothing for him but a cup of soup and a slice of someone's apple cake.

'How do you stand it?' she asked suddenly. She shook her head. 'I shouldn't have said that. A silly thing to say.'

He looked at her. His eyes were very clear despite the weariness and the mud. 'Not silly at all.' He glanced around the crowded platform. 'I go back home, miss.'

She frowned. 'I don't understand.'

'Sorry. I'm not one for expressing myself well. I just . . . well, I keep home in my mind. The hills. The trees. Even the blessed sheep. Sometimes if I can't sleep, I imagine I'm fencing. You know, digging the holes, seeing the colour of the dirt — the good rich dirt we've got on the creek flats.' He gave her a faint grin. 'By the time I get the first two posts straight I'm snoring fit to blow the roof off.' He shrugged. 'Don't say it's not hard, sometimes. Wish I had a photo. I've got one of Mum and Dad, but not one of the old place. Never thought of having one taken, I suppose.'

'I've got one of Glen Donal,' Midge said.

She reached into the bag on her belt and pulled it out. He took it. She shivered slightly as she saw his hand, the black under the nails. Was it Gordon's blood?

He was smiling now. 'You know, it could be home. Same hills. Yours are higher but, I think. That snow in the background up there? Same paddocks. Same sheep, almost.'

'That's Dougie's prize ram.'

'He looks a good 'un. Good chest on him. Look at that nose too. He knows he's an aristocrat. How many bales —' He broke off. 'Listen to us. In the middle of a bloody war — pardon my French — talking about sheep.'

He held the photo out to her.

'Keep it.' It suddenly seemed such a small thing to give him, after he had been through so much.

'I can't take your photo!'

'Please. It would mean a great deal to me if you did.' She tried to find the words. 'To know it was with you. I . . . I sometimes think I'm at home too. It would be . . . well, like sharing it with a friend.'

Suddenly she remembered the chocolate. It was in her apron pocket. She had thought she might share it with Gordon. 'Here, take this too.'

He looked down at it, embarrassed. 'Miss, there's no need.'

'There's every need!' she said fiercely. 'You were there! You helped him, tried to save him!'

'Miss, I think you need to rest. Go back to your hotel, just for a while.' He looked over at Beryl. 'She's had a shock. Can you take her home?'

'No!' Midge said. 'I'm all right. Really. I must get on here. There's so much to do.'

'I wish there was someone to look after you for a change,' he said quietly. He took the chocolate from her and held it awkwardly. Then, as someone beckoned from the station doorway, 'I'm sorry, miss. That's Johnno, me mate. He wangled me a lift. I really have to go. But you look after yourself. Promise?'

'I promise. You . . . you stay safe too.'

'I will, miss. Miss Macpherson . . . would you mind if I write to you sometimes?' Another small, tired smile. 'About sheep, maybe?'

'I'd like that,' she said softly. 'Goodbye.'

'Goodbye, miss.' And he was gone.

Chapter 7

Dear Miss Macpherson,

It was good to get your last letter. It was interesting what you said about how your father weaned lambs at two months old. Makes sense. I'll tell Dad to give it a try in my next letter home. Ours are bigger-framed merinos than yours, I think. They have to go a good way to find enough tucker sometimes, so I reckon they need to be stronger than yours. But what we gain in hardiness we lose in the fineness of the wool. I think you Kiwis have a lot to teach us about record-keeping though, and that stuff about bluestone salt licks was interesting. I've copied that out for my dad too. What does your brother think of dressing with phosphate? We haven't done it yet but Dad is thinking of giving it a go.

We were to be given a breather last week, just a one-hour parade in the morning and a football match in the afternoon at which attendance was compulsory. But the lads made it known that they didn't take to watching a ball thrown about. So the colonel gave us five hours of marching instead, just to show us Aussies he meant business. Most of these officers wouldn't know a trench if they fell in one. They've no idea what the men have gone through.

The next day he had us marching again, just for the exercise, nine hours with only a break for a quarter of an hour. The Pommy captain had a fresh horse and didn't see cause for us to have more time to look at the flowers. We marched through two villages, very narrow unsanitary streets. The farmers here don't live on their acres but all make a village together. But they seem to do a good enough job of it. We passed some cabbages as big as watermelons and some well-pruned vines in the front gardens. All of this with the noise of the guns behind us or in front of us, it was impossible to say.

Well, that is about all from me. I finally had a day's leave yesterday and got into town. Me and Johnno found a little shop where the French were Australianised enough to sell le toast et la bière instead of café françois. I also found la grande cathédrale — and six thousand sandbags all around it! You will see how my French is improving! Miss Willis who taught us back at Biscuit Creek would be impressed. Did I ever tell you Mum made me do correspondence school for a few years too? Think she hoped I'd be a teacher or something, but it never really stuck. The farm is all I ever wanted, just like you.

I hope all is going good at your canteen. They give us Anzacs medals sometimes as long as we don't cheek the officers. I reckon you girls deserve one too.

Respectfully yours,
Harry Harrison

18 September 1916

Dear Aunt Harriet,

Thank you for all your fruit cakes and please thank all your friends in the VAD group too. You should have seen the men's faces when we gave them cake as well as bully beef sandwiches!

This has been a good week. We received a trainload of other comforts to give out as well, so were able to provide socks and gloves and toffees, and some lucky men also got either a pencil or a magazine.

What they keep asking for though is soap. So if your group is able to do anything along those lines, I know so many would be very grateful. Ethel has written to her father asking for soap too, but he is doing so much for us already I am not sure that he will agree to send soap as well, especially as he does not deal in soap and may not be able to buy it cheaply. Is it rationed now, as well?

Please give my special love to Uncle Thomas, Michael, Bruce, Julia and Grace, and know that I am well and your loving niece,

Margery

It worked, Midge thought, as she held a pannikin of cocoa to the mouth of a man whose empty bleeding eye sockets she would have shrunk from a year ago. More and more these days she followed Harry's advice: shut her eyes for a brief moment, so a small part of her was suddenly at peace in the eternal world of grass and mountains. A mob of deer flowing down the hillside, the honking wild geese above the river. Even here, sometimes, a breath of snow seemed to waft, not from any French mountain but from home. White faces watched her, set by months of drabness cut by weeks of horror. But now, she was able to glimpse a ram as it sniffed at the spring ewes, or see a hare nibble at the seedlings, its whiskers twitching.

Sometimes she thought of Private Harrison; wondered if he too was watching the same things, remembering the distant worlds they shared, so different and so much the same.

It was enough, mostly, to get her through her shift.

Midge sat at the narrow dressing table in the room at the hotel and pulled her brush through her hair and pinned it up again into its sensible bun. Was that really her, she wondered, that white-faced girl in the mirror?

I'm tired, she thought.

Not just tired from a year without enough sleep, of trying to nap through the daytime noises as they had today, but tired of unvarying routine, of gaslit nights and stretchers, or daylight and fresh-cheeked young men with little idea what they were going into. Winter was coming, their second in the canteen. Frostbite cases again soon, she thought, as well as wounds.

It was strange to look back at the schoolgirls they'd been only eighteen months before, longing for excitement, to be part of it all, worried that the war would be over before they got to it. It had never occurred to her that the romance would turn into an aching repetition of cutting and stirring, serving and unloading.

A year ago, the feeling of being indispensable had lent her energy. But they had more volunteers these days: friends from school, nieces or granddaughters of Aunt Harriet's friends, or Lady George's.

What would she do if she left here, even for a holiday? Aunt Harriet, for all her kindness, was still mostly a stranger. Auntie Lallie was busy at her casualty station.

If Ethel or Anne decided to visit back home she could go with them. But she would be a stranger there too. And Ethel and her genius for organising *was* essential. She'd been up before the others this afternoon, despite the hours they had put in the previous night, to send another host of telegrams appealing for more donations for 'my boys'.

And Anne . . . Midge glanced over to where Anne was spreading a thick white paste on her face. Anne showed no signs of wanting to go home.

'What is that stuff?' Midge wrinkled her nose. 'It stinks.'

Anne looked up from her silver-backed hand mirror. 'Puréed garlic.'

'Garlic!'

'Madame says garlic is splendid for spots. She spread

garlic on her daughter's spots and her daughter was married within the year.'

'To the fat man who's a prisoner in Germany?'

'Well, he probably isn't fat now he's a prisoner of war. And that's not the point, darling. The point is that finally one is almost totally, entirely spot free! Mummy is going to be thrilled. A daughter she can present at court with pride. Of course Mummy is far too busy to worry about that sort of thing now. But still . . .'

'Anne . . .' Midge hesitated. 'You're not thinking of going home?' Life would be unendurable without Anne, she thought. Ethel was preoccupied, and the others . . . well, they weren't Anne.

Anne looked at her in surprise. 'Of course not, darling.' She laughed and put her mirror down. 'One didn't come to France just for a spot cure, after all. Come on. Madame promised an omelette yesterday.'

'An omelette! Where did she get the eggs?'

'She's been giving the hotel's dishwater to the widow Bodin for her pigs. And in return Madame gets six eggs a day, of which we are to get two in return for being properly sympathetic about Madame's bunions and the difficulty of getting good endives with the Boche in Belgium.'

'She's not complaining about the endives again?'

'She is. "The best endives come from Belgium, *mademoiselle*, as everybody knows . . ." '

After the omelette was duly eaten, accompanied by thin chicory coffee and a slice each of the heavy sour bread that was all civilians in France could get these days, they made their way across the road and through the station courtyard to the platform, carrying the clean aprons that Madame's brother's sister-in-law washed and starched and ironed each day. The shadows were already turning into darkness; the lamplighter just starting his round through the town.

The platform was empty, apart from the station master's wife, slowly brushing the cobwebs from the office windows, and a cat, curled up as though war, trains and the imminent invasion of her territory by hungry soldiers was beyond all possibility.

Ethel was at the canteen already, instructing one of their new volunteers in the art of making one loaf of bread stretch into thirty sandwiches. Ethel looked different from a year ago, thought Midge, thinner, every movement quick and decisive as though there was no time to waste a single gesture.

'Haven't you sliced bread before, lass?' she was saying patiently to the new helper. 'You wet the bread saw first, then you slice from one side, then turn the loaf over and cut from the other side. Otherwise you end up with doorstops, all thicky one side and thinny the other. No, there's no butter. This isn't the Ritz and we ran out of marge last week.'

'Darling, did you have any breakfast?' Anne asked.

Ethel looked up. 'Breakfast? I can't remember. Do you know those blighters forgot to drop off our powdered milk? We'll have to make do with what we've got — half-strength, or quarter-strength if there's a rush.'

'Eat,' said Anne firmly. 'Madame sent you a ham roll.'

Ethel took the roll and bit into it absently. 'You remembered the aprons?'

'Darling, I always remember the aprons. Now, stop fussing and eat your nice roll — well, your quite nasty roll come to think of it.'

Midge fastened her apron and let the talk wash over her. How many nights like this had they lived now?

Slowly the platform began to fill up with stretcher cases and wounded men. The next hospital train was due in an hour.

It looked like being an easy night, Midge decided. The vehicles in the courtyard were just the usual ambulances, with no trucks or carts roped in to help. No push or major battle at the moment, then. Just the usual stretcher cases that needed to be shipped to England or Paris: men unlucky enough to be caught by stray shrapnel or unwary enough to show their heads above their trench; men with trench foot; the shell-shock cases the army insisted on calling 'neurasthenia', denying any possibility that the war itself might be to blame for the screams and terrors.

'Wuff grff?'

Midge looked up as a familiar doggy figure bounded through the men on the platform. Dolores sat in front of her expectantly, her tail wagging. She had put on weight the last few months, partly from begged cocoa, but also from the crusts the men fed her. No matter how hungry they were, it seemed that a crust was a small price to pay for the familiar homelike smell of dog and a large wet lick across the chin.

'You're going to need a corset if you get any fatter,' Midge told her. She reached for the bowl they kept for Dolores these days, and filled it with cocoa. At least it kept the big dog from sticking her nose in the men's pannikins.

Down at the other end of the station Jumbo accompanied a small mob of men onto the platform, their faces covered in damp cloths. Jumbo, Slogger and Boadicea must be picking up gas cases tonight, Midge thought. Mustard gas caused temporary blindness; the only relief was watersoaked bandages over the eyes till the men could get better help in England.

Jumbo settled her men down against the waiting room wall, then reappeared with Slogger, each carrying one end of a stretcher. The girls put the stretcher down by the other men. Jumbo knelt and smiled and gestured up at the canteen, obviously asking if the men would like a drink. Midge nodded to their new assistant.

'Better start taking trays down the platform — the stretcher cases can't come and get it, and the men who've been gassed can't see. They may need you to hold their pannikins while they drink too. No need to hurry. Just let them take their time.'

The girl nodded. Her name was Lena, Midge remembered — there were now so many volunteers it was hard to keep them straight. She had five brothers, three in Flanders, two still young enough to stay at home.

'Hello, old thing.' Slogger's voice sounded flat and strained.

Midge held out a pannikin of cocoa. 'Here. You look like you could do with it.'

'Thanks.' Slogger reached out, then looked on helplessly as the pannikin slid from her fingers. The hot cocoa splashed across Midge's apron.

'Oh bloody hell!' The girl suddenly began to cry. 'I'm sorry. I'm sorry, I just can't help it.'

Midge glanced down at Slogger's hands, then stared. Even by the dim lantern light she could see they were red and oozing pus.

Jumbo ran up to the counter. 'Darling, I told you your hands were too bad to go out tonight.'

The tears turned to hiccups as Slogger tried to swallow the sobs, then giggles as Dolores started to lick up the muddy dregs of cocoa. 'They're not as bad as they look. Well, all right, they are. Trouble is, one's hands are always wet and raw, and we're always handling infected wounds.'

'How can you drive like that?' Midge asked.

'I can't. Except one has to keep going, doesn't one?'

Midge stared — at the hands; at the face, white and pinched with cold and exhaustion. 'Can't you do the driving?' she asked Jumbo.

'Me?' Jumbo shook her head. 'Never learned.' She looked at Slogger helplessly. 'If Slogger can't drive that puts me and Boadicea out of action too. We don't have any spare drivers at all at the moment.'

Midge came to a decision. 'I can drive.'

'You can?' Slogger looked at her suspiciously, despite the pain and exhaustion. 'Are you sure? Really drive?'

'Yes. I used to drive all the time back home. In New Zealand.'

Slogger hesitated, obviously unwilling to trust her beloved Boadicea to a novice. 'Yes, but these roads — they're not roads at all mostly. There's mud and ruts and —'

Midge laughed. 'I used to drive our Ford across the paddocks to pick up a sick sheep! And you should see the tracks about Glen Donal after the rain. I remember when the causeway was washed out for weeks and . . . well, anyway. I can drive. And I'll take over if you like.'

Slogger looked half relieved, half anxious, despite her pain. 'You can be spared here?'

Midge nodded. 'I'll go and fix it with Ethel,' she said quietly. 'You sit down. And then I'll drive you home.'

Chapter 8

(undated)
Glen Donal
New Zealand

Dear Miss Margery,

I take up my pen to write to you because Campbell isn't one for writing much and besides he was out late last night with the lambs we being short-handed with so many men away. But you aren't to worry, nor Mr Dougie nor Master Tim neither, as all is good here, which is what Campbell wanted me to let you know.

You will be glad to hear I have been giving your poor mother's silver a good polish regular, and the curtains closed in the front rooms so the carpets and the furniture covers won't fade while you are away. I was going to send scones because your father always said I had the lightest hand with scones in the South Island but Mrs Maxwell says that her Angus says scones are like rocks by the time they get to him and the same goes for sponge cakes. So I have sent you each a fruit cake and some of my special tablet. I sent some to Master Tim too in hopes that wherever he is it may find him.

Well Miss Margery I think that is all — just to let you know that you three are in our prayers every night and morning and Campbell says to tell Mr Dougie and Master Tim that he is taking good care of the place and it will all be waiting for them just as when they left it.

Yours respectfully and
with our love,
Mrs Maggie Campbell

4 October 1916

My dear niece,

As you will see, I have been transferred to No 15 Casualty Station. It is only a day's drive from your canteen and I trust that before long I will be able to take a day's leave and see you. At the moment though there is no leave for anyone. We are terribly understaffed, as always. It breaks my heart sometimes to refuse the girls their half-day off a week. But even that is impossible with the number of casualties we are getting.

I am giving this to an officer who will be passing your canteen on his way home. His wound did not appear serious at first, but it seems that the nerves of his hand have been damaged as he is

unable to use it. Perhaps they will be able to fix it in England —
but I very much hope for his sake and his family's that it proves
stubborn and that he is transferred to lighter duties. But this way
at least the censor will not be able to make his usual scribbles over
my address!

I heard from Dougie last week, though the letter must have
taken many weeks to reach me.

I have also been asking if any of the men who were at Gallipoli
have any knowledge of Tim, as you requested. I did find one who
said he knew him, a Corporal Mather. I do not want to get your
hopes up, my dear, as the poor chap was very feeble and I do not
put much trust in anything he might remember. But he seemed to
think he saw Tim with a group of four men taken as prisoners of
war by a Turkish captain.

I am afraid I have no time to write more. Things are so very
strained here. I will give you more details when I see you next.
But please, please do not put too much reliance on this, as I think
it likely that poor Corporal Mather was simply trying to remember
anything to please me.

Your loving aunt,
Sister Eulalie Macpherson

~❦~

Midge slid across the leather seat, behind Boadicea's
steering wheel. Dolores bounded happily over her, then
settled down on Slogger's and Jumbo's feet.

How much did she really remember about managing a
car, Midge wondered. And no matter what she had assured

Slogger, driving an ambulance along the dark and rutted roads would be different from puttering across the village in the Station Master's car.

Almost without thinking her hands turned the ignition key, then pushed 'spark' to up and 'gas' to down, and turned the battery switch to 'bat'. The battery began to buzz. Contact! She quickly slid out of the driver's seat and round to the front of the car and grabbed the crank handle, pushed in and brought it up, then grabbed the radiator wire and pulled till she could hear the familar sound of gas being pulled into the engine. She let go of the wire. Now around and around with the crank handle . . .

The engine coughed twice, then burst into life. She raced back to the driver's seat, adjusted 'spark' and 'gas', and threw the switch over to 'magneto'.

The engine hummed.

Jumbo grinned. Her freckles danced across her nose. 'I see you and Mr Ford are well acquainted.' The smile slipped as she glanced at Slogger. The girl's face was damp with sweat. 'Down, Dolores! Come on. We'd better go.'

It was strange driving again. The rumble of the engine, the vibration so different from a train. The headlights were pools of light cutting through the darkness, illuminating scenes suddenly then leaving them behind. Hedges, the ghostly outline of a ruined tank, more hedges, then suddenly a line of men in greatcoats, boots and gas masks like a tribe of insane grey grasshoppers.

Guns spat and growled somewhere in the night, closer and louder than they'd been at the railway station.

'That's the turn-off to our headquarters at the chateau ahead,' said Jumbo. She turned to Slogger. 'We'll drop you off first before we do another pick-up.'

'I'm fine,' said Slogger tightly.

'No, you aren't.' Jumbo flinched slightly as Midge clashed the gears.

'Sorry. I'm out of practice.'

'You're doing well. It's a talent,' said Jumbo lightly, her tone contrasting with the concern on her face as she looked at Slogger. 'I don't suppose I'll ever get the skill.'

Boadicea trundled along the chateau's driveway. It was wide and had evidently once been well gravelled, though now the ruts were appearing and the gardens on either side were ragged. Midge drew up outside the wide stairs leading to the front door.

Jumbo slid out the other door. Dolores bounded out happily and galloped up the chateau steps. 'Come on, old thing,' she said to Slogger. 'You wait here,' she added to Midge. 'Keep the engine going. I won't be long.'

The two girls followed Dolores.

Ten minutes later Jumbo ran back down the stairs, Dolores prancing at her side.

Midge leaned over and opened the door for them. 'How is she?'

Jumbo shrugged as Midge let in the clutch. 'Bad. She'll have to go back to England. There's no way her hands can be treated here — we just don't have the extra staff to look after her. Look here, do you think you can stay on for a while as driver? The last girl whose hands went septic was away three months. I'd hate to keep old Boadicea out of the action for that long.'

Midge felt her heart leap. An ambulance meant travelling, a greater chance to ask questions. A change.

'Yes. I'd love to.'

'You won't be so keen after a few days. And nights,' said Jumbo drily.

Midge glanced at her. 'Then why don't you head back to England with Slogger?'

Jumbo shrugged. 'Can't let Boadicea down,' she said lightly. 'The old girl was wasted as a butcher's truck. The clearing station is to the right,' she added. 'One more lot for us tonight, I think. Then we'll see about getting you digs at the chateau.'

The word 'chateau' had conjured grandness, gilt furniture perhaps, and giant quiet rooms.

The reality was different.

An entrance hall more like a waiting room, with desks and an army-style telephone. A middle-aged woman with salt-and-pepper hair took down her name, address and next of kin and qualifications — none; but 'Captain Nancy' didn't seem to mind.

'Age?'

Midge hesitated. 'Twenty-three.'

Captain Nancy smiled. 'Amazing how many girls just happen to be twenty-three. Don't worry, my dear. You don't have to be twenty-three to serve with us. We're a private outfit. It doesn't matter how old you are, as long as you can do the job. Come on, I'll show you to your room. Down, Dolores! Jumbo, take the dratted beast down to the kitchens, will you?'

A staircase that curved into a ceiling of faded murals: archangels and trumpets and a forest of vines behind; another staircase and then another, each one narrower as they climbed.

'Convalescent senior officers on the first floor,' said Captain Nancy. 'They're in purple silk pyjamas. Convalescent junior officers on floor three, in lilac —'

'Silk pyjamas?'

'The Duchess's idea. To keep up morale. We're supposed to dress formally at night too. Do you have an evening dress?'

Midge shook her head.

Captain Nancy smiled. 'Most of the ambulance staff don't either. Just means you'll take your meals in the staff quarters, not the main hall with the Duchess and officers. Here we are, the attic . . . not as bad as it sounds. I've put you in with Slogger and Jumbo. There's a trundle bed for tonight, but you can use Slogger's bed tomorrow. She's in the infirmary now but she'll be up to get her things so best leave it for tonight. Baths are down in the washhouse in the courtyard — there's a sign out the front. Hot water Tuesdays and Saturdays, but if you get a dose of the creatures just say the word and Cook'll heat you up a tub. Lice,' she added, at Midge's confused look. 'Most of the men are crawling with them. The casualty stations mostly clean them up, but if they're sent straight on without treatment they can be pretty whiffy. Best to strip off and scrub before you spread them to the rest of us, and put your clothes out for boiling and a hot iron. Which reminds me, you'll need a uniform — report downstairs at 7 a.m. Lacey will be on duty then, and can show you the ropes. We do pick-ups from several stations — depends on what's needed. Do you know your way round here at all?'

Midge shook her head.

'Never mind. You'll pick it up. Chamberpot under the bed — we each empty our own, Jumbo will show you where. Candles and matches on the dresser. No fires up here and no more blankets, I'm afraid, so if you're cold just sleep in all your clothes. That's what most of the girls do. Any other questions?'

'Does Dolores sleep up here too?'

Captain Nancy grinned. 'She sleeps by the fire in the kitchen. That dog's no fool. Sleep well then.' She hesitated. 'You'll find it hard at first. All the girls do. Just remember, a good cry does wonders. Don't bottle things up either. We're a fine crew here. No matter what you've seen or gone through you'll find the others will stand by you. Goodnight, my dear.'

Midge opened the door. The room was small, the wallpaper faded and curling at one corner, the low roof sloping over the two small beds.

She pulled the trundle out from under the bed by the window. It was already made up: the sheets, thin patched linen; the blankets thin and patched as well.

She wondered what the convalescent officers' rooms were like, as they slept in their purple silk pyjamas.

And then she slept as well.

Chapter 9

SOMEWHERE IN FRANCE

1 October 1916

Dear Miss Macpherson,

I hope you are well, and your new job isn't too much for you. But I think you are the sort of person who wouldn't shirk whatever came your way.

We've just come back from up at the front again. My word it was crook. Exactly the same trench we were in last time; same mud, same dead trees only a bit deader if you take my meaning.

I saw one of the new 'tank' things a few days ago. They call them 'motor monsters' and my word that's the right name for them. We took a couple of Fritz prisoners yesterday and one of them could speak a bit of English. He kept saying 'Germany is kaput' so I think they have really got the wind up.

We've been in a right pickle here and no mistake. No, not from Fritz but because Johnno has lost his teeth. Maybe you remember Johnno? Anyhow they were a fine set of teeth. He only got them just before we sailed. But the silly blighter took them out when we were doing bayonet practice and now he can't find them. Well, he says some blighter pinched them but I can't see it myself.

He can manage without them now, especially as the food parcels from home have been pretty good. But once we go up to the front again he'll be done for as you need a good pair of teeth to eat the biscuit which is about all they give us to eat. Most times there isn't even any tea to soften the biscuits in. One poor bloke was nearly starving when he got back last time — his teeth broke when one of the dugouts collapsed. He said he'd rather have lost a toe than his teeth!

It's funny to think we are going into winter, while at home the new grass will just be starting and there'd be more lambs than you could poke a stick at. Dad says the lambing rate has been good this year — lots of twins, though the dingos have been a problem, what with so many men away. I told him how big Glen Donal was and he was just amazed. He thought New Zealand was all little farms, not great big spreads like yours.

What do you think of all this talk about conscription in Australia? I reckon it should be left to those who want to come and they can tell that to old Billy Hughes with my love. I tell you what, I wouldn't want a younger brother of mine coming over here, not now. I still think that the cause is right, don't get me wrong. But the English generals don't care how many of us they send to die. We're just numbers on a map to them. I hope I haven't offended you, Miss Macpherson. But a lot of the men feel much the same as I do. We have been fighting back and forth over the same bit of ground for so long. How many men can die for a couple of miles of mud?

There is one more bit of news I am leaving till last, but it doesn't mean much, just that all the better blokes are gone! But I can sign myself now,

Yours respectfully,
Corporal Harrison

10 October 1916

Dear Corporal Harrison,

I hope you are well. It is wonderful about your promotion. Your family must be so proud!

I am starting to get used to being here. The work is pretty heavy. Mostly we pick up stretcher cases from the casualty clearing centres, not the battlefield aid stations. The orderlies are supposed to load the stretchers for us. But there are never enough orderlies, and anyway Jumbo and I can manage by ourselves. Jumbo's real name is Augusta, by the way. Her father is vicar of Buttermere-in-the-Marsh and a noted classics scholar. Jumbo passed the Oxford entrance exam, but gave up her place to work here. She has done her VAD exams and is teaching me a lot.

We work eighteen hours a day sometimes, but other times we can even have a morning or afternoon off, as long as we stay on call. Most of us spend the time in the kitchen where it's warm, doing our mending or writing letters, but some of the girls are fiends for card games.

Everyone goes to bed or gets up at the strangest times, depending on where we are needed. But I suppose that is something you are all quite used to! And after a year at the canteen I don't mind having breakfast in the afternoon any more.

The kitchens here are like a giant cave — it takes ten minutes just to go from one end to the other! The ceiling is low like a cave too, and there are flagstones on the floor. All it needs are some small dogs to turn the spits in the fireplace (NOT Dolores — she'd eat the dinner), though these days there is a big coal range there instead of a roasting ox.

The cooks keep a big pot of coffee on the stove all the time for us ambulance staff, and there are plates of what passes for bread these days always on the sideboard. It's made of ground acorns and bran with a touch of potato, I think, with a scrape of oily white margarine. Or we can have rat stew any time of day or night instead.

I don't think it really is rat — the small bones look more like rabbit. But I wouldn't put anything past these cooks. The stuff they serve up in the dining room for the officers and 'ladies' — the Duchess's friends who help look after the convalescents — is quite different. They have silver cutlery up there — great big heavy old stuff, I've seen it. The Duchess brought over two of her gamekeepers to shoot wild boar — it's illegal in wartime to shoot other game in France, but the boar do too much damage to leave. Wine is brought up from the cellar every night. There is even a small flock of sheep in one of the fields to provide fresh meat. I go and visit them when things get too bad, just to say hello.

I like all the other drivers. The girls and women all live in the chateau, up in the attics like me. The men live out in what used to be the stables. The other drivers and crew are all older than me, but very friendly. They all have brothers in the army, except for Lacey. She was married to a lieutenant in the Guards but he was killed a week after their wedding, so she came here.

The girls were a bit hard to understand at first. They all have nicknames and they call their ambulances by a pet name too. So when someone says 'I'm just going to have a chat to Grunter', it might mean they're going to see their best friend or that they're planning to give the engine an overhaul. Meals are called 'duff' or 'giving a curtsey to the rodents' and going to sleep is called 'toddling off to the attics' because that is where most of us have quarters. It's a bit like being back at school in a way. There are lots of practical jokes too. But it really does help to keep laughing.

We're finally formally attached to the Red Cross but our unit is still run pretty independently. Most of the running costs are met by the Duchess herself, with donations from her friends in England. A few of the staff get small wages, especially the doctors and registered nurses. But the rest of us survive on allowances from our families, except for Kanga. She was a nursing sister in Sydney. She paid her way over here from her savings and really finds it hard going. But the other girls make sure they share any chocolates and things like that with her, and replace her worn-out shoes with: 'These old things my sister sent; darling, they pinch my toes terribly, CAN you use them?'

Nearly all the patients here are 'ambulatory' — able to walk around the gardens with the 'ladies'. They get to dance to the gramophone in one of the reception rooms too. (Not the ballroom

— that is fitted out as a surgery.) According to the Duchess, dancing is SO good for morale.

I've only met her once. She is striking — lots of wild red hair and white arms with lots of bracelets and the most beautiful clothes. She always has a couple of her dogs with her, even when she visits the wards in one of the hospitals. But she is away most of the time, as she is opening a big convalescent centre in Flanders. And thank goodness she has taken Dolores with her! The last time I took her out she had an argument with a poodle (Dolores won). She kept getting fleas, too — and worse.

Well, I think that is all from me now. There's been a call for Leggy and Woogles so I think Jumbo and I will be called out next. I'm going to be sad to leave here when Slogger gets back, in spite of the hard work.

With best wishes,
Midge Macpherson

P.S. They call me Midget!

~✥~

5 NOVEMBER 1916

Midge ran up the kitchen stairs after Jumbo, taking care not to slip. The autumn afternoon light was dim and the stairs were stone. More than one tired girl had injured herself on their slickness.

Captain Nancy sat at her desk in the entrance hall. Did she ever sleep, wondered Midge. She gave the girls a tired nod. 'Usual station. Fast as you can. Gas cases,' she added shortly, handing Midge a rough map.

The gas cases were the worst. Mustard gas meant blindness, and burnt lungs and skin. Phosgene gas was even worse; a foul yellow liquid bubbled from the men's rotting lungs till they died. Men mostly suffered their wounds silently. But the gas cases screamed.

Jumbo bit her lip. 'Mustard or phosgene?'

Captain Nancy shrugged. 'You'll find out when you get there.'

Boadicea was in the courtyard, ready to go. (Midge's last task before bed was to check her oil and petrol and cover her bonnet with a rug.) Jumbo cranked while Midge pressed the starter. When the engine turned over, she ran around to the passenger's seat and climbed in.

The grey skies grew lower as they drove along the muddy road at a steady twenty miles an hour. By the time they reached the cluster of tents that was the casualty station the mist hung just above the trees.

Guns grumbled in the distance, punctuated by the whine of rockets. They sounded closer than they had yesterday. But sound travelled further in the mist, thought Midge. Probably the battle lines were no closer really than they had been before.

Midge shivered as she drew up behind a horse-drawn ambulance — slowly, so she didn't startle the horse. If only the Duchess had issued her drivers with thick sheepskin coats like the regular ambulance drivers had, instead of lady-like capes and cloaks. She watched as the stretchers were loaded onto the ambulance in front, then hopped out to help Jumbo with the stretchers destined for Boadicea. They could only fit two today, instead of four. Gas cases needed a tent of dampened sheets above them; bedclothes or even bandages would stick to their burnt skin.

Both men were unconscious, to Midge's relief, either from pain or chloroform. She and Jumbo secured the stretchers, both marked with the red line that meant 'priority', then Jumbo climbed in next to them.

'Go easy, old girl,' she warned.

Midge nodded. Any jolting would be agony once the men regained consciousness. But it was hard to keep Boadicea steady on the rutted roads. Now to get them to the hospital train before they came to.

Two hours and three flat tyres later, her arms ached from the awkward hand pump. Her hands were numb with cold — except for the blister on her thumb.

Jumbo peered out of the back of the ambulance. 'How are you going?'

Midge gritted her teeth as the tyre expanded to its full size and sat itself back on the seat of the rim. 'Nearly there. Every dratted horse that used this road in the last hundred years must have dropped a nail.'

Jumbo spoke softly. 'I think we need to hurry. One of them doesn't look so good.'

'Oh, heck. I'll do my best.'

Surely nothing else could go wrong tonight, she thought. The mist drifted down as she pumped the crank again. Not the thick yellow peasoupers she had known at her aunt's, but a grey mist that curled like smoke between the branches. Darkness gathered around them as Boadicea rumbled forward again towards the station and the hospital train. One mile, two . . .

Suddenly the headlights failed. Midge braked again.

Jumbo called from the back. 'What is it?'

'I don't believe it! The headlights have gone now. The damp must have spoiled the carbide.'

'All Greek to me, Midget.'

'The carbide fuels the lights. Jumbo, I'm sorry, I can't drive without lights. You'll have to walk in front with the lantern.'

She expected Jumbo to object. But instead there was the sound of her sensible shoes hitting the roadway, then the feeble gleam of light in the fog in front of them.

'I'll go as fast as I can,' she said. 'Just try not to run me down.'

'I won't,' Midge promised.

Boadicea crept along the road. At last a light struggled through the darkness — the first of the village houses. Midge suddenly realised her hands were trembling with tension. But not far now to the station. She glanced down at the watch pinned to her cape. The men would make the midnight hospital train.

If they were still alive.

They were. One was conscious, muttering and shuddering beneath his tent. The other's breath came in long hoarse pants.

She wanted to ask Jumbo, 'Do you think they'll make it?' But the men might hear. Midge forced the smile onto her face, just in case they glimpsed her from their tents.

Someone called from an ambulance on the other side of the station courtyard. 'Cooee! Jumbo, old girl, could you lend a hand?'

It was Kanga. Jumbo ran over, then hurried back to Midge. 'Kanga's got a shell-shock case in with her others. Poor chap tried to throw himself out back there. Shrapnel wounds too. Must have shipped him before they realised he was out of it. Can you cope without me? Don't think Kanga and Spangles can manage alone. He's upsetting the others.'

Midge nodded. The shell-shock cases were supposed to travel by themselves, with a male orderly. Sometimes the men were quiet, staring out at nothing. But other times they attacked anyone nearby — or themselves.

'I'll ask one of the girls at the canteen to give me a hand with these,' she said.

'Thanks, old thing. Look, I'll head back with the others if you want to chew the fat with your friends for a few minutes. I'll meet you back at the casualty station.'

'Midge!'

Midge grinned. Anne wore her usual skirt and fitted jacket under her long apron. She looked taller, and thinner. But it suited her. And her skin was . . .

'Still spotless, darling,' said Anne happily. She looked around the platform. 'No Horrid Hound with you today?'

Midge raised her voice as the train clattered into the station. 'In Belgium, thank goodness.'

'As if poor Belgium didn't have enough to cope with! The Boche and Dolores too!'

'Look, could you give me a hand with the stretchers?'

'Of course, darling. It's going to be a quiet night once this lot are gone — unless you've heard otherwise?'

'No big push on that I know of. Oh, it's good to see you!'

'You too! Do you have time to come back to the hotel? I'm sure Madame would love to make you one of her omelettes.'

Midge shook her head regretfully. 'I need to do another run tonight for the morning train. Damn and hell . . .' She gazed across the courtyard, but Kanga and Spangles' van had left.

'Darling, you are swearing wonderfully! One is quite, quite proud of you.'

'No, really, I've just realised. My headlights went and Jumbo's driven off with Kanga. We only made it because she walked in front with a lantern. I'm stuck here till the fog lifts. Or morning. Damn, damn, damn.'

'I don't suppose it's all that hard to carry a lantern,' said Anne drily. 'I suppose one can get a lift back tomorrow?'

'Easily. But, Anne, it'll take hours to get back to the casualty station. That's three hours' walking, at least. And it's cold. And wet. And —'

'And we can enjoy sprightly conversation as we go, yelling to each over the engine noise. No, really, darling, I'm glad to help.'

Midge hugged her quickly. 'You are an utter, utter brick. Come on, we'd better unload my poor chaps before the train goes without them.'

Midge watched Anne trudge along the road, the mist like flour sifting about her head. Boadicea's engine grumbled. She didn't like low gear. Somewhere across the fields the guns rumbled too. They *were* closer, Midge thought suddenly. One or both of the armies must have decided to make a move.

Trucks passed them coming the other way, their headlights vanishing too quickly to be much use. A rocket screamed across the night and then exploded somewhere in the darkness, so strong the windscreen rattled.

What was happening out there, wondered Midge.

The fog thinned, and finally vanished, leaving a moon sailing like an orange above the fields. A hunter's moon, she thought involuntarily, remembering the night Gordon died. The sort of night when officers safe in their dugouts ordered men to creep across no-man's-land with wire cutters, trying to slip through the barbed-wire entanglements to surprise the enemy.

'Anne?'

Anne's voice floated back. 'Yes, darling?'

'I think I can see enough by moonlight now if we go slowly.'

'Thank goodness. Any slower and all the snails in France would have overtaken us. And one's feet are —' She stopped. 'What's that noise?' she added sharply.

'Aircraft.'

'Ours or theirs?'

'Don't know. Blow the lantern out. Now!'

Midge gazed around at the shadowed fields. Surely there was somewhere they could shelter? Never a ditch when you needed one.

The aircraft was almost above them now. Midge could just make out the markings beneath the wings.

Enemy.

She started to scramble out of the car. Suddenly she knew what animals must feel: the terror of the moonlight that showed up hunted things.

The shock wave hit her before her feet touched the ground, pushing her back onto the seat. She heard Anne scream, from shock or pain she didn't know. The world went black as debris rained down onto the windscreen. Dimly she heard the plane's engine die away.

Had the pilot tried to hit them? Or was the plane damaged, trying to get rid of its explosive cargo before it ditched? But what mattered was it had missed. Boadicea was safe. And her, and Anne . . .

'Anne? Anne, are you all right?'

No answer.

Midge peered into the moonlit shadows. 'Anne! Speak to me!'

'I'm all right.' Anne's voice was faint.

'Are you sure?'

Midge struggled from the truck. Boadicea's windscreen was cracked, she noticed vaguely. There were new scratches on her paint.

'Where are you?'

'Here.' The voice was coming from just beyond the bonnet. 'Darling, it's cold. Cold and damp. Is it raining?'

'No . . . Anne, I can't see you —'

Midge stopped as something rose from the road in front of her. Something black. But it wasn't black. It was blood.

Anne put a hand on Boadicea's bonnet, as though to steady herself. 'I'm wet,' she complained faintly.

Midge stared, speechless, at the ruin of Anne's face.

Chapter 10

Dearest Midge,

Well, one's home and surviving. Just. They got all the shrapnel out except a little behind my ear. A souvenir, so to speak, like those hideous Toby jugs that say 'A Present from Bournemouth'. The doctor said you probably saved my life. Just now one isn't quite able to be glad that it's been saved. Does that sound too, too ungrateful?

Everyone is being very tactful. My old room is full of amputees but Mummy settled me in the old tower. One needs two good legs and sound wind to climb up to the old tower. But at least one can be quiet there.

Mummy has put me to nursing the burns cases down in the ballroom. I think she decided that they were so used to grotesqueries they wouldn't be shocked by my face. One would think they'd rather see a classic English rose complexion that would remind them of what life was once and might be again, not a mirror of what they face themselves. But the men are very kind, and very grateful for any kindness done for them.

Wilkins, our old butler, feels it worst. He nearly cried when he first saw the scars. Well, he did cry, but being Wilkins he couldn't wipe the tears so they just trickled down his nose. I try to keep out of his way so I don't upset him too much.

It's funny, I just don't care about anything any more. The revolt in Russia and the win at Gaza and the poor people sunk in that hospital ship — I make all the right noises at the breakfast table. But the war has just gone on too long. Or I've gone on too long. What use am I anyhow? No, don't mind me. I am destined to be 'good old Auntie Anne, a rock to her nieces and nephews'. Unless this war goes on forever and gets them too.

Don't mind me. I've just got the pip, that's all.

Well, that's all now, my dear. Keep the cocoa pouring and all that now that Slogger is coming back to reclaim her beloved Boadicea.

Your loving friend,
Anne

Slogger ran an affectionate hand down the dusty side of Boadicea. 'You've looked after the old girl then?' Her fingers were still red and shiny with scar tissue, but at least the hand no longer oozed pus.

'She's done us proud.'

Midge was surprised to realise how much she'd miss driving the ambulance. Slogger had been supposed to go on holiday with her family in Scotland, and hadn't been due back for another fortnight. But 'Three months of playing the dutiful daughter was two months too many,' Slogger had said. 'And when Mother started telling me "how lovely you look, dear, now your hair is longer" — well, that was the last straw. A girl can stand just so much tea and scones and bandage-rolling.'

So now Slogger was back, and her driving job was gone, thought Midge, as she wandered from the courtyard into the entrance hall office. She needed to give the uniform back. And send a telegram to Ethel, to make sure there was a bed for her at the hotel and a place on the canteen roster again. The trees in the courtyard were covered in green. Spring was here.

It would have been good to stay. Each ambulance journey might be a short trip into hell, but it was also a slap in the face for the devil. The ambulances and their drivers brought a glimpse of hope and comfort into a world of mud and death.

How could she ever have thought war glorious — that necessary battle against the Hun — back in those impossibly far-off days at school? Midge wearily tucked strands of hair back into her bun.

Captain Nancy was on the phone. She held up a finger to indicate she'd only be a minute. 'No, I'm sorry, sir. Yes, sir, I do realise. But we just don't have any spare drivers. Yes, sir. No, sir. No, I can't take a driver off one of the ambulances. Yes, I do know who you are, sir, but I just don't have a driver free . . .'

'I'm free,' said Midge. 'Slogger got a lift back with Dimples and Char ten minutes ago.'

Suddenly she couldn't face going back to the canteen again, having her life bounded night after day by the hundred yards of hotel, station and its courtyard. It was spring! At least in the ambulance you got to drive through the fields, see trees and hills.

'Excuse me, sir.' Captain Nancy put her hand over the mouthpiece. 'Believe me, ducky,' she said, 'you *don't* want this job.'

'What is it?'

'Driving Colonel Mannix over to Number 15 Casualty Station. He's going to inspect the medical facilities down there. His regular driver's sick.'

'Number 15? My aunt's down there!'

'The nursing sister? Gawd help her if she's under Colonel M's command. He can very well get one of his men to drive, you know. He's one of the wandering hand brigade.' The phone emitted a tinny yapping. Captain Nancy sighed. 'On your head be it. But don't say I didn't warn you, ducky.' She uncovered the mouthpiece. 'Sir? I seem to have found a driver for the colonel.'

Midge had expected a military vehicle. But the car was a burgundy Ford, its controls and engine thankfully familiar to her, the upholstery a matching shade of wine-coloured leather. There was even a small silver vase on the back of the driver's seat, though it was empty.

She stood by the car uncertainly. Her bag was on the roof rack. Captain Nancy had warned her that she would need to stay overnight, at least. She'd cleaned out her room at the chateau, but still wore the grey serge skirt, cape and jacket. It didn't seem right, somehow, to wear her own, all too obviously civilian clothes.

The air thickened around her, not quite rain but not dry either. Midge shivered, then slid into the driver's seat. Where was he?

An hour passed. Midge was beginning to wish she'd filled her thermos and grabbed some sandwiches from the kitchen. The rain grew heavier. No spring shower, this. Soldiers marched along the road, then vanished into the mist. A rooster crowed in the distance. It was strange to think of farm lives going on despite the war around them.

Finally a door slammed. A man approached: the colonel, Midge assumed. He was in his fifties, perhaps, red-faced, with a neat grey moustache and what Tim called a port-and-cigars nose. A young lieutenant scurried at his heels, holding an umbrella over the colonel's head. A man with a captain's insignia strode a pace behind.

The colonel stopped by the passenger's door. 'Ahem.'

'What? Oh, sorry, sir.'

Midge hurried out of the driver's seat and round to the other door. Her shoes squelched in the mud. She opened the door, and held it while the colonel climbed in.

'Sorry, sir,' she said again.

The colonel chuckled amiably. 'Never driven an officer before?'

'Only as patients, sir.'

'You'll soon get the hang of it, Miss Er . . .'

'Macpherson, sir.'

The other two were waiting expectantly. She opened the back door for them to get in too, then trudged back to her side. The rain dripped down her collar as she began the start-up process. She glanced behind. Were any of them going to offer to turn the crank for her? But the colonel was looking impatient and the captain and lieutenant were checking a list. She sighed, and squished back through the mud again.

The rain meant she had to concentrate. It was market day too. Even with the war, produce still must be bought and sold. The Ford edged around carts, an elderly man with a sack of potatoes on his shoulders, two old women tottering under a crate of chickens. If she'd been alone or with Jumbo she'd have offered them a lift, even if it left them cramped. But you couldn't do that with a colonel.

She let the conversation flow over and around her while she focused on her driving. To begin with it was about the movement of supplies — exactly what she didn't know. Bandages? Medicines? It was all shipments, dates and numbers.

A couple of pigs loomed out of the rain, herded by a small girl in a faded and wet blue dress. By the time she'd guided the car around them (the pigs staring, unimpressed; the girl waving shyly, disappointed that none of the men waved back) the conversation had changed.

'Most important thing,' declared the colonel, 'is to stop all this shell shock tommyrot. Have to put a stop to these doctors putting "shell shock" on the field medical cards.'

'Excuse me, sir.' Midge couldn't help herself. 'Why?'

The colonel stared at her, as though amazed that she could speak. For a moment she thought he was going to rebuke her. Then he patted her knee. His hand was white, apart from the dark hairs on the fingers. 'Hard for little girls to understand these things! You see, my dear, shell shock counts as a war wound. Man can get a pension, don't you know, for a war wound. But all these cases, why, it's funk, that's all.'

'So, it's just to save money?' said Midge tentatively.

'Not at all,' said the colonel stiffly. 'Blighters just too scared to do their duty. From now on medical officers are to write "Not yet diagnosed, nervous".'

'But . . .' Midge remembered the screams on the platform; the shell-shock case who had tried to throw himself out of Kanga's truck. Her hands clenched in anger, so hard the nails cut the skin. 'Surely the men with shell shock really are sick. They can't help themselves.'

'Nonsense. Why should one blighter try to run away when his friends can take it? Bad for morale, all this nerve business. Can't let men shirk their duty. Who knows what would happen.' The colonel's face grew redder. 'You leave military matters to those who know, Miss Er . . .'

He made an obvious effort to change the subject. 'You get any shooting last winter?' he asked the captain.

For a moment Midge assumed he was talking about the war. But the captain shook his head. 'Not much, sir. A few pigeons and a brace of rooks.'

'Ha! Bagged three dozen pheasants in one morning last time I was down at Hillington.'

'Oh, well done, sir,' the captain replied.

The colonel looked complacent. 'A fine bag. You shoot, Miss Er . . .?'

She tried to speak normally. 'Miss Macpherson, sir. No, sir. Well, a little, sir. Mostly just potting rabbits, at home.'

'And where is that?'

'The South Island of New Zealand, sir.'

'You're a colonial! I'd never have known it.'

It was meant as a compliment. She said, 'Thank you, sir.' How was it possible, she thought, to despise a man so much? How many men like this were wandering through the war while the men she'd tended were dying?

The colonel smiled at her, as though his approval was a favour. 'What brought you over here, my dear?'

Explanations lasted through two villages and past a broken-down truck, its wet soldier cargo smoking by the side of the road. Midge expected the colonel to ask her to stop and help, but he didn't.

Finally he looked at his watch.

'Time for a little *déjeuner*, eh?'

'Excellent idea, sir.' That was the captain.

The colonel peered out of the window, through the rain. His moustache twitched in anticipation. 'If I remember rightly there's a hotel. Old Piggy Harbord and I dined here once, oh, a year ago. Jolly fine dinner they gave us too. *Quiche de Nancy, foie de mouton à la patraque.* Got a good memory for that sort of thing. You like French food, Miss Er . . .?'

'Yes, sir.'

'That's the ticket. Jolly good. Ah, yes, there it is. Hôtel la Mère Brabant, the sign with the goose's head. Better not park her in the street, Miss Er. Never know with these foreign blighters. Fingers all over the upholstery. Leave the car smelling of garlic, like as not. Ha, ha! Let us out here, then you can park it in the courtyard. That's the ticket.'

The hotel was large, with a terrace along the front, too grand for red geraniums. Wet orange trees stood in barrels. Midge drew the car up by the dripping sign. This time she remembered to turn the engine off and get out first, to open the door for the colonel, and then the others in the back. They dashed for the doorway, out of the rain. Midge sighed, and slid in to start the controls before turning the crank again.

The courtyard at least was cobbled, with a minimum of mud and any horse droppings swept away. An elderly ostler opened the car door for her and promised what she hoped was an oath to guard the car from all garlic-smelling fingers. It was impossible to know which was the hotel's back door, so she squelched round to the front again and up the stairs to the door.

A girl stared at her as she slipped inside. A wet-looking girl, with damp hair and a smudge of mud on one cheek. It was herself, she realised, reflected in the gold-framed mirror on the wall opposite. She leaned closer, brushed what moisture she could from her hair, and wiped off the smudge.

'Er, *déjeuner*?' she enquired at the desk.

A bark of French answered her and, more usefully, an elderly man with a white cloth over one arm ushered her tactfully down the corridor towards a smell of onions.

Her stomach rumbled. Breakfast, with its cup of coffee and sour bread, was a long time ago.

The room was large, made even larger by the mirrors on the walls. Gold-framed mirrors, gilt-edged columns, tables dressed in white and silver, the cutlery heavy and expensive. A smell of chicken and the tang of wine. Her stomach muttered in satisfaction.

The two men stood as she approached. It surprised her, after the way they had treated her as their servant in the car. But perhaps, she thought, etiquette in hotels was different.

'That's the ticket,' said the colonel meaninglessly as she sat. His glass was already half empty. A waiter — also elderly, like so many of the civilians in France these days — glided over and filled the glass again.

It was strange to unroll a damask napkin again, to sip red wine from crystal. How could such luxury still exist? For men like the colonel, she supposed, glancing across at him.

'Ah, let's see.' The colonel perused the menu. His moustache twitched again. 'Mimosa soup. Sole *à la maison*, no, make it supreme of pike *à la Dijonnaise*. Sweetbreads *à la Napolitaine*. Leg of mutton *à la Muscovite*. Potatoes *mousseline*, green peas. Salad *Bagration*.'

The soup was rich, a taste of chicken with beans and chopped hard-boiled eggs. The pike was even richer, the fish itself almost unrecognisable in its creamy, winey sauce. She had thought the mutton might bring a scent of home. But it too had the tang of herbs and garlic, and its juices oozed pink, not grey. Only the peas were familiar. She would have liked a second helping — not from hunger, as already she felt slightly ill from the unaccustomed richness of the food, and her head spun from the wine. But simply because their greenness was the only sane and familiar thing in this meal.

The colonel held forth between mouthfuls, and filled her glass again. 'Drink up, Miss Er. I like a girl with a hearty appetite. Ha, ha! You'll like the salad. Only the French can make a good mayonnaise. Salad cream has nothing on it.'

'Do you have salad cream back where you come from, Miss Er?' asked the captain. They were the first words he had addressed to her.

'Yes, sir.'

Is it because of men like you, she thought, stupid men, ignorant men, men in charge because of who they are, not what they are — is that why so many have to die?

The colonel patted her knee. His hand stayed there, fat and white and hairy. 'Come, come, Miss Er. You can be a bit more forthcoming now. What do you say, Ferguson? Cheese?'

'Definitely, sir.'

'That's the ticket. And the little lady would like an ice?'

'Sir . . .'

'Tut-tut. All little girls like ices.' He squeezed her leg, then, thankfully, took his hand away. He gestured at the waiter. 'An ice for *mademoiselle*. *Bombe chocolat*, eh? And the cheese board. Port or madeira, Ferguson?' He answered his own question. 'Madeira, I think. You ever drunk madeira, little girl?' His moustache twitched even more this time.

'Sir . . .' She clutched her napkin. The room was spinning. 'I think I've had enough. I have to drive this afternoon.'

'Drive? What?' He shook his head. 'Tell you what. Yes, tell you what, rain coming down too hard to drive now. Stay here tonight. Damn good dinner they give you here, pardon my French, Miss Er, ha, ha. *Poulet estragon*. Had squabs here last time with what's-his-name, salmon too, damn good sauce, hollandaise, pardon my French again, Miss Er.' He patted her leg again.

He was drunk, she realised. And so was she. She had never drunk more than half a glass of wine before, to toast the King at Christmas or on someone's birthday.

She had a sudden vision of Corporal Harrison's friend with his ill-fitting false teeth soaking his hard biscuit in the filthy water of his trench. The hungry men on her platform, thousand after thousand of them, grateful for their cocoa and their bully beef sandwich. Suddenly she couldn't take any more. The hot room. The smell of too much food. The smell of cigar that wafted from the colonel's clothes. The heat of his hand on her leg. She pushed back her chair. Instantly the waiter was there to help her.

'If you'll excuse me for a moment . . .' she began.

The colonel's hand squeezed, then blessedly let go as she stood up. 'Certainly. Certainly. Off you pop, little girl. Yes, we'll stay here tonight. Really get to know each other, eh?' He gazed around. 'Where is that madeira?'

She escaped, into the cool of the corridor, out onto the terrace and into the rain.

The rain had lessened to drizzle. The clouds were low, the mist hovering about the trees. The cold shocked the nausea away.

What was she to do now? Impossible to go back in, to that man and his moustache and his bally madeira. Equally impossible to just drive off. The car wasn't hers. Nor, she realised gratefully, was the responsibility hers either. What could the colonel do? Ring up and report her? She wasn't even officially a member of the ambulance unit. Probably he couldn't even remember her name, and she could trust Captain Nancy not to remind him of it. She could just walk away.

But where to? The hotel was isolated, with no other buildings nearby that she could see. And if she took a room here the colonel would find her. She could refuse to come out, of course. But it would be unpleasant and cause a scene.

She trod slowly along the terrace, then back into the courtyard, and asked for the car in halting French.

She lifted out her case, then hesitated again. No, there was nothing else for it but to take a room. Pretend that she was ill, perhaps, and hope her French was up to convincing the maid to give a suitably dismissive message to the colonel.

She was just about to mount the hotel's front steps when a vehicle loomed out of the mist. For a moment she thought it was one of the trucks they had passed on the road. And then she realised it was a car, much like the one she had been driving, but with a red cross on the side. Impulsively she stepped into the road and put up her hand.

The car jerked to a halt. 'You all right, miss?'

Her heart thumped. She had been hoping the driver might be familiar, even another woman. But although he was a stranger, at least this man spoke English.

'I'm sorry, my car has broken down. I don't suppose you could give me a lift?'

The man shook his head. 'Sorry, miss. Orders. We're on our way to the casualty station. All our lot's been ordered to report there. Big push on last night, I reckon.'

She knew what that meant. Thousands, tens of thousands, dead, dying, wounded. But Aunt Lallie was at the casualty station, she thought vaguely through her spinning head. If I find Aunt Lallie I'll be all right. Whatever the colonel was going there to do, she doubted he'd be inspecting the nursing staff. Not if there'd been a push last night and the wards were full of wounded. Not the colonel with his madeira.

'Oh, the casualty station is perfect. That's where I was headed before I had to stop.'

'Hop in then, miss. You're a nurse?' he added.

'Ambulance driver,' she said. 'The Duchess's unit. Relieving anyway. But the regular driver is back now.'

'Well, they'll welcome anyone with a pair of hands where we're going.'

The engine flared again. The car took off, as jerkily as it had stopped. It wouldn't have jerked like that if I'd been driving, she thought, leaning back against the leather seat and shutting her eyes.

She wondered how long the colonel would wait, her untouched chocolate ice melting at his side.

Chapter 11

15 April 1917

Dear Miss Macpherson,

I hope you are well.

I got the parcel you sent. Thank Miss Carryman for the chocolate — I don't know how she got so much but tell her the boys are grateful. Not much to report here. A general out from Blighty came to give us a pep talk today. They want to send us back up the line. Some of the boys threw clods of dirt at him. You would have laughed if you had seen it. But I reckon we will be going anyway. I'm going to take a good long look at that photo you gave me before we go, just in case there isn't time to look at it again once we get to the front. Come to think of it, that ram of yours has a bit of a look of the general. Reckon the sheep has more brains, but.

Oh, and Johnno has found his teeth. Or someone's teeth, because he swears there is an extra tooth he never had before. I'd offered to chew his food up for him, but you know, the so and so wasn't even grateful.

Well, I am not one for putting pen to paper much, Miss Macpherson. I have never written so much before in my life as I have to you, I reckon, even when Mum made me do that correspondence school. But you can't know what your letters mean to me. I read bits of them out to the others, and they think you're just bonza too. I am glad that you are out of it and going back to the canteen. There is only so much a body can take. You know Miss Macpherson I reckon sometimes you get used to looking after others so much you forget about yourself.

I hope this finds you well as it leaves me.

Yours sincerely,

Harry Harrison (Sergeant!)

—◦◦◦—

The casualty clearing station was tents and men, trucks and mud and chaos; a temporary hotchpotch that looked as though it had grown, mushroom-like, from the dirt around it. The sound of guns rumbled in the distance, like thunder that forgot to end. Each truck brought more men, and made more mud and chaos.

Men lay on stretchers on the muddy ground. Men carried stretchers, some wounded, but still able to stagger. Men leaned on each other, the blind supporting the lame. Men passed by in grey coats and muddy uniforms, their badges startlingly white in a world of drab. The vivid flash of blood was the only colour in the landscape.

'A new push' the driver had said. A few words by men like the colonel, a long way from the battle lines, translated into this.

Midge had been standing, staring, for minutes now since the ambulance had left her at the first row of tents. Slowly, the chaos before her eyes resolved into some sort of order.

Ambulances and trucks bringing stretchers, presumably from the battlefield itself; men waiting, like wet sheep in a pen before shearing, but these men were grey, not white, dappled with mud and blood, men with bandages, sitting or standing, those with less serious wounds, she supposed. Waiting, waiting, waiting for help to save their lives, their sight, their limbs. Trucks leaving with the stabilised wounded, so few out of so many, off to hospitals in Paris or England.

The sagging damp tents over there must be the wards and offices, she thought, or perhaps living quarters for the medical staff. There was no way to tell which. She shifted her case from one aching hand to the other and squelched over the boards laid in the mud to the first tent, and stepped inside.

The tent itself was long and grey and not quite waterproof, so what had been steady rain outside was transformed into fewer but larger drips that dangled off the tent's roof and plopped onto the planks that had been roughly laid to make a floor over the mud.

It wasn't an office, nor was it a ward or dormitory. It was, she thought afterwards, more like the waiting room of hell.

Two rows of tables. Ordinary tables, like the kitchen table back home. But these were draped with sheets, not a tablecloth, and decorated with blood instead of teapots, and on each table, instead of saddle of mutton or a plate of biscuits, was a living, bleeding man.

Women in stained grey aprons bent over them; men in once white coats worked with bloody hands; here and there a nurse in a still-white cap and veil hurried from table to table.

One glanced up at her, her attention still mostly on the bloody arm she bandaged. 'What are you doing here?'

'I . . . I'm looking for Sister Macpherson.'

'New are you? Well, there's no time for paperwork now.' She nodded to a smaller table along the back of the tent. 'Clean aprons over there.'

'I'm not a VAD. Or a nurse, either.'

'Well, what are you then?' Even as she spoke the woman's eyes slid over to the next table. Someone is dying while she deals with me, thought Midge.

'I was an ambulance driver —'

'Good enough. You can help Mr Fineacre. He's on the end table.' And she was gone.

Midge moved in a dream to the back table. What was she doing? She couldn't stay here. Not untrained. What would Aunt Lallie say?

The legion of wounded outside rose up before her.

How could she go?

Midge put on the apron.

Mr Fineacre was Uncle Thomas's age, tall and thin and clean-shaven, a white coat over his uniform, slightly bulbous pale blue eyes in a shadowed face. He nodded, and held out a large pair of scissors. 'Cut.'

The boy on the table stared up at her. His face was white, his eyes even whiter in the bruises around them. For a moment Midge thought Mr Fineacre meant she was to use the scissors to operate, to cut flesh and bone. And then she saw the scissors in his own hands as he began to cut away the top of the boy's uniform.

'Start at the side,' he said shortly. 'Then we'll lift the shirt off. I think the stomach wound's the only injury but we need to check. Can you hear me, lad?' he asked more gently.

The boy nodded, an infinitesimal movement, as though even that was agony.

'Where do you hurt?'

'Not hurt,' said the boy. Midge stared at the bright blood on the shirt she was cutting. 'Cold. Just cold.'

'Ah. Well, we'll warm you up again.' The man's voice was reassuring. He looked over at Midge. 'Ready?'

Midge nodded. She smiled at the boy automatically, the practised smile she had learned at the canteen, in the ambulances. She remembered Slogger's words. No matter how bad it is, you have to smile at them. Together she and Mr Fineacre peeled the blood-sodden garment from the boy. He gasped. His eyes rolled upwards. Midge looked down.

Blood boiled upwards, slowly, sluggishly, around a bulge of purple intestine. Mr Fineacre reached over and picked up a wire cup covered in gauze. He held it over the boy's mouth and nose. He began to drip a solution from a large brown bottle.

Drip . . . drip . . . drip . . .

The chemical smell seeped up through the scent of blood and disinfectant.

The boy's breathing changed. The gasps relaxed, turned deep and steady.

'Ready!' called Mr Fineacre.

Immediately another man stepped over from the next table, his gloved hands blood-covered. A woman in a nursing sister's cap stepped over with him.

Midge looked enquiringly at Mr Fineacre.

'He's the surgeon,' said Mr Fineacre tersely. 'Only one we've got. Our job is to get the boys prepared for him. Ready for the next one?'

The body on the next table was a man, forties perhaps, skinny. One foot dangled below his trouser leg, held on by tendons and shreds of bone. Amazingly, he was conscious, even through the long minutes it took to cut off his trousers, till finally he too closed his eyes as he breathed in the anaesthetic.

Slowly they fell into a rhythm. Cut and strip together, then Midge pulled any remnants of cloth from the wounds with a pair of tweezers while Mr Fineacre dripped on the chloroform.

Cut, strip, drip . . .

Cut, strip, drip . . .

All around them the surgeon cut, stitched; nurses handed instruments, bandaged; VADs fetched and swabbed. As soon as one man was bandaged, an orderly lifted the stretcher under him and took him out, while more orderlies carried in another.

It was unending. Unchanging, body after body, wound after wound, till suddenly you focused again and saw the faces, the individuals not just 'the wounded', every one with a sister like me, thought Midge, or parents perhaps at home. Each one with a life that had been shattered, the next moments perhaps deciding whether they lived or died.

Oh, Tim, she thought. Tim, Dougie, Gordon, Harry . . . Cut, strip, drip . . .

What was happening outside, Midge wondered. Her wrists ached. Her feet were beyond cold. Only her fingers were warm, cutting and stripping the still-living flesh. Was the 'sheep pen' of men growing smaller? Or would they have to keep working until each battlefield was emptied?

Where was Aunt Lallie?

Thirst and hunger came and went. There was no food, no drink for any person in this tent, no time for either. Even a sandwich snatched would cost a man his life.

Cut, strip, drip . . . The world narrowed to this tent, to this table, to her hands wielding the scissors.

'I demand to see the surgeon! I demand —'

'He will be here in a moment, Colonel.'

Midge woke from her daze. It couldn't be.

It wasn't. The man on the table in front of her was not

the one she had left at lunch . . . had it only been today? How long had she been here?

'I demand . . .' The words were muffled as Mr Fineacre held the mask over him. 'Mwwf, wff.'

Drip, drip, drip . . .

To Midge's horror the man tried to sit up. Bone showed white as blood streamed from his shattered shoulder. One arm hung awkwardly, as though it wasn't sure if it still belonged there or not.

Mr Fineacre waved his hand. Two orderlies ran over. They stood either side of the table and held the colonel down. He was a big man, and they were short and thin. Despite his wound they had to strain.

The colonel's good hand tore the mask away. 'I demand —' he began again. A dribble of blood trickled from his mouth.

Mr Fineacre pressed the mask back on. He dripped on more chloroform, more quickly now.

Drip, drip, drip, drip, drip . . .

'He's not going under,' whispered Midge.

Mr Fineacre bit his lip. He kept on dripping. None of the others had taken even half as much as this, thought Midge. The colonel kept on struggling.

Suddenly he stopped. The waving arm went limp. The orderlies stepped back.

'Oh, God.' Somehow it seemed like a prayer, not swearing. 'He's stopped breathing!' called Mr Fineacre. 'Someone, help him.'

'Can't, old chap.'

It was the surgeon at the next table. A shattered leg lay at his feet. As he moved sideways Midge could see the arteries he was tying in the leg stump, the flaccid body of the man who only this morning had been walking.

'Help me!' Mr Fineacre shook Midge's arm. She jerked the colonel's one good arm while Mr Fineacre pressed his chest. Suddenly the colonel took a gasping breath.

'We've done it! Next table,' said Mr Fineacre.

They moved away just as one of the orderlies called, 'He's gone again.'

Mr Fineacre grabbed the colonel's arm again. But it was obvious he was dead.

'Is he . . .? Did we . . .?'

'I gave him too much anaesthetic.' Mr Fineacre's voice was flat.

The world shook. She took hold of the table till the dizziness passed. 'It's my fault. I'm not a nurse.' Was that her voice babbling? 'Not even a VAD. I didn't know what to do . . .'

She felt like running. Hiding. Her ignorance had killed a man.

'I'm not a doctor either. I'm the chaplain.'

Midge stared at him. Mr Fineacre managed a smile. There was gentleness in it, but no humour. 'That is the third man I've killed this month. But I've helped save a lot more. So have you. We do what we have to. Come on.'

She followed him to the next table. To table after table. The darkness thickened outside the tent. Someone lit lamps and hung them from the dripping roof. They hissed and spat when the drops hit them.

Table after table. Cut, pull, drip . . .

Midge kept wielding the scissors. There was no energy now to do anything but cut. Cut, pull, drip . . .

Something crawled under her sleeve. Lice, she thought, with a shudder of repugnance. They must have been crawling out of each uniform she touched. But there was nothing she could do about them now.

Cut, pull, drip . . .

Something changed. For a while she was too tired to realise what it was. And then reality filtered through the weariness. No more orderlies and stretchers. Instead two wounded men would stagger in, carrying a third between them. Sometimes they staggered out again to wait their turn for surgery; at other times they slumped onto the rough wooden floor till a table became free.

Mr Fineacre saw her stare and shrugged. 'We usually run out of stretchers during a push,' he said shortly. 'You can't send the boys in an ambulance without a stretcher. Can you carry on, my dear?'

'Yes,' said Midge.

Cut, pull, drip . . .

'Margery!'

Snip, tug, pull . . .

'Margery! Margery, look at me!' The voice was used to obedience.

Midge looked up. 'Aunt Lallie,' she whispered.

Aunt Lallie looked just the same. Just the same but different. Blood on her apron, but her hands in their rubber gloves were clean. She must have just washed them.

'Rest,' said Aunt Lallie.

'But I can't —'

'Rest.'

There was a tent. This too had the wooden floorboards and the drips that crept down your neck. But it had beds instead of tables: six of them, a few feet apart.

There was water in a bowl, and disinfectant and a wooden bucket for her louse-infested clothes. She washed her hair twice, wringing out the moisture as best she could without a towel, then sponged herself, starting with her top and moving lower, hoping she had got every one of the 'greybacks' as she went. She put on clean clothes — day clothes, not a nightdress. Her body screamed for sleep but her mind knew any rest was unlikely to be long, and probably disturbed.

There was cocoa in a tin mug, thin and lukewarm.

The guns cracked and thundered in the distance. Were they nearer now? The dark about the tents was lit by lanterns. The red flares further off were shells. Impossible, she thought. So many wounded here, and they are still fighting. Each second shattered more young men.

The beds were only stretchers, hard and narrow, with two thin blankets, no barrier to the cold. It didn't matter. She drank, she lay, she slept. There were no dreams. Exhaustion didn't leave energy for dreams. She woke to Lallie's voice, her hand on her arm.

Daylight; sunlight instead of rain. The smell of mud. The sweet scent of blood. The sound of flies and, when she looked out between the tent flaps, there was a pile of arms and legs.

Aunt Lallie pressed another mug of cocoa into her hand.

'I have to go. My dear, can you carry on?' Lallie's voice was a strange mixture of family and professional, thought Midge.

She had to sleep. She had to escape to a world where there was grass, and peace and normality . . .

'Yes.'

'Good girl.' Lallie patted her shoulder, hesitated, then bent down and kissed her cheek. Her lips were cold. 'We'll talk later. This has to ease up soon. It has to . . . I am so glad to see you,' she added softly. 'There's more hot water in the bowl. Latrines are two tents down. Get some rest and a bite to eat, then report to the tent you were in last night.'

She walked to the tent flap, then turned. 'This isn't surgery, my dear. It's butchery.'

She left.

There was no sign of Mr Fineacre in the tent's grey morning light. Midge recognised most of the others though, their heads still bent over the bloody operating tables. She wondered if they had slept at all.

How long had she slept? Three hours? Four? She hadn't bothered to find breakfast. Last night's sandwich was still a nauseous lump in her stomach.

A young woman in the grey serge dress and long apron of a VAD beckoned. Midge made her way through the tent, the others seemingly oblivious to everything but the broken bodies on the tables.

'Can you take over here?' the VAD asked.

'If it's nothing complicated.'

The woman shook her head. She was working alone. 'You were here yesterday? Same as before then. Cut the uniforms off. Check pockets. You know the drill.'

'Check the pockets?' Mr Fineacre hadn't mentioned that.

'For letters, that sort of thing. One chap had a live grenade two days ago. Silly blighter. We might all have been for it.'

Midge wondered guiltily how many letters she had discarded. But if there had been any grenades at least they hadn't gone off.

'Thanks. I'm done for. I've worked twenty hours this stretch.'

Midge stared. 'How can you stand it?'

The woman shrugged. 'Captain Salter, he's the surgeon in the corner, worked twenty-three hours yesterday. Two hours' sleep and he's back again. No one else wants to work so near the lines. See you later.' She was gone.

'Sister . . .'

It was the man — no, boy — on the table. 'Sister, is it bad?'

She managed a smile. 'You'll be all right.'

'Can't feel my leg.'

She checked automatically, then began to clip the bloody sleeve from his shirt. 'It's still there. It's your arm that's hurt.'

'Can't feel my leg,' he said again, as though he hadn't heard her. 'Can't march without a leg. They'll send me back to Blighty, won't they, Sister? Can't march without a leg. Tell them to send me back to Blighty.'

'Shh. I'll tell them.'

'Name's Pete.' The voice was mumbling now. 'Tell them Pete has to go back to Blighty. You tell them now.' His eyes closed.

Midge hesitated, the scissors in her hands. Something was wrong. Almost instinctively she felt around the unconscious boy's head. Yes, there was a lump on one side.

'Thank you, Miss . . .' It was the surgeon, his face as pale as any of his patients as he moved from the table behind onto hers. He began to examine the boy's arm. 'Aye, we can save this, I think. Sister, could you pass me —'

'I . . . excuse me . . . I think he's hurt his head too.'

The surgeon looked up, as though seeing her for the first time. 'What's that?'

'He seemed . . . dopey. Sleepy. And there's a lump here on his head.'

The surgeon's fingers followed hers, then lifted the boy's eyelid.

'You're right. Could be concussion. Could be a haemorrhage. Not much we can do except get him to Paris and hope he makes it. Sister, make a note to give him priority, will you?' Then, as Midge moved to the next table, her scissors in her hand. 'Well spotted, Miss . . .'

'Macpherson,' said Midge. 'Miss Macpherson.'

She smiled down at the man on the new table and began to cut again.

Snip, snip, snip, smile and snip . . .

She had thought that after a while the faces would blur, as they had for a while last night. But they didn't. Each one stayed with her. It was as though her memory was telling her that it was important not to lose each one. The lives in front of her might be short, so each second must be remembered, the final moments most of all.

'What's your name?' A whisper from a muddy face.

'Margery.'

'My sister's called Margery . . .'

Mumbles of pain, of hope, of terror. Whispers, a clutch on the arm. 'Don't let them send me back. Sister, don't let them send me back . . .'

One boy gazed up at her. 'He's a good dog,' he said clearly. 'The best.' His eyes rolled back into unconsciousness. Was he dreaming or remembering, thought Midge. She hoped whichever place was good.

Body after body. As soon as one table was clear the body from another stretcher took its place.

Snip and smile, snip and smile . . .

'My teeth . . .' A man with half a hand stared up at her. She bent to hear the murmur. 'What was that?'

'Don't let them take my teeth.'

'They won't take your teeth, I promise. They're just going to fix your hand.'

'No, miss. These teeth!' To Midge's horror the two remaining fingers tried to probe into the man's mouth.

Suddenly she understood. 'Your false teeth!'

'That's right . . . can't eat wi'out me teeth . . .'

She remembered Private Harrison's friend's battle with the hard biscuit of the trenches. 'I'll take your teeth out. I promise we'll keep them safe.'

'They're good teeth. Never had teeth as good as these.' The white bone where his fingers were missing finally found his jaw. He gave a startled shriek. His face turned blank and unconscious.

She fished the plate of false teeth from his mouth, hesitated, then used a bandage to tie them to his one sound arm. At least when he woke up he'd have his teeth, and rescue from the war now too.

Snip, smile, snip and smile . . .

And suddenly a table was empty, then two, then three. What were the orderlies doing? She staggered outside, trying not to trip on the uneven planks.

'What's going on? Why have you stopped bringing them in?'

'That's it, miss. For the moment.' The orderly only came up to her shoulder, with the wizened face of a monkey. 'You go and have a nice cuppa char now, miss,' he added comfortingly. 'That's what you need. A nice cuppa char.'

'Tea sounds wonderful,' said Aunt Lallie, appearing out of the long tent next door. 'And let's see if we can't find some food.'

Chapter 12

16 April 1917

My dear Margery,

I hope you are well, as your uncle and I and the family are here.

I hope you are not worried at the reports of the zeppelin raids. The zeppelins look quite fearsome floating up in the sky to be sure — much larger than you would think and so quiet. But no bombs have fallen near us. Flora's family though have been burnt out by the incendiaries — you remember Flora, our parlour maid?

We have agreed that her two younger sisters can come here and share her room and help in the kitchen. They are rather young for service, only eight and ten. But they seem to be good girls and there is really nowhere else for them to go.

I have never seen two children eat as much as they do though! You would think they had never seen meat before or even jam or milk. From what Flora says they have been living on bread and lard and dandelion leaves and mashed potatoes. But even bread is so expensive now, it is difficult for poorer families to feed their children.

Your uncle says that the children line the street outside the factory each evening when the workers leave, begging for the crusts from their sandwiches or a piece of stale cake. Mrs Southey, the vicar's wife, is planning a soup kitchen three nights a week in the church hall. We plan to boil the soup in coppers so it will be quite like your canteen! Sadly the hall is used the other nights, but it is for the Red Cross and the Prisoner of War Society so one cannot complain.

I do hope you are keeping well and dressing warmly in this cold weather. I am so glad you will be going back to the canteen. Sometimes I wonder if we should ever have allowed you to go to France. But we are very proud of you, my dear, as proud as of our boys in uniform.

Your loving aunt,
Harriet

'Better call me Sister Macpherson.'

They were in another tent, or perhaps it was a hut — the walls were canvas, the floor the same rough boards as before, but this building at least had wooden posts and a tin roof. There were tables and chairs and orderlies collecting mugs and plates, and a smell of stew, which tasted disconcertingly like that served at school. The pudding tasted like school's too, a slab of flour and suet and what might have been a crust of half-burnt jam. But Midge was too hungry to care. Aunt Lallie had eaten hers with the efficient dispatch of a woman who knows that meals are necessary, and must be taken when and where you can.

'Then I can stay?' Midge said. 'I know I'm not trained. But I can help cut off the uniforms, make the beds . . .'

Aunt Lallie shook her head. 'My dear, I'm sorry. This isn't like the Duchess's operation. We have rules . . . Oh, here is Captain Salter.' She stood up as the surgeon Midge had seen in the tent came in. 'Captain, this is my niece, Margery Macpherson. Margery, Captain Salter.'

'Miss Macpherson.' The man's face was thin above his uniform, his eyes red-rimmed. The hand that held his mug of tea looked surprisingly soft and white.

'I was explaining to my niece that she can't stay here. Much as I would like her to,' added Aunt Lallie.

'She's your closest relative, isn't she, Sister?'

'The only one with half a brain,' said Lallie drily. 'Or any gumption.'

Midge looked at her, surprised. She had never wondered what Aunt Lallie wrote to her cousins, or even if she wrote to them at all.

'Well, Miss Macpherson, your aunt is right. This is an official army operation. I know things are different in some of the volunteer brigades. But here we need paperwork. And more paperwork. How old are you?'

'Twenty-three . . .' The familiar lie faded as she caught Aunt Lallie's eye. 'Nearly eighteen.'

The surgeon lifted his mug to sip his tea. The tea slopped as his hand trembled. He grasped it with both hands to steady it. 'Which means you're seventeen. A good many years away from being eligible for overseas work.'

'I've already worked in France for over a year now. My friends and I run a canteen . . . and I've been driving an ambulance.'

'Not the Duchess's affair?'

Midge nodded.

'They do good work.' He shut his eyes for a second, then opened them with an obvious effort. 'No, Miss Macpherson, I am afraid it's impossible for you to stay here, either officially or unofficially. It's my responsibility to make sure things are done properly, you know. I have no choice but to ask you to make arrangements to get back to your friends as soon as possible. Let's see . . . shall we say in a couple of months?'

'A couple of months?'

His eyes crinkled as he smiled. 'Yes. Do you think you will be able to make the necessary arrangements to travel by then?'

'Yes, sir. Thank you, sir.'

'Good. And if anyone from headquarters arrives, Sister Macpherson, you will of course inform him that your niece is in the process of leaving.'

'Certainly, sir.' Aunt Lallie smiled. 'Thank you,' she added quietly.

'My pleasure. Now I am going to sleep for a fortnight. Or however long the Germans give me.' He turned to go, then looked back. 'By the way, good show about that head injury you spotted. Your niece has the makings of a good nurse, Sister.'

He smiled again, and was gone.

'He's nice,' Midge said.

'He's a good man,' said Aunt Lallie softly. 'I wish we had a thousand like him.'

'Aunt . . . do you have to go back on duty straightaway?'

Aunt Lallie glanced at the watch pinned to her uniform. 'Not for another twenty minutes.' She patted Midge's hand. 'I'm afraid we won't get to spend much time together, my dear. But it's so good to see you. Just out of curiosity,' she added, 'how exactly *did* you get here?'

Midge explained. Then: 'Aunt . . . in your letter you said that you met a man who thought Tim had been taken prisoner. Where is he? Can I speak to him?'

Aunt Lallie shook her head. 'Not possible.'

'I know I can't go and talk to a soldier on duty. But I could write to him, meet him when he's next on leave.'

Aunt Lallie sighed. 'I'm sorry. I thought I explained — I was more than usually tired when I wrote to you. He's dead.'

'Oh,' said Midge.

'Sepsis. Infection. There was nothing we could do. Just stay with him. It was a quiet time, so I sat with him that night. Just let him talk. It's what they need, sometimes. All you can do for them. He spoke about Gallipoli, so I asked him about Tim. Just for something to say. I didn't really expect him to know anything.'

'And he told you he had seen Tim captured.'

Aunt Lallie nodded. 'With three others. But Margery, don't make too much of it. He was dying. In shock. Rambling half the time. He just wanted to make a connection with the nurse sitting with him. If I'd asked him if he'd seen the King at Gallipoli he'd probably have said yes.'

'But it might be true,' said Midge stubbornly.

Aunt Lallie sighed. 'Yes. It might be true.'

Midge sat silently for a moment, then looked back at her aunt. 'You're right. There's nothing I can do about it. Now what can I do to help here?'

'I'll take you to Miss Pleasance. She's the most senior of the VADs.' Aunt Lallie smiled wryly. 'I'm sure she can find a job for you. Probably the worst on the station. You may regret ever coming here.'

'No, I won't. I'm glad.'

Aunt Lallie laughed. 'Oh my dear, I'm glad as well.'

Chapter 13

Dear Ethel,

Sorry to vanish again, old thing — I hope I haven't left you in the lurch. It's a long story, but I'm staying down here with my aunt and lending a hand where I can for a couple of months. Would you mind awfully sending any mail down here?

It's impossible to describe this place. Well, if I tried the censor would blank it out anyhow. Everyone works to exhaustion. No one's had home leave for over a year. The sisters work fifteen-hour days, except when there's a push up the line, when they work longer. But they still couldn't find me much to do at first — it seems I don't even know how to make a bed properly! We don't even have any floors that can be scrubbed — it's all planks across the mud. And as for washing dishes — well, that's done by the orderlies and it would be quite improper for me to help them!

Finally they decided to give me a VAD's apron and headdress, but I wear them over my ordinary clothes, partly because I'm not official and partly because there wasn't a spare VAD skirt!

I mostly push the trolley of bandages and saline around while the nurses do the dressings, and go and fetch sheets and things from the packing cases that are all we have for cupboards. They have to be propped up on wooden chocks to stop the damp spreading up into the linen. They've got me ironing too — a hot iron is the only thing that kills the lice eggs, and of course we have to iron all the bandages before we reuse them. At least I get to stand next to the stove when I iron. It gets so cold here — the wind blows right under our tents. I am very glad I missed winter here. Aunt Lallie says her hot water bottle had ice in it a couple of months ago, so you can imagine what my toes are like sometimes.

It's wonderful that America is coming into the war, isn't it? Though Captain Salter, our surgeon, says that it may be a long time before any American troops can get here, especially with all the submarines. I think we are all afraid to hope too much, these days. Sometimes it seems like the war will go on till every young man in Europe is dead or maimed and every woman beaten to exhaustion. I can't think when I last saw anyone who wasn't just deep bone tired.

Well, that's all I have time for now. Maybe they'll promote me to bedpan duty today! See you soon.

Your loving friend,
Midge (Ironing
Champion of France)

The days became routine.

There were no spare beds, so she slept in Lallie's while her aunt was on night duty. She had thought it might be awkward sharing a tent with nursing sisters, rather than where she belonged with the VADs. But it seemed the nurses accepted her as Lallie's niece, someone outside the hierarchy of the wards, where a lowly VAD wasn't allowed to use the same staircase as a sister, much less share her tent.

Even during the 'off' times the station was never quiet. All day the road was full of trucks and cars and horse carts — many official army vehicles, but others either commandeered or belonging to one of the volunteer organisations. Ambulances bringing the wounded or taking patients to the hastily set-up hospitals in commandeered chateaux or schools; cars, trucks carrying troops to 'somewhere in France'. At night the traffic was lighter but seemed heavier, as the headlights lit up the road and shone down into the wood below and on the military cemetery that stretched to the trees.

There were funerals every morning. Never very long — a prayer, then the body consigned to the muddy ground, the sound of the bugles drifting on the wind, the shots of the last salute of the firing party, Mr Fineacre stepping from grave to grave with the same efficiency and compassion he showed in the operating tent.

The first days there had been a hundred funerals a day or more; but even now, when there were only ten or so, Mr Fineacre still got through them at a speed which would have distressed his parishioners at home.

'Funerals are for the living,' he explained one day. 'There are rarely any families to grieve here. The dead are in God's arms now whether I say a long prayer or a short one.' He shrugged. 'These days the living need me more.'

One end of the cemetery was mud, the white crosses the only brightness. But the other, where the graves were months rather than weeks or days old, was a mass of flowers — poppies and yellow mustard flower dancing between the wooden crosses as though to replace the flowers that mothers, wives and sisters might have brought, or the bright dresses of the women who were far away.

Midge pushed the tea trolley along the bumpy duckboards laid on the mud between the tents. One more ward to do. This tent held the 'temporaries', the boys whose wounds weren't bad enough to be sent to hospital but who needed a few days care before they were sent back to their units, or those who needed extra care before they could be shipped off to the hospital trains.

The tent flaps were open, despite the cold. As always, the neatness of these temporary wards was startling after the mud and noise outside. Two rows of grey beds had their grey blankets, each with their edge of sheet firmly tucked in with every corner looking like it had been sliced out of cardboard. The nurses might not win their battle with death, or stop the chaos of the war. But here at least they kept control. Grey faces on white pillows.

But there the uniformity ended, for these faces were anything but the same. Bandaged eyes or foreheads, pads fastened across the hair, other faces unmarked. But all the eyes had shadows, and all — except for those who might never see again — were trained on her.

And then a voice. 'Blimey, it's Miss Macpherson!'

The voice was vaguely familiar. And then she saw him, sitting up in the bed, marring the neat creases. 'Corporal — I mean, Sergeant Harrison.'

He propped himself up on an elbow and grinned. 'What are you doing here, miss?'

She hurried down the tent towards him. 'Hiding from a colonel.' She was surprised at her feeling of joy. It was just pleasure at seeing a familiar face, she told herself.

His grin grew wider. 'You've got my sympathies with that, miss.' His mouth grew grim again. 'He didn't . . . try anything, miss? Some of those Pommy top brass would . . .' He hesitated, as though the words he'd been going to say might not be suitable for a lady's ears.

'He commandeered me to be his driver, that's all. And I don't want to be commandeered.'

'Too right. You want to stay clear of Pommy colonels.'

Her gaze took in the bandage on his arm. 'But what about you?'

'This?' He shrugged his good arm. 'Bit of shrapnel. Second time I've caught it in that arm. The doc fished it out. Give me a few days and I'll be good as new. Hey,' he added, as a new thought dawned. 'I sent you a letter last week. It's your birthday tomorrow, isn't it?'

'Is it?' It was as though a breeze from another world

washed through the tent door. She grinned at him. 'For some reason I haven't been thinking about birthdays.'

He looked at her sternly. 'It's not right, forgetting something like your birthday. You need someone looking out for you. Too right you do. Someone to bring you flowers and . . .' He hesitated, obviously trying to think of other appropriate gifts. 'A box of handkerchiefs and things.'

She smiled. 'My old governess back home sends me handkerchiefs. And I can't see where anyone can get a bunch of roses in early spring here.'

'Is that your favourite then? Roses?'

He suddenly seemed conscious of the interested gazes on either side, and grinned again. 'I'm forgetting me manners. Miss Macpherson, I'd like you to meet Jacko.' The boy in the next bed bobbed his head. 'He caught it in the knee and in the stomach. He don't do things by halves, Jacko. That's Nipper. He lied about his age, just like your brother. And this big galoot is Davo.' The man with the bandaged eyes raised a hand. 'He got a dose of mustard gas, but don't you worry about him, they're taking that handkerchief off his eyes any day now.' The voice was just a bit too convincing.

'All this socialising's very well,' someone muttered. 'But she's going to be in for it if old Tin Drawers catches her yacking to us.'

'Tin Drawers?'

'Sister Macpherson. She's a tartar all right.'

'She's my aunt.'

Jacko snorted, which made him cough. 'No way,' he choked. 'Sisters don't have families. They're made out o' India rubber in the factories.'

'Shut up, you donkey. Beg your pardon, Miss Macpherson. Oh he . . . 'eck, here she comes.'

'Have you finished the teas yet, Miss Macpherson?'

'Nearly, Sister.'

Midge winked at Harry, aware that Aunt Lallie was watching. She'd need to be careful, she realised. It was strictly against the rules for VADs to talk to the patients beyond the absolute minimum needed to care for them. Sitting with a dying man was excusable. Chatting to men almost ready to go back to their unit wasn't. Any misbehaviour would seriously embarrass her aunt.

But it seemed cruel not to be able to talk to a man who had been risking his life for his country, to do something to show friendship. Perhaps she could slip him another biscuit with supper. There might even be time to talk unobserved for a few minutes.

How did Aunt Lallie stand it, she wondered, as she pushed the tea trolley over yet another warped plank of wood. The discipline, the exhaustion, day after day . . .

But as it turned out there was another push that night — a gas attack, the shells fired into the trenches to burn flesh and eyes and to maim. There was no time to visit the wards, or even think of Harry. Another night stripping uniforms, cutting them into shreds before lifting them off to try to minimise the pain when the cloth stuck to gas-burnt flesh.

It was dawn before she got to bed; afternoon when she woke, guilty that she might have slept too long. With no regular duties there was no one to wake her. She washed her face quickly in the icy water in the canvas bucket and reached for a clean apron, then hurried out towards the wards.

'Can I take that for you?'

The VAD relinquished the empty tray to her gratefully. 'Would you? Collect the rest for me too. You're an angel. I'm all in. I've still got the fomentations to do too. There's just the trays to collect from Wards Two and Three now, and then the prisoners' dinners.'

The prisoners were wounded Germans, in a special hut under guard. To Midge's surprise the men regarded the prisoners with sympathy, bringing them cigarettes and even precious chocolate.

'I can manage,' she said. 'Go on. You look dead beat.'

'Talk about walking wounded. My feet are about to fall off.'

Midge began to clear the trays, tent by tent. At least it wasn't bedpans.

She hesitated when she came to Harry's tent, guilty that he might think she had forgotten him. What if he had grown worse during the night? She only had his word, she thought, that it was just a minor shrapnel wound. Maybe there was sepsis, or even gangrene . . .

But he was still there, propped up on his pillows, his tanned face brown against its whiteness, staring at the doorway. Watching for her, she thought with a pang that was half happiness and half guilt.

'Miss Macpherson!'

'Shh.' She glanced around then hurried up to him. 'I'm not supposed to fraternise.'

'This ain't fraternising. Me and the boys just wanted to wish you happy birthday.'

She'd forgotten. Again. Her eyes filled with tired tears. 'Thank you.'

Harry reached under his pillow. He pulled out something long and flat and folded into two.

'What —' she began.

'Don't let Sister see it!'

'Why not?'

'Because it's made out of one of her precious charts,' said Jacko from the next bed. He must have been coughing in the night, for the dish next to his bed was filled with blood and sputum, and his eyes were rimmed with shadows. But he still grinned at her. 'Well, open it.'

The chart, complete with someone's medical notes and temperature recordings, was on the outside. She turned it over.

It was a vase of roses, the vase and stems sketched in black pencil, the flowers in red. They were small — not long-stemmed florist's roses, but the sort that might grow in a cottage garden, rambling over a fence.

'It's from me and the boys,' said Harry awkwardly.

'But how?'

'Davo did it. He's an artist back in civvie street.'

She glanced at the man with the bandaged eyes.

'He did it from memory, like,' said Harry a trifle

anxiously. 'We handed him the pencils and sort of gave him instructions.'

'Pack of useless drongos, beg your pardon, miss,' added Davo. His face, with its bandaged eyes, seemed to stare a little to the right of where she was standing. 'You do like it?'

'I've never seen anything like it,' whispered Midge.

It was true. The drawing was rough in places — a flower that didn't match a stem, the vase lopsided on the paper. But how could pencil lines glow like that, as though the flowers were still touched by sun? As though a hand had only just picked them from a garden far away.

'Still think they should have been bigger. You know, real proper ones. And we should have coloured them in,' said Jacko. He held out a hand — a not very steady hand. 'Here, pass it over, miss. We can soon fill in the bits.'

Midge held the drawing to her. 'No! It's the most beautiful, I mean the most wonderful present . . .' Her voice broke.

'I think she likes it,' remarked Jacko.

Harry looked at her in concern. 'Jeepers, we didn't mean to make you cry.'

Midge sniffed and pulled one of Miss Davies's handkerchiefs out of her apron pocket. 'No, it's so lovely. And after everything you've all been through you thought of this . . .'

'Should've given you a medal, not a picture of some flowers,' said Jacko. 'Reckon all you sisters should get medals. You're dinkums, the lot of youse.'

'Miss Macpherson, haven't you done the trays yet?'

It was Aunt Lallie. Her apron was as starched as her manner.

Midge clutched the drawing to her. But Aunt Lallie didn't seem to see it. 'I'm just getting them now, Sister.'

'See that you do. It's nearly time for the temperatures.'

Midge tucked the drawing under her arm and bent to get Harry's tray.

He said quietly, 'We chose roses 'cause that's what you are, Miss Macpherson. A rose, among all us thorns.'

She straightened. 'I . . . I think that is the nicest thing that anyone has ever said to me. And this is the best present ever.'

She looked up to find Aunt Lallie's eyes still on her. She began to carry out the trays, hearing Aunt Lallie's firm step behind her. Her aunt said nothing till they were outside the tent and walking down towards the mess tent. Midge waited for the rebuke. But Lallie said nothing, until Midge had unloaded the trays onto the tables by the orderlies' tubs. And then it was just, 'Happy birthday, my dear.'

'I —' began Midge.

'You thought I'd forgotten?' Aunt Lallie smiled. 'Come and sit down.'

The tables in the mess tent were strictly for the nursing and medical staff, not the VADs. Once more Midge was aware of her uncertain status. She put her sketch on her lap as Lallie pulled something out of the pocket of her apron. 'I'd like to give you this.'

It was a locket, small and square, like a tiny book on a silver chain. Midge opened it. A boy and a girl stared at the camera. They were six years old, perhaps, seated on a small plush sofa, their arms around each other. Neither smiled, but they looked happy, as though they were waiting for the photographer to finish so they could get back to their game.

Like me and Tim, thought Midge. She even had a photo at home almost the same.

'Your father and me,' said Aunt Lallie.

'I can't take this!' It must be unbearably precious, Midge thought, to have travelled with Aunt Lallie all this way.

Lallie shrugged. 'I can see it whenever I shut my eyes these days. I . . . I had your father for longer than you, my dear. I wish I could give you my memories of him too. It's best that you have it. Besides, I wanted to give you something.' She smiled. 'When was the last time I was with my favourite niece on her birthday?'

'I can't remember.' Midge slipped the locket around her neck so it hung under her apron, and smiled. 'Yes, I can — when you came out to New Zealand on holiday.'

'Those were good months. You were all so happy. Have you heard from Douglas lately?'

Midge nodded. 'I got a letter last week. Doug's letters never say much. Just that he's well and all that. You know he was made a captain.'

'I do. You must be proud of him.'

'Yes.'

Midge was silent. Somehow she wondered if Captain Douglas Macpherson was still the brother she knew. Perhaps, she thought, Margery Macpherson wasn't the sister he had once had either. Would Tim have changed too? Even if he were still alive, the laughing boy she'd known would have gone.

He has to be alive, she thought. Surely I'd feel something if he were dead! Suddenly she wanted to ask Lallie if she'd known when *her* brother died. But the words didn't come. Besides, she didn't want to think about death today. Her fingers touched the precious roses on her lap. She wanted to think of flowers . . . and mountains . . . and the world after the war. But what was the use of having an 'after the war' if there was no Tim and their plans to go home to?

'Aunt Lallie, will you come out to us again after the war? Please come! To Glen Donal, I mean.'

'Perhaps.' Her aunt looked at her shrewdly. 'So you still plan to go back to Glen Donal?'

Midge looked up, surprised. 'Where else?'

'You might have married by then,' said her aunt drily.

Midge hesitated. 'There was a man . . .'

'But he was killed.'

'How did you know?'

'So many are. You wanted to marry him?'

'I don't know,' said Midge frankly. 'I liked him. More than that, maybe. Or I might have, if we'd known each other more. He was . . . nice. A kind man.'

'The sort you could have breakfast with?'

'Yes. That sort of man. But he was regular army and I'd have been an officer's wife. I don't know if I'd really have wanted that. Running the house, having tea with other officers' wives. I need space about me. I want Glen Donal,

Auntie. Ever since I was forced to leave I've known I have to go back there. I want the mountains and the smell of trees and the shearing and the lambs. It's who I am. What I am.'

Her aunt was silent for a moment. 'If Tim is really missing and Dougie doesn't survive, the property will be yours. Have you thought of that?'

Midge flushed. 'Yes. But I could manage it all, Auntie. I know I could.'

'I believe you could. Though you may have a battle getting others to accept it. But if Dougie survives Tim, Glen Donal will all belong to him. My dear . . . have you ever thought you might tire of sharing someone else's life? Being Mrs Solicitor or Army Officer? Being the sister of the man who owns Glen Donal? Never someone in your own right, but just in relation to a man.'

'Is that why you're a nurse?'

'Partly. It may be an uncomfortable life at times, especially now. But it's my own life. Not a shadow of someone else's.'

'I . . . I don't know. I never thought of it that way. I couldn't be a nurse, Aunt Lallie. Not forever.'

'You may find it hard to go back to just being Dougie's sister, after the war,' said Lallie softly. 'Even if you and Tim do go out on your own, what will happen when he marries? No one will really take you seriously as a farmer, my dear. They'll look at Tim, not you, for the decisions. I think many of the women who have served in this war will find it hard to step back into the background.'

Midge frowned. 'Yes, but —'

The world erupted. Noise so loud it wasn't noise at all, but only shock, propelling her into Aunt Lallie's lap, then both of them onto the ground, the table tumbling after them, the noise turning into echoes, each almost too loud to hear, and then retreating, to be replaced by human screams.

'Margery.' Aunt Lallie's voice was calm from somewhere underneath her. 'Are you all right?'

'Y-yes.'

'Can you get up?'

'Yes.' She sat; felt rather than saw Lallie unfold herself next to her, pushing the table back, then using it to help her stand. 'You're all right too?' It hurt to talk. No, it hurt to hear. Her ears buzzed. A pain was beginning, deep inside her head. Her fingers hunted blindly for the paper with the roses. Yes, here it was, unharmed. 'What was it?'

'Rocket.' Aunt Lallie's voice was still calm. No, not calm, thought Midge. Controlled.

She watched as her aunt straightened her cap and cape, then walked swiftly out of the mess hut. Midge limped after her. The screams were coming from outside.

The pain had turned into a headache. Every noise was too loud but also not loud enough. She rubbed her ears as she stumbled out the door, but it made no difference to their ringing. And then she ran.

Along the duckboard path, stumbling and tripping because the explosion had tilted the rough boards. Everyone else, it seemed, was running too.

What had been the main surgical tent was now a crater, rimmed with black. Part of the tent hung over the lip, leaving the surgical tables exposed, like beds where someone was changing the sheets. One was even upright, though the patient it had held was gone. The other tables were crumpled, some with one leg standing, some with two, some with a shred of body and some with . . .

'Margery, go back.'

'But Aunt —'

'Reassure the patients in the other tents. Tell them it was a single rocket, or a bomb perhaps. But there is no danger. Tell them they are safe. You understand?'

'Yes.'

She stared at the crater again, her eyes drawn unwillingly, unable to let go. And then she turned into the nearest tent.

'A stray bomb, or a rocket. I'm afraid I don't know more.' Smile, she thought, smile. Nothing works like a smile. 'No, the front isn't any closer. Really, it's all right,' to a young man who was moaning into his pillow. The nerve cases were the worst, she thought. You could touch the others' wounds. But the nerve cases were far away, back in whatever horrors they had witnessed.

'Miss Macpherson! You're all right?'

It was Harry, his face grim. His hair flopped over his forehead. His hands looked poised to grab her, if necessary, out of harm's way.

'Yes, I'm fine. You shouldn't be out of your bed.'

He relaxed slightly. 'You're sure you're not hurt?'

She straightened her cap. 'I'm sure. Please, Harry.'

She had used his Christian name, she realised. But it didn't seem to matter now.

Into the German hut, answering the guards' questions too. It was harder, this afternoon, to look at the faces of the Huns, to know what their countrymen had done. But she kept on smiling, telling Korporal Schmidt so he could translate for the others. 'A rocket or a bomb. But you're safe now.'

Korporal Schmidt nodded. He hesitated. '*Fräulein* . . . your friends perhaps were hurt?'

'I don't know,' she said. 'I don't know who was hurt.'

'*Fräulein*, I am sorry. It is war that does this, not men. War takes men and turns them into war. I am sorry. My English is not good.'

'It is quite good,' she said automatically.

He nodded. 'Thank you, *Fräulein*. I will tell the men.'

Funny that an enemy could be so kind, she thought vaguely.

The air smelled sulphurous outside. She stood with her eyes shut and let the breeze play on her face till a gust of wind crept up from the trees. Freshness and green leaves . . . She opened her eyes.

A VAD stood staring into the crater, a bowl of theatre instruments forgotten in her hands. Miss Hardersley, thought Midge. She was engaged to a captain in the Guards. Her brother had died at Ypres.

Midge ran over to her across the duckboards. 'Do you know who was hurt?'

Miss Hardersley nodded. There were tear tracks in the dust on her face. But the tears had dried. 'Dead,' she said flatly. 'Not hurt. Matron called the roll. Sister Samuels, Alice Glennings. She . . . we were at school together, you know. Did our training at the same time.'

What could you say, thought Midge. There were no words of comfort that Miss Hardersley hadn't used herself a hundred times.

'I'm sorry,' she said softly.

Miss Hardersley nodded again. 'Corporal Anderson has concussion and a fractured tibia, but they say he'll be all right. He was helping with the stretchers on the far side when it happened. And they can't find Mr Fineacre. No one knows if he was in there helping with the surgery or somewhere else.'

'I . . . I'll go and look in the graveyard. Sometimes he's there.'

'Yes. Maybe.' The girl looked down at the instruments in her hands, as though she'd just remembered them. A few more deaths, but the struggle to keep men from dying went on. 'Matron will skin me,' she muttered as she hurried off.

Midge walked slowly down the duckboards, past the plot of rhubarb one of the orderlies was cultivating (no one knew what he fed it with. No one, said Aunt Lallie, quite wanted to ask) and down the hill to the graveyard. Shadows dappled the crosses as the breeze washed over flowers and the grass.

But Mr Fineacre wasn't there.

The replacement chaplain arrived next afternoon. Midge stood with him among the dancing flowers while they consigned Mr Fineacre to his final home, with the boys he'd tended.

─◈─

Letter from the Reverend Mr Fineacre to his son, Terence. Sent 5 June 1917.

My dear Son,

If you read this it will mean that I have died for the cause for which I left your mother and yourself. I know that it will be many years before you are able to read this letter. I have written it so you will have your father's voice one more time. You were too small, I think, to remember me when I went away. I also feel that I need to explain to you why I am no longer there for you.

My dear Son, please never feel that I abandoned you. I did not want to go to this war. Others did, for adventure and to see the world, or because times have been tough and they longed for regular money and honour to call their own.

It is impossible to tell you, my dear boy, how much I wanted to stay with you and your mother. Even if I left this war tomorrow you would be a big boy, almost four by the time I saw you next. I have missed your first steps and your first words and all the other things that a parent can hold dear in his memory.

So I must tell you why I left you and it is this: when your country calls you, each man must do his duty if he can, or for the rest of his life know that he has failed his land in her hour of need. The men here need me more than any parishioner back home; they need far more than I can ever give. But when things are bad, all you can do is your best.

There are many things a father needs to teach his son, but I have only a few words to give you now. Even though I am a clergyman I've never been very good with words. I would like to tell you how to dream of a better world, how to do justly by your fellow man. But I hope that as you travel life's road you will find others who will show you these things as I have not been able to. I hope, too, you will read the words of Our Lord and find the inspiration and the clarity on which I have tried to build my life.

Life is so very short, my son, no matter how long you live. Fill every minute of it. Be a comfort to your mother, and know this is the last prayer of your Dad.

Your loving Father,
Colin Fineacre

She was still by the new white cross inscribed with Mr Fineacre's name when Harry found her. Up on the nearby hills guns puffed white smoke. The trees up there were skeletons, black, not green. Spring didn't touch the world up there. Men moved, almost too small to see.

We are the ants of war, she thought. Tiny, industrious, helpless in others' scheme of things.

The guns' rumble was even louder today. The casualty station would have to move again soon, and fast, if the battle came closer.

'Miss Macpherson?'

She didn't turn. 'My name's Midge.'

'Are you sure you want me to call you . . .'

She did turn then. She saw hesitation in his face, the knowledge of the gap between them: his 'cockie' farm against the rolling valleys of Glen Donal; the sergeant speaking to a 'lady'; a gap as wide, almost, as between Anne and her imaginary footman.

'I'm sure,' she said.

'You've been crying.'

She nodded.

His hands hovered again, helpless, as though he wished to touch her but knew he couldn't. Then he reached into his pocket and pulled something out.

'Here.'

She felt something pressed into her hand. She looked down. It was the photograph she had given him (was it really only a year ago?) on the crowded station platform after Gordon's death.

'I can't take this, Harry! I gave it to you.'

'I reckon you need it now. Please, Miss . . . Midge. I want you to have it. I want you to look at it just like I have this last year. To see that cocky expression on that ram's face and know that somewhere far away there's still sheep being born and shorn and dogs barking and creeks flowing. Good things. Real important things. More important than all this.' His hand took in the mud, the crosses, the torn and wasted hills.

She looked down at the photo. And suddenly he was right. She could see the trees, the silver glint of water. She could even smell the mountain's snow and grass.

'I can see it without the photo. I want to be able to think of you looking at it,' he added softly. 'It would mean a lot to be able to think of you doing that.'

She slipped the photo into her apron pocket. 'Thank you.'

She held out her hand to him. He took it. His hand was warm and rough and very comforting. He wasn't wearing his sling, she realised. He would be heading back to his unit soon.

'Will you be all right?'

It was a silly thing to ask a man going back to savagery among the trenches, but he understood what she meant.

'She'll be right, Miss . . . Midge. And I'll imagine you looking at that photo too. You don't mind?' he added a bit anxiously. 'Me imagining you while I'm out there?' He was still holding her hand.

'No. I don't mind. I . . . I'll keep writing.' She wanted to say more, to give him more. But what else could she give him now?

'I'm glad,' he said simply.

Someone would see them, she realised. She pulled her hand away reluctantly. 'I'd better go. We're so short-staffed.'

He nodded. 'I'll stay here a bit. Say goodbye to the padre. He was a good bloke. He did his best for us.'

It was as good an epitaph as any, she thought.

She looked back as she neared the tents. He was still watching her. He lifted his hand in a half wave as she went in.

Chapter 14

12 June 1917

Dear Miss Davies,

    I'm sorry I haven't answered your letter before. I have been moving round a bit and your last letter only just reached me. Please thank the children for the scarf— tell them I love the bright colours. Thank you too for all the news of home, and the cuttings from the newspapers. They mean a lot to me. I can just imagine you on your new bicycle!

    As you will see from the address on this letter I am lending a hand for a few months at the casualty clearing station where my Aunt Lallie is stationed. It is a nightmare of a place and this war is a nightmare too. We lost over 100,000 men in the last 'push' they say, and gained perhaps a mile of ground. From the cuttings you have sent me I do not think anyone at home can realise just

186

how bad things are here. Our men keep going with such courage despite orders from England that even to me seem such stupidity.

There is no more news of Tim yet, I'm afraid. We have kept hoping that we might get a letter either from him or the Red Cross to say that he is a prisoner. But there has been no word. Mail takes such a long time to get through from the prison camps though, and so many letters get lost when ships are sunk or trains bombed. I'm sure that is why we haven't heard from him. Dougie continues well. He is stationed far from where I am, though, in Belgium. I would love to see him, but none of our boys have had more than a couple of days' leave since they have been stationed there.

I hope you are well. I am well too, apart from a little trouble with my hands. But all of us have that over here — our hands are constantly damp and we always have to battle infection. But it is nothing serious.

Your affectionate pupil,
Midge Macpherson

'Sister!'

Midge put down the letter she was writing and looked up. It was the boy from Harry's ward — Nipper, that was his name.

'What are you doing out here? And you shouldn't call me Sister. I'm not a nurse, remember?'

The boy shook his head, too sunk in misery to understand her words. 'We're going back tonight,' he whispered.

Midge said nothing. What could you say?

'I . . . I don't want to go.'

Suddenly he was crying. He looked even younger, his eyes red, wiping his nose on his sleeve. How could they ever have thought this boy was twenty back in Australia, thought Midge.

But of course they hadn't. They hadn't cared.

'I thought it was so grand, lying about my age. I thought . . . Miss, I can't go back! Can't you say I'm too sick to go? Please, miss, I'll do anything.'

'Nipper, I'm sorry. They wouldn't listen to me. I can try with my aunt if you like.'

But she knew it was no use. How many pleas like this had her aunt already heard? There was no choice, for her or Lallie or this boy. You fought with the others. If you ran, they shot you — not the enemy, but your own side. And if you screamed in terror, or shook hands with the enemy as you gathered in your dead, they wrote 'lack of moral fibre' — LMF — in blood upon your forehead.

'No. Don't say nothing to Sister. Please.' The boy wiped his sleeve across his eyes one more time. 'I know what she'd say. I'm sorry, miss. I really am. Miss, will you write to me? Same as Harry?'

'Yes. I'll write.'

'And, miss, when we march out tonight, will you wave to me at the gate? Please? It won't be so bad if there's someone to say goodbye.'

Midge felt her own tears prickle her lashes. 'I'll be there.'

The men marched out at dusk. Grey uniforms in grey light. Grey faces too. These weren't men eager to face the enemy, full of the romance of the battle. These were men who had been there and knew what they would face, who had lost faith in most of the men who ordered them.

But still they sang. It was 'A Long Way to Tipperary' tonight, and if you shut your eyes and listened only to the voices and the beat of marching boots, you might almost think that they were happy.

Nipper was halfway down the line. She waved and smiled, the practised smile you gave to men when your heart felt it would rip in two.

She caught Harry's eye and waved to him as well. She tried to make her smile genuine; something real to give him, not the practised cheer. She touched the pocket of her apron where she kept the photo, and saw his glance of understanding.

'Wish me a Blighty One next time!'

Who called that? What was his name? There were so many. Bluey, that was it. She smiled. She smiled and waved and smiled . . .

'You don't get used to it.' She hadn't noticed Aunt Lallie come up beside her. 'We patch them up and then we send them off to die. They know it and we know it.'

She touched Midge's arm lightly. 'Come on, my dear. There's time for a cup of tea before the rounds.'

Midge tried to put her smile in place again. 'Does tea help?'

Aunt Lallie looked at her strangely. 'You know, my dear, I think it does. Especially if you drink it with friends.'

Another week. The guns drew even closer. She'd have to leave, she knew, when the casualty station moved to safer territory in two days' time.

She kept the drawing of the roses in her bag, wrapped in her spare petticoats, the photo in her apron; looked at them both before she went to sleep and when she woke. Harry was right. They were a reminder that somewhere there was another life: beauty, growing things, lambs being born and flowers to fill vases. Pikelets with butter and jam on the verandah, looking down towards the river . . .

'Miss Macpherson!'

'Yes, Sister?'

It was Aunt Lallie's friend, Sister Atkins.

'Miss Macpherson, would you do Sergeant Ross's dressing this evening, please? Nurse Rowan will show you how.'

'Yes, Sister.'

Midge frowned. She had never been allowed to do dressings before. And Sergeant Ross was one of the bad cases, too bad even to ship out to one of the hospitals.

She found Nurse Rowan already at the sergeant's bedside, the tray of dressings beside her. The sergeant lay on his stomach, but he turned his head on the pillow as she arrived.

'Ah, so ye're the treat Sister promised me!'

'I'm sorry?'

The man laughed. It was a faint sound, more like a dog panting, but it was still a laugh. 'A lass from home.'

'Scotland?'

'I am not! It was my father who was from Scotland. I'm a Kiwi, like yerself.'

'I see.'

It began to make sense now. The comfort of a voice from home. And then Nurse Rowan moved and the reason became even clearer. This man was dying.

His buttocks had been shot away. But where there should have been red flesh was pus — yellow pus, green pus edged with black, already seeping into the new dressings. A tube ran down from his side, but instead of the usual clear fluid it ran green and brown. A perforated bowel.

Nurse Rowan gave her practised smile. 'Just keep changing the dressings when they become sodden,' she said. 'Hypochlorous acid quarter of a per cent solution.' She took the man's big hand in hers. It was a large hand and looked like it should be brown. But it was now pale and the fingertips were blue. 'You behave yourself for Miss Macpherson.'

'Aye,' he said. 'I will.'

There was a chair by the bed. Midge glanced at him. He must know what that meant — only the most serious cases had a chair. She sat and lifted off the already sodden dressings. The man's eyes closed briefly, but he made no sound. She dipped the new dressings in the solution and laid them on.

'Where are ye from?' His voice was deep, but faint.

'The South Island. Glen Donal. It's a sheep property, up in the high country of Canterbury.'

'Ye've never seen the North Island then? The Bay of Islands?'

She shook her head.

'Oh my, Sister, ye have to see the Bay of Islands. The most beautiful place on all the earth. Those islands . . .' He shook his head slightly, apparently without either the words or strength to describe it.

Once again she pulled off the pus-soaked dressings, laid on new ones. He was quiet. She wondered if he was asleep or unconscious. The last, she hoped. It was so much easier when they felt no pain or fear. But his eyes were still shut when he added, 'There's a song that tells it all. Wasn't supposed to be about New Zealand, but it is. It's a Scots song. My mum sings it but I never caught all the words.'

'How does it go?'

He hummed a moment. It could have been the drone of an aircraft for all the tune it carried.

She shook her head. 'Can you remember any of the words at all?'

'"Islands of rain and sun." That's what I remember.'

'I do know it!' Joy rushed through her at having something to give him. 'It's "The Skye Boat Song" . . . No, it's the other one, "Sing me a song of a lad that is gone" it begins. But it's the same tune.'

'That's it. Can ye sing it, Sister?'

'I can.'

His breathing seemed to grow quieter. 'I'd like it fine if ye could sing it.'

She tried to keep her voice as soft as possible:

'Sing me a song of a lad that is gone,
Say, could that lad be I?
Merry of soul he sailed on a day
Over the sea to Skye.
Mull was astern, Rum on the port,
Eigg on the starboard bow;
Glory of youth glowed in his soul:
Where is that glory now?'

Her hands changed the dressings as she sang on. He was smiling. Despite the pain his hands were relaxed on the white sheet.

'Give me again all that was there,
Give me the sun that shone!
Give me the eyes, give me the soul,
Give me the lad that's gone!
Billow and breeze, islands and seas,
Mountains of rain and sun.'

'That's it,' he breathed. 'They're there waiting for me, aren't they? The islands of rain and sun?'
Her voice caught in her throat. 'Yes.'
'Sing that bit again.'

'Billow and breeze, islands and seas,
Mountains of rain and sun,
All that was good, all that was fair,
All that was me is gone.'

She was silent. The ward was quiet too. Had they all been listening, she wondered. Finally he said softly, 'Sister, am I dying?'

'I'm not a nurse. But I think so.'

'I think ye're right.' He was quiet for a while and then he said, 'Can ye do something for me?'

'Of course.'

'Tell the others not to blame themselves. Tell them they did their best. Tell them to live their lives. That's what's important. If only one of us makes it out of this, tell him not to waste it.'

'I'll tell them.'

He hadn't said who the others were. But it didn't matter, she thought. She would tell them all, every boy she could.

'Will ye sing again?'

The voice was even fainter now. His eyes closed. He wasn't asleep. The breathing was too shallow. Nor was he dead, for the blood and pus still flowed. So she sat there, changing the dressings, knowing it was futile. She sang until he died.

Two more days to go, she thought, as she went to get a VAD to help her lay the body out for burial. Two more days till I am away from here.

She shouldn't be glad to go. She should want to stay, to help. And if the choice had been hers she would have.

But every fibre of her being longed for sunlight on the mountains, and a breeze that didn't smell of rotting flesh, of blood and death.

Chapter 15

Casualty Station 15
France
1 July 1917

Dear Harry,

I wish we could have had another chance to talk, to tell you how my very best wishes go with you and hopes for your safety. I didn't even really get a chance to thank you properly for the roses. They are so beautiful. I will write to Davo too, to thank him again. I do hope they can help him in England. My aunt said that there is a good chance of saving the sight in one eye at least, and maybe even both of them.

You are right, you know. I keep looking at the photo and your roses too, and no matter what happens here it doesn't seem to hurt so much. I think of you too, and your kindness, and that helps as well.

Things are much the same here. You should have heard the cheering though, when we heard that the first American troops had landed. Oh, and I have to tell you the remark of one young Tommy here, when he heard about the splendid progress of General Allenby and the Australians in the Holy Land. 'Well, all I can say is them shepherds won't half have to watch their flocks by night with them Aussies about!'

Tomorrow I will head back — I was going to say 'home' but of course home is far away. Back to the canteen and Madame and the hotel. I am so looking forward to seeing Ethel again. I wish Anne could be there too. I think she is one of the closest friends I have ever had. When this is over it is going to be so hard talking to the other girls I knew at school, or friends at home. It's as though Anne and Ethel and I — and you, of course — are part of a world the people at home can never share or understand.

It is so good to be able to write to you, you know. Dougie doesn't really like me being here, and my aunt and uncle would worry if I told them what it is really like. I always feel better after I have written to you. I hope you don't mind my scribblings! You can always use my letters to line your boots if they are too long!

I met a couple of Australians who had been at Gallipoli a few days ago, but none of them could remember Tim. It's really the New Zealanders I need to ask, but most are stationed too far from here. But if you meet any and are able to ask I would be so grateful. Somehow I am so sure that he is all right. Did I tell you we are twins? I can just imagine his grin if he knew how much I was worrying. 'Silly old chook,' he'd say. 'You should know I always land on my feet.'

I will write again when I get back to the canteen.

Your affectionate friend,

Midge Macpherson

P.S. *It's grand that the season has been so good back in Australia.*
Please give your parents my best wishes when you write next.

⁓◎

It was hard to leave Aunt Lallie. Life seemed fragile now; bright meetings that the war could so quickly burn away. Aunt Lallie seemed so small standing in the makeshift courtyard, even in her sister's cap and cape. She lifted a hand in farewell. Midge waved back, leaning forwards to reach the truck's window, then sat back in the tiny space behind the front seats.

'Capable woman, your aunt.'

The woman's voice was American, the vowels longer and more melodic than Midge was used to. The Model-T Ford truck belonged to the American Fund for French Wounded, but the driver and her companion wore no uniform, not even the sensible grey serge skirt and coat that so many of the female volunteers adopted. Instead the driver's white shirt was topped with a tie and what looked suspiciously like an embroidered smoking jacket. To Midge's shock, what had looked like a skirt now appeared to be a form of loose pantaloons that hung skirt-like when the wearer stood, but separated into trousers as soon as her feet touched the pedals. Midge had seen women in trousers before — a bicyclist had passed the school wearing bloomers and of course there was Slogger and the men's trousers she wore. But she had never seen women in trousers made especially for them.

'A fine lady,' agreed the driver's companion. In a world of uniforms and serge and aprons, her dress had the ruffles of a debutante, with the big frilly sleeves that had been fashionable before the war. She shoved her hand between the front seats and held it out to Midge in the back. 'I don't think we've been properly introduced. My [She pronounced it 'mah'] name is Cecilia Harrington. Of the Charleston Harringtons. And this is my dear friend Eliza Dintwhistle, the artist. I believe you may have heard of her?'

'Ah, no, I'm sorry,' said Midge. 'I don't know much about art.' She shook Cecilia's hand gingerly. It still seemed odd to shake another woman's hand. 'I'm Midge,' she added. 'Midge Macpherson. Well, it's Margery really but most people call me Midge.'

'Midge! Why, that's so cute! Eliza, don't you think that's cute?'

Eliza looked up as the gears clashed under her hand. 'Cute as a button,' she agreed.

'Your aunt told me you and your friends run a canteen, Miz Macpherson,' Cecilia went on. 'Why, I do think that is fine. And what were you doin' before the war?'

'I was at school in England,' said Midge, embarrassed.

'Well, of course you were. Sometimes my mouth just runs away with me before I think. Cissie, I say to myself, you just think now before you go rabbiting on, hear? Isn't that right, Eliza, darling?'

Eliza grinned. 'You said it, sweetheart.'

'Eliza and I have this dinkiest li'l flat in Paris. You should have seen Paris before the war, Miz Macpherson. So many artists and writers that you couldn't move sometimes without trippin' over one. Eliza, darling, look out for that man an' his pig — there, you've frightened the poor beast. I despair sometimes, I really do, Miz Macpherson. Eliza just has no sense of the road at all.'

'Nonsense.' The truck's gears clashed again. 'Don't you worry, Miss Macpherson, you're safe as houses.'

'Safe up here maybe, darlin', but how about those poor sufferin' creatures on the road? Miz Macpherson, don't say you're not *terrified*, absolutely terrified, by this mad creature's drivin'?'

'Well, I —'

'Just insane,' said Cecilia, patting her friend's arm. 'Why, I remember back in Paris, we were on our way to a luncheon with the Baroness Peirlot — do you know her, Miz Macpherson? Such a charmin' lady. She paints too, you know, these just perfect watercolours. And what should Eliza do but . . .'

Midge settled back against the wooden panels of the truck. It was going to be a long journey.

They stopped for lunch at a small hotel.

Cecilia beamed as she studied the menu. 'Isn't this the duckiest li'l hotel?'

Midge gazed around at the small stuffy room. The wallpaper was of faded roses, the tablecloths were mended at the corners, but there were bright poppies in the tiny vases on each table. Even better, there was no smell of damp cabbage and old socks, which had been the companion to all their meals at the casualty station.

'The French really understand food, don't you think so, Miz Macpherson?'

'Yes, I —'

'They make food important, don't you agree? Cooking is as much an art as paintin' and sculpture and writin'.'

'Except you don't cook, Cissie.'

'But I eat, darlin'. I'm a very good eater. Never trust a man who isn't a good eater, that's what my daddy always used to say, bless his heart, and I think the same goes for women too. You do like your food I hope, Miz Macpherson?'

'I —'

Cecilia beamed at her. 'I *knew* you would. Now, what will we have? Spinach soufflé, I think. Picasso always loved our spinach soufflé, didn't he, Eliza? He's on a strict diet, you know, Miz Macpherson. No red meat but lots of spinach. *Trois croquettes de jambon et trois pêches flambées, s'il vous plaît,*" she said to the waiter. 'And, my dear, a bottle of Moselle, do you think?'

'Sweetheart — not a German wine!'

'Oh, how silly. There's my *darned* mouth runnin' away with me again. Oh dear . . . Miz Macpherson, forget I said that terrible word, will you?'

* 'Three ham croquettes and three peach flambées, please.'

'Darned or Moselle?' Eliza was obviously practised at interrupting the flow of her friend's conversation. Then to the waiter: '*Chablis, s'il vous plaît.*'

'Now aren't you dreadful? Isn't she dreadful, Miz Macpherson?' Cecilia drew a breath. 'Eliza! Over there!'

'What, sweetheart?'

'That man. I declare, that man is German! Look at those clothes! An escaped German prisoner!' She beckoned wildly to the maître d', then launched a flood of French at him.

The man bowed politely. '*Pardonnez-moi,*' he began. The rest was too fast for Midge to understand.

'What's he saying?' whispered Midge.

Eliza grinned. 'The poor man owns the hotel. He has just been released from Germany where he was a prisoner of war. That's why he's wearing German clothes.'

Suddenly a man in the uniform of a French captain appeared in the doorway. He surveyed the room, then crossed over to their table. '*Mesdames*, your pardon.' His English was strongly accented but understandable. 'The truck in the entrance to the court belongs to you?'

'It does,' said Eliza.

The man bowed again. 'I am afraid, *madame*, that it is blocking the exit so none of the carts can get out. I am afraid I must ask you to back it out.'

'But we can't do that!' cried Cecilia.

'But, *madame* —'

'Like the French army,' declared Cecilia, 'we never retreat!'

'What she means,' said Eliza more calmly, 'is that I have never learned to reverse.'

Midge put down her napkin. 'Perhaps I could reverse it for you?'

'You clever girl! You can drive? Why, Eliza, isn't she just the cleverest thing?'

Yes, thought Midge, it is going to be a long day. But it was also just what she needed after her weeks in the wards.

Chapter 16

Dear Miss Macpherson,

I hope this reaches you. Sergeant Fraser is going on leave and said he will drop it at your canteen. Keeps it from the censor any rate! I hope you can read it all right too — I had to borrow this pencil off a cobber and it's blunt as all blazes.

A strange thing happened yesterday. We were ordered to explore part of a captured German trench. They are usually just like ours mostly, but this one was different. It must have taken in some old farmhouse's cellar, because we turned a corner and there was this spiral staircase going down into the dirt.

Ozzie Baker had a candle and some matches. I went down first. I didn't like it, I can tell you. The smell nearly knocked me over. The stairs led down to a concrete cellar with a pile of Germans dead on the floor, all starting to decay. And there was a bucket half full of fat and a copper with the mangled remains of a German.

Well, I felt like losing my dinner. You hear so much about the barbaric German practice of boiling down their dead for their fat. But I had never believed even the Huns could do that. Then here it was in front of me.

Ozzie and Johnno were coming down behind me and making noises about the smell. I was just about to tell them to go back and we'd make our report when suddenly I saw that the corner of the copper had been blown away and I saw things different.

What I reckon is those Hun boys were cooking something in their copper and that was what the fat was for. And then a shell or bomb entered their cellar and hurled one man into the copper and the rest to eternity. It made me remember that Korporal back at casualty and how he was a white man and how easy it is to hate people that you don't know.

Well, that is enough philosophising for now. I hope you don't mind my writing to you like this. I can't write to the family at home. It is not just the censor but they just would not understand. Sometimes I think it is not right to write such things to a girl like you, but then I think about what you have seen which is equal to anything I have seen, and I think of what my mum has gone through too and I think sometimes women are tougher even than us men.

But I am glad you were not in that trench.

I hope you are well and that this finds you as it leaves me.

Yours very truly,

Harry

It was dark when they reached the hotel. They had detoured to see a German tank stranded in a field, the truck bumping over the bomb-ridged earth.

'Now you come and stay with us in Paris as soon as you have leave!' called Cecilia as Midge leapt out of the truck, then reached in and hauled out her bag. 'You will, won't you?'

There was no use trying to explain that there was no one to give her leave. Nor did it seem likely that either hostess would be there — Cecilia had told her that they were headed up to Brussels to organise the distribution of American donations. Instead Midge waved as the truck rumbled off, then picked up her bag and walked towards the hotel. She had sent Ethel a telegram to say that she was coming, and had asked her to make sure there was a bed for her. No matter how crowded the hotel was, Midge was sure Ethel could organise anything.

The hotel's geraniums were just the same, the bay tree in its pot, the same 'chien méchant'* sign leading to the courtyard. Back where I started, she thought.

It was almost like coming home.

The days consumed themselves.

A year ago, every face seemed burnt on her memory, every injury, each suffering man on a stretcher on the platform. But now it was as though the whole world was

* 'Beware of the dog.'

war and suffering. Pain and mutilation were normal, not remarkable. The days were cocoa, stirring the pots so the milk frothed, slicing the bread, opening can after can of bully beef, the smell forever in her nostrils so she thought she could never eat beef again, even Madame's *pot-au-feu.*

But when the *pot-au-feu* was there on the table, flanked by carrots and tiny pickled cucumbers, she ate it. If she didn't there would be no energy tomorrow to stir and slice and serve, to harangue bakers and train guards. The hotel meals were the brightest part of the day; not just the food, good even after so many years of war, but the chance to laugh. No matter what the joke it was impossible to laugh on the platform; not with the fresh faces of young soldiers going to horrors they hadn't yet imagined; the pain-racked faces of those returning on their stretchers. There were Harry's letters, too. Though they came from the trenches they brought a breath of home.

Christmas came, and the first of the winter frostbite cases. Puddings arrived from England, where Aunt Harriet's friends had again sacrificed their fruit and sugar ration for months to make puddings for the boys, stuffed with sixpences as well as love. Every Australian had a billy can, too, packed by volunteers back home, filled with chocolate, razor blades, toffee, cans of sardines and potted meat, notebooks, beef stock cubes, socks or mittens. Red Cross warehouses across France and Belgium were stocked with Christmas crackers, Christmas cards, nuts, tins of sweets and garlands to decorate the hospital wards.

* Beef stew

Midge had managed to find time to knit Harry socks, and Dougie too. They were a bit lopsided, but they were all she could think to give, apart from a tin of small cakes she had coaxed Madame to make.

Even the station canteen was decorated this year, though not with the mistletoe one hopeful Tommy had offered Ethel.

'One kiss is all well and good, lad,' she'd told him. 'But ten thousand Christmas kisses from all the lads are too much for any girl.'

More fresh volunteers had joined the canteen. Anne's maid had returned with her to England, and the maid Aunt Harriet had sent had gone home too while Midge was with the ambulance brigade. But three friends from school had arrived to take their places, and the daughter of an old friend of Aunt Harriet's.

It was an easy day today, thought Midge, as she gave another stir to the copper of frothing milk and cocoa. Stirring the cocoa was everyone's least favourite job. Somehow the milk always splashed and the cocoa fumes left your face feeling greasy. But she'd been slicing bread yesterday, and serving the day before, so it was her turn with the whisk today.

For once the war seemed far away from their railway station; no uniforms to be seen. Even the far-off guns seemed quiet, with the wind in the wrong direction to carry the shudders across the town. A boy in a rough smock herded half a dozen noisy geese along the green grass by the railway track. Down past the platform a pair of nursemaids pushed perambulators. An old woman in a tattered shawl carried her buckets towards the village pump.

Ethel bustled over to her and peered down at the copper. Ethel always seemed to bustle these days.

'No troops coming through today,' she said. 'There'll be a hospital train in the early afternoon, but that should be it.'

'Only one lot of cocoa then?'

'Should be plenty.' Ethel had lost most of her northern accent these days, as though she no longer had time to bother with it. She hesitated, as though wondering where to bustle to next, then added, 'I've been thinking we need to open another canteen, down at Mont Claire.'

'There's no train station there, is there?'

Ethel shook her head. 'The trucks stop there though. These days more troops are being trucked than come on the train. I'll drive down tomorrow and see the mayor. If we can agree . . .'

Midge watched Ethel's glowing face and let the words wash over her. For all Ethel used the word 'we' she knew it would be all her friend's organisation. Ethel might have been a dunce at needlework, and poor at games. But she thrived at organising.

'You should have been a general,' she said suddenly.

'What?' Ethel stopped her description of the church hall that would make a perfect canteen headquarters and grinned. 'If they'd let women be generals we'd have sorted out the war in the first six months or, better still, not had it at all. Now look, lass, how about we —'

She broke off as a man in a blue post office uniform pushed his bicycle onto the platform. '*Les demoiselles anglaises?*' he called.

The station master pointed at Midge and Ethel. The man nodded his thanks. 'Mademoiselle Macpherson?' He stumbled over the strange-sounding surname.

'*Oui, monsieur.*' Midge's hand shook as she took the proffered telegram. Green . . . There was only one reason for a green telegram these days.

'Midge, darling, what is it? Who is it?'

Midge lowered the piece of paper. 'Dougie. It's . . . it's from Aunt Harriet.'

'He's not . . .?'

'No. "Severely injured" — that's all she says. "Douglas severely injured. No 1 Military Hospital, Dover. Come immediately. Aunt Harriet." Ethel, he can't be —'

Midge stopped. She had been going to say 'can't be dying'. But of course he could. What made her brother different from the tens of thousands — the millions — already dead?

Glen Donal, she thought. What will happen to Glen Donal if Dougie and Tim are both gone? And then the certainty: I can take care of it. I can do it.

'There's the passenger train at a quarter past eleven.' Ethel took charge. 'You hurry back and pack. I can hold the fort here while you call Millie to take your place. Hurry, lass! I'll get Madame to pack you a hamper too, or you'll starve by the time you get to Blighty.'

~❦~

The men in the next carriage were singing. Drunk, she supposed, soldiers off on leave. There was no first class carriage on this train. She sat crammed between an old woman with a big covered basket that smelled of turnips, and a small pale girl with bare legs, and shoes too big for her.

'If you want the old battalion,
I know where it is,
If you want the old battalion,
I know where it is,
It's hanging on the old barbed wire.'

Madame had packed cold chicken. It had been months since she'd had chicken. But she couldn't eat it. She passed it to the child, who gazed at it like a treasure before she began to eat. Instead Midge watched the fields of France fly by: fields of cows, of cabbages, lanes of marching men.

The land of war, she thought. And I'm leaving it.

But England was a land of war as well. Convoys of ambulances filled the streets, and lines of Woodbine-smoking Tommies, laden with packs and rifles. The railway waiting rooms were now canteens, strangely like theirs. There were only so many ways you could run a canteen, thought Midge vaguely, or feed men reliably and quickly.

Noticeboards — *French Money Exchanged Here for Troops in Uniform Only* — dotted the platforms.

She found a taxi with difficulty, the horse thin and dispirited. Even the people on the street seemed dull-eyed. Notices in shop windows declared *No more potatoes*, *No tea*, *No butter*. A bread shop's windows were boarded up. Had they been broken by the starving, she wondered.

If only the horse would hurry. She could run faster than this. But people would stare at a running girl, and it was too far to run all the way. All the horses in the streets were plodding. No oats, she supposed, all kept for the horses of war.

She listened to the clop of the horse's feet. Tim and Doug, they seemed to echo. Tim and Doug and Tim and Doug . . .

At last the cab drew up outside the hospital. It seemed so solid, so purposeful, after the makeshift hospitals she was used to. She paid the cabbie, then asked her way to Dougie's ward. It was strange to be a visitor, after working with the wounded so long.

'Can I help you, miss?'

The man was a VAD. The only other male VADs she'd seen had been elderly, but this man was young. It was only when he offered to show her the way to Dougie's ward that she realised he was crippled, both legs in splints to the knees, so he walked in a twisting shuffle.

'In here, miss.'

The room was long and high-ceilinged; proper beds, linoleum on the floors, all as different as possible from the rough tents of Aunt Lallie's field hospital. But one thing was the same: the rows of beds, each only a couple of feet apart. The men with faces of pain and nightmare; the brown, black or red of their hair a startling splash of colour against the whiteness of their faces and their pillows.

She found Dougie halfway down the ward. He was asleep. His face looked thinner and it had lost its tan. His pyjamas looked new. Midge wondered if Aunt Harriet had sent them, or if the hospital provided them. His hands lay motionless against the stretched sheet, above the cradle that protected the stump where his leg had been.

There was no room to sit between the beds. No chairs to sit on either. She stood at the foot of the bed for a while.

Another woman sat on the edge of a bed further down the ward. She wore a 'best'-looking hat, with a small veil and a feather, and shoes that looked like they pinched. The man in the bed held her hand, rather than the other way around, as though he was the one to give comfort to his wife. He too had a wooden cradle under his blanket, but his was larger. Both legs then, thought Midge numbly. How will his wife bear it?

But at least her husband was alive. War couldn't take back a man who had no legs.

There were no other visitors. Families who couldn't afford to visit their wounded could take their telegrams to any police station to get a railway pass, and stay at the relatives' hostel near the hospital. But too often jobs still needed doing, young families had to be tended. Perhaps, thought Midge, there would be more visitors later in the day.

The smell was too familiar. Ironed bandages and disinfectant, old blood and the sweet stench of infected flesh.

Tim, she thought. Where are you? Please, Tim! If Dougie dies . . . don't leave me all alone.

A voice behind her said, 'Here, miss.'

It was the VAD. He pushed a wooden chair towards her, its seat polished by innumerable skirts of women like herself. She sat gratefully, still staring at her brother.

'Will he . . .' That wasn't her voice, she thought. She forced herself to speak firmly. 'Will he live?'

'I reckon he will, miss.' The man's voice was gentle. 'He's made it this far. You can tell mostly. Sometimes they give up when they see what's happened. But he's a fighter. Know what his first words were?'

Midge shook her head.

'"I always liked the right one best anyway." On account of it was the left one they cut off, miss.'

'I . . . yes, I see.' She tried to smile.

'A chap who says somat like that is going to pull through, you take it from me, miss. And, miss, he's got a good big stump there.' He saw she didn't understand and added, 'If there ain't much leg they can't fit an artificial one, you see. No room for the harness. But Captain Macpherson here, he's got a fine big bit o' leg left.' He hesitated. 'Miss, it's all right, you know. You don't need two good legs for a bit o' good in life. You take it from one who knows.'

She nodded numbly.

He bent down conspiratorially. 'How about I find you a cuppa char, miss? Sister won't be this way for half an hour. I reckon a cuppa char would do you the world of good.'

'Yes. Thank you.'

She had accepted automatically, but the tea did make her feel better, the heat restoring her. He had even added precious rationed sugar and placed a biscuit on the saucer. She was just finishing it when Dougie's eyes opened.

For a moment he stared at her without recognition. And then he smiled. It wasn't much of a smile. But for the first time Midge believed the VAD's assertion that her brother would survive.

'Midge, old girl. What are you doing here?'

She could taste her tears as she tried to smile back. 'Just seeing what you've done to yourself.'

She reached for his hand. He squeezed hers, then pulled away. Shadows, she thought. She had seen them on the faces of so many men. Now Dougie wore them too.

'They all died, you know, Midge.'

For a moment she thought he was delirious, then she realised what he was saying. 'The men you were with?'

'Sometimes I think I should have died with them.'

'Don't be ridiculous! None of them would thank you for that!'

He shut his eyes. Not in weariness, she thought, but to shut her out. 'You can't understand.'

Suddenly she was no longer the helpless little sister. The strength she'd learned in France flowed back to her.

'I understand more than you think! I'm not your sheltered baby sister any more. I've been there, Dougie.'

'Handing out tea and cakes.'

'Cocoa and bully beef sandwiches actually. But it was more than that. I drove an ambulance. I spent months helping at a casualty station near the front line. I may not have gone up the line myself, but I've nursed men who have. I've heard their stories, changed their bedpans, helped gather up their arms and legs and hands, sat with them till they died.'

She shut her mouth, suddenly aware that she had said too much. How could she have talked about lost limbs and dying to her brother lying legless in the bed?

His eyes were open again. He looked at her curiously. 'Well,' he said. Impossible to know what he meant by it. His mouth twisted. 'So you want a story, little sister? I'll give you one.

'We were in the trench. You know what a trench is like? It's mud even in summer, but you don't mind the mud. It's rats as big as poodles, and hands and feet — the bits blown off your men, the bits the rats have chewed. It's stepping on what you think is mud and suddenly it explodes in your face and you realise it was a man buried underneath and you've got his guts all over you. And all you can feel is relief it's not a shell. You think: arms still present, body all right, legs both there.'

She felt that she would faint. 'Dougie, you don't have to —'

'I have to tell someone. If I don't I'll never get away from it.'

She clenched her fists so hard they hurt. 'Then talk,' she said softly.

'Four of us shared the room. Four officers, four beds. A room? Mud and broken timber, but at least we had beds. I was asleep when the order came to stand to. You don't take your clothes off when you're up the line. Not even your boots. I grabbed my gas mask and rifle. I staggered out. I was half asleep. And they were on us. Bullets going every which way and dirt flying and men screaming. It wasn't quite dawn but there was enough light to see.

'I yelled, "Stay together, boys." And, God help me, they followed me. Followed me because I was an officer. I led them round the back of the dugout and up and over. My only thought was to get out, get out before they gassed us or we were buried.

'It was impossible to see anything up there. Smoke and mud and it all looks the same anyway, the craters and the ruined trees. But they were watching me, following me, trusted me, God help them. So I called, "This way," and we began to run.

'There were ten of them maybe to start with. No time to count them. No time to think. One by one they died. The men carried the wounded while they could till they dropped as well. I hung one chap across my shoulders. That saved my life, I think. A shell hit us in the back, blew half his head away. But when I dropped him I saw the wound in front too. He'd been dead when I hauled him up.

'We came to the barbed wire. You know what an entanglement is like? Only five of us now. We struggled through it. Barbs tearing at our uniforms, our skin. All the while the mud was still flying, the smoke was like a yellow fog. The sun was coming up now; I knew it would shine on our helmets. I hadn't really felt terror till I saw the sun. And then I did see a helmet shine but it was one of them, a Hun. He was crawling through the wire towards us and then he saw us too. He aimed his rifle. It hit Reg Donaldson —'

She didn't mean to interrupt but the words came out. 'Donaldson?'

He nodded. 'Donaldsons at home. Sam's nephew. He'd been in my lot all along. He started to scream. Not words. Just screaming, screaming. The Hun was still tangled in the barbed wire. He knew he had no chance now. He yelled "Kamerad" and tried to put his hands up. I shot him in the face.

'Reg was still screaming. Screaming and screaming. And all I could think of was how to shut him up so the Germans didn't find us. We tried to pull him along but you can't in the barbed wire. There was so much noise. I think he was dead when we left him. Oh God, Midge, I hope he was dead. I keep thinking over and over. Maybe he wasn't dead at all. Maybe I'm just trying to change my memories. If I could ask the others . . . but I can't.

'Anyway. We got through.

'The machine guns were sweeping the ground now. The rest of the Huns must have been close. They got me in the leg and I fell into a shell hole. That was what saved me, I think. I saw the others dive into another hole.

'I looked down at my leg. The blood was pouring out so I tied my hanky to make a tourniquet. There was water in the bottom of the crater. I think I had some idea of hiding in it but it wasn't deep enough so I began to dig. I piled mud over my body, over my face.

'I heard one of my men yell out, "Captain, where are you?" But I didn't answer.

'And then the German voices, and then the screams.

'And I just lay there. Lay there in the mud. The Huns went past and the bullets kept on flying and then . . .' He stopped.

'Yes,' she said gently.

'I don't know. I woke up at the aid station. I'd lost consciousness, I think. Our blokes pushed the Huns back and retook that stupid, stupid piece of ground. But the others — they found their bodies. All dead in the shell hole. Bayoneted, every one. All dead because of me.'

'Dougie, darling, you couldn't have known.'

'But it was my job to know! Don't you see, you stupid girl? It was my job to lead them and I failed and so they died! And there is nothing — nothing — you can say that will change it or make it better. Nothing.'

She sat silently, watching him pant with the exertion of it all. Some of the men down the ward were looking at them curiously. Others ignored them. They must have heard it before, she thought vaguely, remembering the screams from the wards she'd worked in. Just one more man remembering the agony.

He grew calmer, and looked at her. 'Sorry, old girl. For calling you stupid.'

'It doesn't matter,' she said gently. 'And you're right, Dougie. There is nothing that will make it better. But you are alive, and if the others could talk I know what they'd say.'

'How can you know?'

'Because a dying man told me.' She shut her eyes, trying to remember. 'He said, "Tell the others not to blame themselves. Tell them they did their best. Tell them to live their lives. That's what's important. If only one of us makes it out of this, tell him not to waste it."'

He was silent. For a moment she thought he was angry. But then he said, 'Don't waste it? What do I do with my life now, Midge, eh?'

She tried to give him one of her practised smiles. It wouldn't come. Instead a real smile emerged. She took his hand again.

'Now? We're going home, Dougie. At last we're going home.'

Chapter 17

Dearest Anne,

It was wonderful to see you down here at Roehampton last week. I can't tell you how much your visit meant to me then, and when you come to see us at Dover. I know how hard it is for you in public, but just to be able to talk to someone — well, you know how it is.

I can't get over how depressed England is. It's not just the hungry children waiting at the factory doors for scraps. Everyone seems grey. So many years of rationed food, I suppose, of reading newspaper lists, of hoping. I used to dream of sunlight on the hills at home. Now I find I'm just longing for the sunlight.

I wish I could persuade you to come home with us, even for six months or so. I know it's partly selfishness — I would so love to have you with me. And I know you are needed where you are. But oh, Anne, England is so cramped, so desperate, and the war is just too near. Sometimes I could hear the bombs when I walked along the cliffs back in Dover.

Dougie's last operation seems to have done the trick. I don't know why I should find the idea of trimming bone so disturbing now — maybe it makes a difference when you know and love the person it's happening to. But the stump is finally healing, and he should have his first fitting for his new leg in about a fortnight. They have even measured his foot to make sure the boot on the new one matches!

It would be easier if Dougie would talk about what's happening to him. But he won't — or at least not to me. And he's made it very clear he doesn't want his sister nursing him either.

Many of the VADs at Queen Mary's Hospital are men — there is so much lifting and carrying with the amputation cases. They even carry the men off to football matches at the weekend! But I met Dimpy Morell in the wards yesterday — do you remember her? She was a year ahead of us at school. She's been a VAD for the past two years. I met Sister Atkins here too, Aunt Lallie's friend. She says that now the Americans are taking over so many of the nursing jobs Aunt Lallie should be transferred to England soon as well. I do hope so — it would be so good to see her again before we go home.

I told Sister Atkins I was going bonkers trying to fuss over Dougie and not being allowed to, and she has put me to work with the neurasthenia cases in the convalescent home. The men call it 'shell shock', but the army doesn't like the term. If a man has shell shock he can get an army pension as it is classed as a war wound, but if he has neurasthenia then he just gets discharged with no help at all, or even sent back to the front.

I met a few neurasthenia patients while driving the ambulance. We had to be careful with them because they could go into these fits and we had to make sure they didn't fall off the stretchers or go banging themselves about. One of them went berserk with a knife, but that was in Mollie Heenan's ambulance, and she had a male orderly and he was able to get the knife away.

The men here aren't violent. All the violent cases are sent to the asylum, poor things. Mostly the men here just tremble and they often stammer so badly it is hard to understand what they are saying. They wet the bed too, and are so embarrassed about it, and some of them have hallucinations and see the most shocking things.

My job is supposed to be to collect the breakfast trays and take the morning milk around. But Sister Atkins says what the men really need is just someone to speak normally to them and reassure them that there really is a world beyond the war. One poor chap was screaming the other day that he could hear the bombs. He was screaming and screaming and wouldn't stop and I couldn't see Sister Atkins anywhere. But Mrs Andrews (she's a VAD here and a real old dear) told him to sit down and drink his milk like a good boy, and all of a sudden he did. Then she explained about how the bombs and noise make you deaf and the deafness makes a ringing in your ears and that was what he was hearing, not bombs at all. She promised he wouldn't have to go back — that is what they are all terrified of — and he calmed right down. I hope it's true — that he won't have to go back, I mean.

I spend each morning with them now, which leaves me the afternoons to take Dougie out in his wheelchair or to pick up things he needs. He is still so fussy about his pyjamas, I just can't tell you. He says to say 'Hello' to you, by the way, and to thank you for the grapes.

Sister Atkins says that all going well it should take Dougie about six weeks to get used to his new leg. It all sounds incredibly fast but that is what is expected nowadays. So I have put us on the list for a passage home. I would like to wait to see Aunt Lallie, but it is so difficult to get a berth these days, and we must take what we can get, especially as Dougie is wild to get back. If we get a passage soon we will go directly to the ship, but if Dougie is discharged before then we will go to Aunt Harriet's. I don't want to be a burden on her though, especially now so soon after Michael's death. And no, darling, this isn't a hint for you to ask your mother to put us up. I know she would, but it is just too far for Dougie on the train.

It must be strange in France now, so many Americans are there. Ethel says she has almost got used to the accents. I keep waiting for her to elope with a nice sergeant-major — it would take a sergeant-major to cope with Ethel these days — but she says she'd rather have a motorbike than a husband. I think she is serious! Has she told you that she has started yet another canteen? That makes the fourth. She sounds rushed off her feet but very happy. At least someone is happy in this wretched war.

Take care, my dear, dear friend. Please, please do come out to us, at least to visit, when all of this is over. I miss you and Ethel more than I can say.

Your loving pal,
Midge

My dear Margery,

I do hope you are well, and that dear Dougie is still progressing steadily. Oh dear, I do not know if I should tell you this — I sent the poor boy a pair of socks I had knitted, just before his accident, as well as a fruit cake, you remember my mother's recipe that we made up every Christmas? Then when I heard from you I felt terrible that I had sent him such a tactless present, all unknowing. But you know what that sweet boy did? He wrote back to thank me, to say the socks would last twice as long now!

Those Christmases seem so long ago already. Dancing Roger de Coverley up and down the shearing shed, and you and Tim and Dougie tobogganing down the grassy hills on tin trays and trying to avoid the tussocks. Oh, I must tell you too — before I left Glen Donal I wrapped all your dear mother's Christmas tree ornaments in tissue paper. You will find them on the top shelf of the linen cupboard. But of course, I will be seeing you both soon, I hope, now you have booked your passage home. Do remember — a saltine cracker or some plain dry toast in case of mal de mer, and strong sweet tea.

Do give my very dearest love to Dougie, and to yourself I remain,

Your loving governess,
Amelia Davies

P.S. The enclosed sugar pigs are from little Diana, the youngest of my pupils now. I am afraid they may be sadly squashed by the

time they reach you, but she says they are for you and Dougie,
with her love. I wrapped them in silver paper, so if the sugar
dissolves I hope it will not stain the mail.

The docks smelled of coal smoke, an echo of the stink of shellfire so vivid that for a moment Midge shivered and felt the hair stand up on her neck. The seagulls screamed above them.

She turned to help Dougie out of the taxi, then hesitated. Dougie hated to be touched these days. He had abandoned his wheelchair and swung his new leg between his crutches. He managed on land well enough, but on a swaying ship . . .

But Angus was already there, an arm out for Dougie to lean on, as the taxi's horse stood patiently, dreaming of oats maybe and the warmth of his stable. Somehow Dougie could accept help from Angus, when his sister's assistance just annoyed him. Perhaps, she thought, it was because Angus had been a soldier too. He'd been a batman till he'd had a touch of gas, and worked as a hospital orderly in London till his coughing grew too bad in the peasouper fogs. He could help Dougie bathe and dress, the intimacies he didn't want a sister near. Maybe, thought Midge, as she watched Angus trying to suppress a cough, it was easier to accept help from someone who had been damaged too.

The *Lady Lyndon* was small, with only twenty passenger cabins. They'd had to wait to get berths — most ships now were used as troop carriers, not for passengers.

Somewhere down in the hold there would be cargo destined for New Zealand; and on the trip back the ship would bring meat, canned or frozen, and the precious wool for uniforms.

She should be interested in whose wool and at what prices. But her mind seemed to have narrowed. All she could think of was home and Dougie and how to get him there.

At other times she wondered if her heart would snap as soon as the ship sailed, the threads that linked her to Tim breaking as the distance between them grew, abandoning him to the war; abandoning Ethel, Harry, Anne . . .

She couldn't think of them. She wouldn't. That was the good thing about duty. Duty narrowed down your world. Her duty now was Dougie.

Her stateroom was small, in first class but right next to the door into second. Second class had fewer stairs and would be easier for Dougie. There were no flowers waiting for her. Staterooms used to be filled with flowers before a voyage. But not these days. Nor was there a hamper of fruit or chocolates, or even a parcel of books. No one these days had time for anything but necessities. But at least she had the room to herself.

Her bag had already been delivered, with its label *Wanted On Voyage*. The stewardess must have unpacked the contents too. She wondered if the woman had been shocked by the bag's poor contents. She had grown out of the dresses she'd worn in her school days, and the clothes she'd worn in France were shabby now, with stains that brought back scenes she wanted to forget. Aunt Harriet's dressmaker had made her two new day dresses, and had taken in one of Aunt's old evening dresses to wear at the ship's dinners. They were enough.

She sat down at the tiny table and stared at nothing. Could she risk a nap? Or should she check on Dougie?

A cup of tea, she thought wearily. That was what she needed. She reached over to ring the bell for the steward. And then she saw them. Letters, carefully propped up next to the ship's stationery in its leather folder. Three of them, one in a familiar hand. Harry's.

She was surprised at the sudden lightening of her heart, as though a bird had started singing.

Somewhere in the back of her mind she had been aware that she hadn't received a letter from Harry since she'd been in England, though she had continued to write to him. She had assumed that his letters simply hadn't found her. Perhaps he had even been given leave finally, like other Australian and New Zealand troops, after their three years of almost continual fighting, and had more interesting things to think about than the wan girl he had met only twice. It hadn't even occurred to her to worry about him. Perhaps your brain had only room for so much worry at a time. Harry had survived so long it seemed impossible he should be seriously injured.

And now she had a letter.

She looked at the envelope. It was stamped, so must have gone through the mail. Ethel must have sent it on, and then Aunt Harriet, and then the relatives' hostel at

Roehampton. It must have been travelling for weeks, or even months. She wondered briefly if it would ever have reached her if it hadn't arrived before they sailed.

She tore open the envelope, her fingers clumsy with eagerness.

25 April 1918

Dear Miss Macpherson, [Harry still couldn't manage to call her Midge, she thought. For him the gulf was still too wide.]

I write to you with hell at my back, because that is what it has seemed like, if hell is brimstone and fire raining down on you.

[She stared at the paper, shocked; not just at the words, but the ragged look of his writing. He had never written like this before.]

Things have been bad, but never like this. It has been the worst week ever for us, over 100 names on the list of missing. Two gas attacks last week. I got my mask and helmet on in time but Nipper didn't. It got Spot too, one of the dogs the men have kept as pets. It was horrible to see him die, but there was nothing we could do to help him. None of us could bear to bury him, just left the poor creature to lie with his paws over his nose. I think three-quarters of those with me last year have been lost. Another two 'victories' and the whole battalion will be gone. In return for 100 lives we have got a few acres of uprooted earth and a ruined village. There was much talk that us Anzacs might finally get let off once the Americans arrived. But instead it has been worse than we have ever known; the officers safe in their dugouts sending us out to die. I think every man here has lost hope of ever getting out of this war alive.

They finally marched us out on Tuesday, the few of us left, ankle deep in mud. We camped close to morning in the ruins, then along the Anzac Light Railway in metal trucks, with our backs to the thunder of the battle we had left and our ears still ringing from the shells.

The ringing never goes away these days. I think it will be with me till I die. I have been lucky so far, but as one by one we are blown away or vanish in the mud I know my time cannot be long away. Cousin Fritz seems to throw larger shells at us these days, but we never know when one might hit and sometimes I think he doesn't either, just throws them when he remembers. It is a stupid profitless war all right, and at times I think that Fritz knows it too, but we are trapped in it with no escape. It is hard to realise we are even still in France. It's all us Aussies and Tommies. Not one of your lot either, though I know they are just up the line from us.

It is funny. Sometimes these days it is as though Australia and all in it have vanished and only here is real. There is no use writing to people in a dream land. But you are real and I can write to you. I know it sounds all very stupid. I hope that you will understand. Sometimes we are all so tired here I don't think there is one of us who makes sense.

I think we will be going up the line again soon. I am giving this to a cobber who's working as an orderly. He got a splinter of wood blown through his foot, the lucky blighter, so won't be going with us. If I don't come through he will send this to you. I want to thank you for your friendship. The only good things we have any more are dreams and hope, and you gave me both for a while.

I tried to think of home the other day, but for the first time it wasn't there. It was like something has sliced it from my memory.

Or maybe it was never there and I imagined the whole thing —
the sheep, the way the fences stretch across the grass. All the colour
has gone from the world. There's no green now. Just mud and blood.

Pay no attention to me, Miss Macpherson. I am tired, that's all.
I hope you find your way back to your place in New Zealand. I
really do. If there is any good left in the world it must be there.
When you get back among the trees and sheep and wide free sky
think of me sometimes. I cannot tell you what your letters have
meant to me. It's funny, but when I started this letter my pencil
almost wrote Rose instead of your real name. I hope you don't
mind but that is how I think of you, the one beautiful thing in all
this war.

.   *Yours truly, always,*
                          Harry Harrison

If I don't come through he will send this to you.
No!

She wanted to scream. Instead she stuffed her fist into
her mouth so she didn't cry out, alarm the other
passengers, the stewardess, Dougie in his cabin next door.

The sense of loss struck her like a blow. To the world
outside she and Harry had been from two different worlds.
But they had understood each other in a way she had never
felt before, even with Tim.

You hardly knew him, she told herself. Just like you
hardly knew Gordon.

But it wasn't true.

There had been a bond, however unlike any romance
she had ever read. She had been happy when she thought

230

of him; had felt safe, even with the sound of shells rumbling all around, when he was near.

He had been through so much, and had survived to smile. What had they put the man through in the last few months to write to her like that?

She should have been there for him, as she had been for Dougie. But she hadn't. Had no right to be, had no way to be. And that loss froze her heart.

She let the letter fall to her lap. The sounds of departure filtered through the window: engine noise, the ship vibrating, the squawk of a seagull far above.

How had he died? Where had he died?

She picked up the second letter, stared at the unfamiliar writing for a moment, then tore it open.

Dear Miss Macpherson,

Please excuse me writting to you like this we have never met but Harry told me a lot about you so I thought I should write now becaus you wont have herd.

Harry court it a week ago but you are not to worry he is not dead the captain told us this morning after parade.

Miss Macpherson it was like this, we was in the trench and theer was this noise and the world exploded and it was dark I couldnt breethe. Then I felt hands grab my ankles and someone pull me out. It was a shell that had landed on the side of the trench burrying us all but not me so much just some cuts and a bruzed face. I yelled Harry is in there but allready they were digging him out with their hands and pannekins and everything they had becaus Harry is a right good cove and I don't think there is one of us he hasnt done something for even giving me his ciggyrettes and wanting nothing in return not like some I could name.

Everyone was digging even Captain Sanders. His hands were all red and bleeding after from scraping at them rocks. There was Harrys arm and it twiched and Bluey yelled he is alive and we scraped where his face should be and thank God he was face uprite becaus we could get his mouth clear and he gave a coff and started to breethe while we dug out the rest of him.

Miss he looked crook as a chook when we dug him out his head bashed on one side and bleeding and a broking arm but they can fix that allright no worries it was his head that was really crook. Bluey and I carried him to the casuallty statin and they put his head in a brase and tied him down so he couldn't move it round becaus he was trying to scream by then I reckkon he didn't know where he was or that we had got him out. And then he went real quiet which I reckkon was good becaus it stopped him moving and the ambullance took him then miss and that is the last I saw of him.

But like I was saying Captain Sanders says that Harry is in England he's got his Blighty One so he won't be comming back which means that he is safe and he deservs it if any of us do for all that he has done and Captain Sanders says that his head will be all right too they say so miss you are not to worry if you dont hear from him which Bluey said that you mite do but Bluey isnt one for writting becaus he left school when he was eight and the teacher was a [a word crossed out, as though the writer had thought better of it and left a blank instead].

Well that is all Miss. I hope you are well and that your brother is better too he is well out of it thats all I can say.

I remain,
Yours sincerelly
and faithfully,
David Gerald Carter,
Private

She shut her eyes briefly. It was as though her heart was finally beating again. Two letters, one of death and one of life.

One more letter still to read. It, too, had been readdressed, had come a crooked way to find her.

Her hands trembled as she tore it open.

21 March 1918

Dear Miss Macpherson,

Harry Harrison said to write this to you. He said you wouldn't like it but you has a right to know. I am not a good writer miss but I will do my best.

I was with your brother right up until the end. That is right Miss, I saw Tim killed there was no mistaking it. I was in the trench at Gallipoli with him and a shell hit us and it caved in. They dug me out miss but Tim caught it I mean he was still under there. I saw his face Miss then another shell hit us and we had to leave so I reckon he got buried a second time. But he was dead the first time. It would have been quick Miss Macpherson he would not have felt no pain so don't you fret about that none.

I am sorry you did not know till now Miss. I reckon they need to

233

tell families more but what can you say so much happened there I
suppose we will never know the half of it even those who were there.

Harry says to say hello he is writing to you too. He is a good
mate miss the best there is.

Yours respectfully,
Private A. O' Bryrne

Midge put the letter down. Pain? Of course Tim had suffered pain. Had any letter written to a dead man's loved ones ever said 'He died in agony'?

But she'd been there. She knew.

Had she always really known? Was that why she'd been so determined it wasn't so, in spite of all the evidence? For her body felt no shock. She had thought that Tim's loss would feel like a hand had been cut off. But she felt . . . what?

Not enough pain, she thought. Suddenly she longed for pain. But it wouldn't come. Instead, she knew, the loss would tear at her, nibble at her, every day that she lived and he did not.

So that was it. The end. Hope gone, plans gone. Tim vanished with so many like him.

'Smiling may you go, and smiling come again.'

Tim, she thought. My darling Tim. Tim of the laughter, Tim with his plans. Three children, tobogganing over the grass. One gone, one crippled. One who had to carry on.

It's not fair! she thought. I want my brother back! I want my Tim! I want the years we might have shared together.

And now? She bit her lip. What a silly question. You carried on.

Slowly she opened the small bag marked *Wanted On Voyage*. She took out the precious picture of the roses that Harry had given her so long ago. Once again she traced the lines of the flowers with her fingertips. Then she wrapped it in its paper once again.

It was over. It was time to take Dougie home. Help him run Glen Donal, help him cope without his leg. It was so much easier, she thought, just to go where you were needed than to plan for any other life.

She glanced out the porthole. The ship had sailed while she'd been reading, slipping away from the wharf with none of the cheers and streamers of peacetime. There was grey sea there now, ruffled by wind and the wallow of the ship.

England was behind them. England and the war and all its horror. There was nothing she could do for Harry now. She couldn't even write to him till they made port, had no way to find out his address. Tomorrow, she thought, Glen Donal will be closer still. Tomorrow and tomorrow, and then we will be there, with no echo of the guns around us.

And Harry? He was safe now too. He would marry a nurse, perhaps, as he convalesced in England, or one of the girls who waited back home in Biscuit Creek. He was out of the war at last. He and she could both go back to their own worlds. Somehow she knew there would be no more letters from Harry now.

He will get home, she thought, to his sheep and his fences and his family.

We have both survived. We are free.

Chapter 18

Glen Donal
New Zealand
24 November 1918

Dearest Ethel,

So the war is over. It is hard to believe it here, at the back of beyond as you call it. But it is hard to believe in the world outside at all sometimes. Even our time in France seems like a dream.

We celebrated with champagne, and the next day Mrs Campbell and I spent cooking and cooking and cooking and we had all the men and the families up at the shearing shed for a slap-up afternoon tea, scones and sponge cake and ginger cake and lemonade and beer. The children put up Christmas decorations, streamers and Father Christmases, which is the best we can do for flags and bunting at short notice. Dougie made a speech and a very good one, thanking everyone who stayed behind and kept the place going. They also serve who shear the daggy sheep bums, but in fact he put it well and I think even meant it.

What was the Armistice like in France? And what will you do now? I couldn't help thinking of you all as I stood there with my glass of shandy making small talk with old Mrs Cameron and the Fraser ladies. Did you all dance on the railway platform? But I suppose you had to be hard at work even after the Armistice, with so many men to go home. I felt a bit useless here, to tell the truth, despite the heroic baking.

Things flow on here just as I always imagined. We had a good lambing this year. The rabbits have bred up since the men were away and there was a landslip on the hills in one of the far paddocks. But all that news is important only to us and can't mean a thing to you over there.

Well, I'd better go. We're off to a tennis party after church. I have a new tennis dress, a most fashionable one with a dropped waist. Suddenly, as soon as we heard the war was over, I felt so dowdy, and Miss Davies has my measurements so she got a dressmaker down in Christchurch to make me up some clothes. There are ribbons and ruches and ruffles and other up-to-the-minute items that I have never heard of before, but Miss Davies assures me are all the rage. Miss Davies found someone to restring my racquet too.

Dougie is even playing tennis, can you imagine? He doesn't do much footwork, but he's awfully good at lunging and his serves are terrific. He looks very handsome in his whites. He is much in demand at mixed doubles, and not just because there are fewer men here now. So many never came home at all, but lots of other men have stayed in the cities. You can't blame them wanting higher wages and more comforts after what they've been through.

Goodbye, old thing. I miss you lots. Don't forget your loving friend,

Midge

~∰~

1st London General
Hospital
8 December 1918

Dear Miss Macpherson,

Excuse a stranger writing to you. We met so briefly in France and England you may not remember me. But after so many years of hearing Eulalie read out your letters it is as though I have known you too. Your aunt was very dear to me. Please forgive any familiarity.

By now you should have received the official telegram, but I know telegrams can go astray. If this letter then is a shock to you, please forgive that too.

I was with your aunt at the hospital when she died this morning. It was an easy death, compared to most. This new influenza strikes one down almost before you know that you are ill. Even yesterday your aunt seemed well, though tired as we all have been for so long. She collapsed on her rounds last night, and I was with her till the end. But I think I have told you that already. Forgive me, my dear. This letter is not as clear as it should be. But I did not want to delay writing.

My dear Miss Macpherson — or may I call you Margery? Because that is how all your aunt's friends have thought of you these many years. Your aunt was a woman to be proud of.

Her last words were of you and your brother. 'Give them my love' she said and then, 'Tell Margery to carry on'. I do not quite know what she meant by that, but perhaps you do.

I hope, my dear, that one day we may meet again, in memory of your dearest aunt.

> *I remain,*
> *Yours sincerely,*
> *Sister Alicia Atkins*

13 May 1919

Dearest Midge,

I am getting married.

I know this will be a shock to you. It is to me.

You know, I used to dream that one day a blind convalescent would come here. I'd nurse him and he would fall in love with me, unable to see my face. A beauty and the beast but in reverse, with me the ugly one, and him unknowing. A nice obscure man, with a lovely manor house and lots of slobbery dogs, who didn't need a wife to show off to the world.

Well, I got Gavin instead. He's not what I expected, Midge. He's not what Mummy expected either. He's an archaeologist, though he was only on one dig out in Mesopotamia before the war took us all. He was in the Australian Light Horse out there too

— not with our lot; a colonial, just like you, though he studied at Oxford — and came here to recuperate from appendicitis, of all things. As he says, to escape the entire war without a scratch then end up with appendicitis is something for the record books.

But he made a full recovery, thank goodness, and by the time you get this we will be married and on our way east again. I gather that when the money for a dig comes through you have to move quickly, and I HAVE been moving quickly, trying to get a tropical kit ready, or whatever one calls a kit for Mesopotamia. No big wedding, just the family and some of the household and Ethel of course and some of Gavin's chums in the local church. I suppose Wilkins will cry again, the old dear, and pretend he isn't.

I do so wish you could be with us, but there simply isn't time. We will be thinking of you so very much, so if you smelled the scent of wedding cake among your mountains a few weeks ago, then that was us.

Gavin doesn't mind about my face. Or rather he minds the pain behind it. But he says that none of us came out of the war unscathed. He couldn't cope with a wife untouched by it all. So somehow my face is right, it fits with what's happened to our lives. His colleagues seem to cope with it too, which is the main thing, and at least out there one won't have to meet lots of staring strangers. There'll just be us and the villagers, and all the glories of Babylon, at least those we can dig up. It's funny. You wanted me to have sunlight and your wide horizons. Well, I'm getting them, just not the ones you planned.

Be happy for me, darling. As happy as your loving friend,

Anne, soon to be

Mrs Gavin Ridgeway

Deepdene
Yorkshire
February 1920

Dearest Midge,

Well old girl, I've sold the blessed bike. A lorry ran into me when neither of us were expecting it. I got off with a broken collarbone but the old bike was a goner and Da had pink kittens and threatened to cut off my allowance. Our George went more boringly on and on about the dangers of women's rights than ever. Our George is making the perfect wholesale grocer. His soul is made of cocoa.

We had a spiffing demonstration outside Parliament House the other day, but the press is getting tired of this chaining ourselves to the railings lark. We'll have to think of something more newsworthy pretty soon. Tattooing 'Votes for Women' on the old Prime Minister's head strikes me as a good one, don't you think? It's all right for you out in the colonies, lass; you've got your votes, but we back home need help!

Look here, Midge, don't you think you should come back and join us? You can't be happy out there playing tennis among those sheep. Come and set up house with us in London. There is so much that needs doing here. We need all the hands we can get.

You remember Dimpy — Moira Garrington-Ffoote? Dimps was a VAD out in Malta and then up our way; one brother caught it at Flanders and the other was gassed; coughing his lungs up in Oxford these days, poor blighter. Dimps has set up a school and soup kitchen for the children in the East End, and we want to get a library going too. Do you realise there are children who have never seen a book in their whole lives? Or eaten more than bread and scrape for dinner? Sorry — I didn't mean to preach to you of all people! But we need you here! Dimps and I plan to take a house in London. There'll be plenty of room for three, or more when we get the volunteers, and . . .

Midge put the letter down and looked out the window. Behind her Harry's rose picture glowed on the wall, above the mantelpiece with Tim's and Dougie's photos, and the miniatures of the three of them Mum had asked to be painted a few months before she died.

Out the window the mountains reached for the sky; a peak of snow trembled gold as the sunlight faded. She could hear Dougie's voice over near the shearing sheds, yelling some order to the men, then the scrape, scrape, scrape of his crutch on the gravel path. Dougie managed to get most places by himself these days. He even managed to drive, pressing the clutch down with a stick to help his new foot.

Dougie had needed her on the ship home; needed her for the first few months at Glen Donal, when the pain of a leg long gone still woke him screaming.

But a month ago Dougie had become engaged to Sylvia Malcolm from Mount Albert. A nice girl, Sylvia; Midge liked her, though it was hard to find much to talk about. The last thing Dougie needed now, as he rebuilt his life, was a sister interfering in the running of his farm. A sister who remembered the days of his agony and the childishness that came with pain.

Dougie's eyes still wore shadows. Every man who'd made it home had shadows. She supposed her face had shadows of its own. And the silence of Tim's voice still echoed through the house, across the paddocks, never mentioned by his brother or his sister, always felt.

Her heart still burned like a sliver of ice had lodged in it when she thought of Tim. Every stair and cupboard at Glen Donal spoke of Tim. The shelf with the old monkey that they'd shared; the banisters they'd raced each other down. The cribs still up in the attic, one his, one hers.

She supposed Dougie's babies would sleep in them one day now.

Tim, she whispered, and pretended she heard a whisper back. 'Sis? Sis . . . Sis . . .'

But it wasn't Tim. It was the wind in the willow trees, the swish of Mrs Campbell's broom. Smiling may you go, and smiling come again, she thought.

Oh Tim . . .

Ghosts, she thought. There are too many ghosts here. The ghosts of our childhood, the children laughing by the stream. The ghosts of Ernie the snigger, dead at Gallipoli, Jock the breaker lost in the mud at Ypres, Will who rode the one-eyed pony that everybody said was mad . . .

She lifted Ethel's letter again. Was that the answer? Become a suffragette back in England rather than a maiden aunt listening to her ghosts at Glen Donal? But England was the past. It had never been her heart's country. Even the blood-fed soil of France held more of her soul these days than the green fields of England. She got up, and began to pace the room. Was she lost too, then, 'missing in action', a ghost herself, all meaning taken from her life with the loss of Tim and all her dreams? Surely there had to be something more she could do with her life; something with meaning; something with a purpose as strong as Dougie's as he hauled his maimed body across the paddocks, reclaiming a future that France had nearly torn away.

Dougie had come home again. But was Glen Donal still home for her?

The paddocks and the mountains still stirred her soul. But Tim's absence cut her like a knife. And Ethel was right. After the last four years it was hard to make do with the routines of roast lamb and tennis parties.

Suddenly she remembered Lallie, her voice harsh with weariness, the beat of the shells drumming across the fields. 'Tell Midge to carry on,' she'd said. Should she become a nurse? Take up Aunt Lallie's cape and veil? She'd had enough of wounds and bedpans. That was the past. That was Lallie's life, not hers. Lallie would never have meant her to stand in her shadow. It had been Lallie who'd urged her to make her own life, not live someone else's. There had to be something more.

Suddenly she noticed her name on another letter, half hidden under the envelopes for Dougie on the salver. The paper was thin and cheap. When she picked it up she saw that the address had been written and rewritten many times across the front; not surprising, as the sender had

244

addressed it simply to 'Miss Rose Macpherson, Glen Donal, New Zealand'.

It was a miracle, she thought, picking it up, that it had found its way here at all.

Rose . . . Surely Harry wouldn't be writing to her after all these years? And he'd always used her real name before. Besides, it wasn't his writing. It looked like a woman's hand, the copperplate slow and careful, as though it had been drafted once then copied to look perfect, each word blotted carefully before the ink could run.

> *Moura*
> *Biscuit Creek*
> *New South Wales*
> *Australia*

Dear Miss Rose Macpherson,

I am sorry to be writing to you out of the blue like this when we have never spoke but I am Harry's mum. Well, Miss Macpherson, you see it is like this.

I know you met my Harry in France when you was working there. I didn't know they had girls in the army. I know you must be brave though if you done that so maybe you won't mind me writing to you like this. Maybe after all you must of seen you will understand.

Perhaps you didn't know that Harry was wounded over there. In the head it was. The doctors said he should be all right now but, miss, he isn't. He doesn't speak at all most days, not at all no matter what you say.

It's not like he is really sick his appetite is good and he works all day fencing, mostly off with the dogs. He smiles at the dogs sometimes but that is all. He has never even smiled at me, his Mum. I can stand that Miss Macpherson. I could have stood it if he'd been killed though in a way it would of killed me too. But I can not stand seeing my boy unhappy. Not just unhappy Miss. Most times its like he isn't even there. Well, Miss Macpherson, you are wondering why I am writing to you about this but it was yesterday Harry's dad harnessed up the sulky to see Lewis's new radio. They got it sent from Sydney special and we took Harry too in case it did him good. I don't know if you have radios in New Zealand but they play songs so it sounds just like the piano and singers were in the room and they played this song called 'The Rose of No-Man's-Land'. It was all about you nurses over in France where you were with my Harry. I remember some of the words. They stuck by me even though I only heard them the once.

'Neath the War's dark curse
Stands a Red Cross nurse
She's the rose of no-man's-land

And suddenly Harry speaks up. He was smiling too. Miss it had been so long since I saw my boy smile. He says I knew a Rose but she wasn't with the Red Cross. And we all stared because like I told you, miss, Harry has never said a single word since he come home. I said who is she Harry? And he said like I should have known, She's Rose Macpherson of Glen Donal in New Zealand. And then he said I hear the guns still all the time. Rose would understand. I said what about the guns Harry? And he said,

Can't speak over the guns. Rose knows. And that is all he said. He stopped smiling Miss. He went away again.

Miss, Harry is my only boy there was another and a girl but they died of the polio so you see, miss, Harry is all I have and next door too their boys died at Gallipoli all three of them and they was relying on Harry to keep their place going as well. So if you can tell us why Harry can't speak or how we can help him I would be much obliged and Harry's dad and the Martins who are next door.

I remain yours faithfully,
Mrs Ellen Harrison

Chapter 19

Wentworth Hotel
Sydney
10 April 1920

Dear Ethel,

I suppose you think I'm bonkers. But I'm not, you know. It's just that for the first time since the war I have a glimpse of something that is worth doing.

Not that I know how much I will be able to do at Moura. If, as I suspect, Harry Harrison is suffering from a combination of shell shock and hearing loss — the noise of the guns his mother spoke about does sound like the symptoms of so many young men driven deaf by the years in the trenches — then I can at least offer some suggestions and reassurance to his parents, and possibly to Harry too. And as you and I know so well, how can anyone *understand who wasn't there? How does that song go? When they ask us, what are we going to tell them . . .*

Well, I was there, and so was Harry. I can't talk about those days to Dougie — he just wants to forget. So seeing Harry, helping him, may give me a little peace as well.

But it's more than that. As you guessed, I've been bored sick. There was something in Harry's mother's appeal about everyone on both farms relying on him that got to me. Yes, I know shell shock, but I know sheep too. Maybe I can help there as well. Dougie snaps if I so much as make a suggestion at Glen Donal.

Dear friend, don't misunderstand, but I have come to realise that I'm not a nurse, or a suffragette. I'm a sheep farmer. It's in my blood. Perhaps these people need help so much that they'll forget I wear skirts, not trousers . . .

~∰~

She sent a telegram to say when she was arriving; not a letter, in case the mail was slow. She bought new clothes in Sydney — including a low-waisted dress, with a pink sash across the hips — not just to look her best but to say 'My life is new now too'. All she wore was new, except for Lallie's locket. She always wore that now. She left the hotel before first light, the gas lamps lining the streets still flaring into the city dark, the road still damp with night and dew.

The car was a Ford, familiar but strange as well. The leather smelled new and felt soft. It had been extravagant buying a new car, when she might use it for so little time, slinking back home a failure. But the salesman had said they'd buy it back from her and it would work out cheaper than hiring. Dougie had accepted she had earned the right to do what she liked with her money now, even though she still wasn't quite twenty-one.

Two punctures in the first four hours, and the radiator boiled on the slope they called the Razorback. But that was nothing after driving an ambulance in France. She had her puncture repair kit, and there was petrol available. She only had to use the jerry cans in the back once, all the way to Goulburn.

Out from Goulburn the grass looked thin; the trees stunted too. Strange trees, with stranger twists and poor drab tops, like they were panting for more soil or rain. Was this what Moura would be like? She shivered. Impossible to think of living here after Glen Donal. This land could never speak to her heart.

She turned from the main road onto another. The land began to rise. Almost indiscernibly at first, the engine hardly labouring. But the air changed; the sweet unmistakable smell of cold and hills.

The trees were taller here, thick-trunked and sturdy, carrying their green heads with pride. They still looked odd. But perhaps you could grow to love them, she thought. Maybe there was a generosity in this soil too.

She stopped when her watch said it was lunchtime. She spread the blanket on the grass beside the road and sat down to force herself to eat and drink, just as she had for all those years in France. A picnic basket and thermos had come with the car, as though to tempt you to buy it with the thought of picnics by the roadside.

The hotel had filled the basket with sandwiches, even wrapped them in a damp damask napkin to keep them fresh. Ham and pickle, tomato and cheese, the bread well buttered so it didn't go soggy; roast beef and cucumber. A thermos of tea, with milk and sugar added, just as she liked it. Three slices of fruit cake in another napkin. How many napkins did they give away to wealthy guests each year, she wondered.

To her surprise she found herself finishing even the cake. She hadn't realised she was hungry.

She glanced at her wristwatch again. It was new, a Christmas present from Dougie. A thoughtful present to a much-loved sister.

Had she really been naive enough to think Dougie would let his little sister help run Glen Donal?

It was time to go. Another two hours to get to Biscuit Creek, then another half-hour to Moura, she thought.

The way grew steeper. A river ran below her, a thin mirror over the sand, edged with the prints of cows and piles of dung. Then cleared land again. A mob of 'roos bounced across the road in front of her, hardly glancing at the car. Laughter bubbled up; impossible not to laugh at creatures so ridiculous.

Biscuit Creek Township was bigger than she'd expected. English trees lined the streets, dappled with autumn leaves, like home. A bank, two cafés, even a dress shop and a jeweller's as well as the stock and station agency, the saddlery, the funeral parlour, the baker's. No garage, but she had enough petrol in the jerry cans. She stopped at the blacksmith's to ask directions. The man looked curiously at the car, and even more curiously at her. But he was polite and helpful.

She tried to ignore the stares as she drove out of town.

Her skin began to prickle. It had all seemed so simple a month ago; even yesterday. Like the war, when you had to make decisions quickly, with no time to regret the ones that you got wrong. Running a canteen, nursing in France — did wisdom and experience in some areas really teach you how to cope in others? What was at the end of this long road?

It was almost like the roads of home, she thought, the dirt orange instead of white. The ruts were the same. Even the hills were the blue of home. She had expected more points of difference, foreignness. But so much was familiar. The scent of long-cropped grass, of sheep manure in hot paddocks. Even the broken-down fences, so like Glen Donal, where the fencers too had gone to war, leaving the wires to tangle and the posts to rot.

A rabbit darted along the roadside, and then another. That was why the grass was so close clipped, she thought. Eaten back by rabbits, so many they were forced to feed by daylight too. Now she looked she could see rabbit holes, and the beginnings of erosion gullies where the creatures had eaten the roots of the grass, leaving the soil to blow and wash away. Had they tried ferrets, she wondered. If nothing was done this land would blow away, rabbit-eaten into dust, the men who could have cared for it lost in

France, in Belgium, along the Turkish coast, or maimed like Dougie, Harry . . .

I'll fight for you, she thought suddenly. Poor abandoned land. I can make you flourish. What about the new barbed wire? Could that help keep the rabbits down? And that ram, panting in the shade of the gum tree — his chest looked too skinny for him to father anything. A few Lincolns crossed with these merinos would mean fat lambs as well as wool, and lucerne down on those creek flats would do for silage . . .

Stop it, she told herself. Tomorrow you might be heading home, embarrassed. Or maybe sitting with a man whose mind was so destroyed that he could never recognise her. Perhaps he even had found another girl to smile at, in the months it had taken his mother's letter to reach New Zealand, and for the journey here.

The road began to rise again. She could see the mountains now — not the white-tipped crags of home, rearing and soaring to the sky. These were gentler, rounder. But the scent in the breeze was the same: the old-tin smell of cold. The sky was the same too, that intense blue you only saw above the mountains. An eagle balanced on the sunlight, far above.

She could breathe here. There was space, just like at home. Space to dream.

What do you think, she asked her brother, and felt Tim smile in the back of her mind. All our plans, she whispered to him. You won't be lost forever, Tim, if I can make our dreams work here.

Twenty minutes past town, the blacksmith had said. Trees drooped above the road, their dangling leaves like long slim fingers. Her heart thudded so hard she felt it would burst out of her skin. Yes, there was the house, about half a mile across the paddocks from the gate, small and unpainted with a corrugated-iron roof; a scatter of fruit trees out to one side and hens clucking on the other. But you could do something with it, she thought. Like leave it for the termites and build another house, a bigger, better one, up on that hill perhaps, for the view.

Money could do so much here. Money, and the experience of a larger, richer farm . . .

She turned into the gate, then slowed down as the car bumped along the track made by horse and carts, suddenly reluctant to arrive. Would they welcome her? Would there be scones, a Victoria sponge oozing red jam and the best china, a lace tablecloth perhaps, the silver teapot? Or had they just wanted advice? Had she only imagined the unspoken invitation in that pleading letter?

Perhaps what she'd thought she and Harry shared was an illusion, born in the strange world of war. Maybe this whole journey, she thought suddenly, was her own form of war sickness. Another ghost, conjured from her loneliness and loss.

The house looked larger close up, but just as plain. Someone had planted two camellias out the front, just starting to bloom, and a ramble of roses along the side fence, the roots holding the dust together into soil as they hunted for some moisture. Even now, in autumn, soft-stemmed pink flowers poked their heads out of the tangle. The afternoon shadows were turning the grass from gold to purple.

And then she saw him. He was out the back of the house, by the plum trees and rhubarb patch, repairing the chook-yard fence. She wondered if he'd been told not to go far today, that a visitor was expected. He wore moleskins and a neat blue shirt. It was strange to see him out of uniform or pyjamas. But somehow the work clothes were familiar too, as though she knew them from decades in the future. His hair was longer. Two black and white dogs crouched at his heels as he slid the post into the hole, his gaze intent and certain.

Her heart clenched. She had planned so long for this moment. There he was, not her imagined Harry, but the real one.

Had she created a dream hero, from memory and roses?

One of the dogs got to its feet and began to bark.

He looked up then. He watched as she stopped the car, opened the door, began to walk across the dust to the gate.

What was he thinking? Did he even recognise her?

Her hands were shaking, from weariness as well as tension. She felt for the locket at her throat, to try to stop the trembling. Her knees felt like marshmallows. Suddenly, she wished she'd dressed differently, not in stockings and heels, the fashionable small hat, but with her hair pulled back and wisping across her face, in her apron with the stains.

His hand rested on the dog's head to silence it. His face was still but suddenly . . . real . . . so she felt a shock of warmth all through her body, and thought 'Why, this is love.'

Then all at once he smiled.

It was a smile of memory, a smile of kindness. The smile of the man who had said, so long ago, 'I reckon sometimes you need someone to look after you too.'

He began to walk towards her. And then he stopped.

The world cracked for a frozen moment as she wondered if he had changed his mind. But he only stepped back and picked a flower from the tangle on the fence.

It was a rose. And as she watched he held it out to her.

Lachlan

At 10 a.m. the street was empty. The shops were shut, even the supermarket that was open every day till late at night.

At ten past ten the SES began to block off the main street, and the side streets too. By ten-thirty the crowd had gathered by R & G Motors.

It felt strange not to be with his unit on Anzac Day. It felt stranger to be in uniform again, after a year at home. For a moment he was back in the jagged hills of Afghanistan. We did good there, Pa, he thought.

And then the present came into focus again, his family, waiting up by the war memorial, Alanna and baby Jack, and Mum and Dad, the familiar paddocks that had drawn him home, just as they had brought Pa home, and Great-Gran.

The drawing of the roses hung on his wall now. Pa had left it to him in his will, and the photo of Glen Donal that still sat on the mantelpiece in the house that Great-Gran had built, where he and Alanna lived now.

Lachie reached into the ute and took out the limp pink rose, then lined up with the other servicemen and women. A few, like him, were in uniform, mostly World War II veterans, thinned by old age so they fitted into the pants and jackets again that had been too tight for years. His was the only beret among the hats. The Vietnam vets wore ordinary clothes, with their medals pinned to their chests.

Behind the servicemen and women came the children, wearing the medals of their grandfathers, great-grandfathers; then the fire brigade, the scouts, the school cadets. And leading them all were the Biscuit Creek Light Horse Brigade, the horses groomed and shiny, the men with feathers in their hats, recreating the heroes of so long ago.

The drums of the community band began to beat.

Boom. Boom. Boom.

It was strange too, marching in the parade as an adult; up the same hill he had marched up as a child, pushing Pa in his wheelchair, the same shops along the street. But there was no wheelchair to push today. This time his body instinctively followed the beat of the march. This time, some of the medals were his.

Lachie glanced at the faces lining the street: people who thought they knew about a war because they'd seen it on TV; boys who read books about army heroes; those who were here for sentiment or memory, or because it was a festival like Heritage Day, with uniforms instead of costumes.

What would you have thought of it all, Pa? he wondered. The politicians' speeches, using the memories of heroes to sell themselves. The TV spectacle. The shadows he'd seen in his friends' eyes, that Mum said she saw in his. What would Pa have thought of Afghanistan? Of Rwanda? We did our best there, too, Pa. We did what we could. The Iraq war?

Pa would have understood, he thought. Pa knew the difference between those who ordered war and those who fought it. 'They called it a noble cause,' Pa had said once, in one of those speeches he sometimes gave after the long silences of his deafness, as they drove home on a day much like today. 'But we were the ones who gave it nobility.

'You go with such idealism. You fight, because doing nothing would be worse. And then you find that wars are run by the same men who run everything else, who make the money, give the orders. All they give you in return is a little bit of glory.

'And the friendship. But that isn't theirs to give.'

The watching crowd was thick about the memorial. Men waved digital cameras; women held the hands of grandchildren and whispered explanations. One couple had pinned rosemary to the knitted coats on their dogs. Mum had that look that said she was crying, but didn't want to let it show. Alanna held Jack higher in her arms, so he could see.

One by one the wreaths were laid — fourteen of them today. A toddler in pink yelled 'Daddy!' as the Air Force wreath was laid. Another child demanded a biscuit. But mostly there was silence.

The wreath from the CWA, all dark green bay leaves and red flowers. The wreath from the Central School, from St Pat's. The wreath from the Light Horse Brigade, the wreaths from Legacy . . .

The naval helicopter roared up the street, just above the roof tops, circled, and flew back across the memorial.

The Last Post's echoes trembled down the silent street. Then it was over.

The crowd moved off to the rotunda in the park, mostly silent still, with murmurs, not loud voices. The speeches were in the park these days, now the crowds were too big to fit around the statue in the street; the hymns, the anthem. Only Mum and Dad, Alanna and Jack stood on the footpath by the memorial now.

Lachie waited. Waited till the street was empty, till his neighbours, friends and strangers had all gone. Just as he had waited with Pa, year after year. Even that last year when Pa had insisted they bring the wheelchair to the hospital (Great-Gran's photo beside his bed — he'd had it in his hands with her locket when they found him that last morning), and insisted too that they bring her rose from the bush by the kitchen door.

Now Lachie laid the rose among the wreaths. It had wilted a little more in his hand, just as it had wilted when Pa carried it. But the colour was still bright, stronger in this drought year than the wet years of his childhood.

'A rose for the Anzac boys,' he whispered. 'Rest in peace, Pa. We shall remember them.'

Sergeant Lachlan Harrison saluted.

Author's note

The Forgotten Army

How many women fought in World War I?

We'll never know. But there were thousands, or even millions — as many, perhaps, as the men who fought there too.

Few women in World War I carried weapons. But these days we say a soldier 'fought' in World War I or II if they were in transport, or administration, and not just one of the relatively small proportion of soldiers who actually faced the enemy. The women of World War I fought in other ways, and often in battles as hard as the men's. And mostly their war was unrecorded. It is only over the past few years, as the diaries and letters of participants in World War I have been published, that it's become possible to glimpse the unofficial war. It is those diaries and letters that show just how many women left their homes and became unofficial volunteers in France and Belgium. Military historians and journalists wrote about the men, the tactics, the regiments. For obvious reasons they left out the stories of the unofficial volunteers. (There is only so much any one person can write, especially when his or her duty is to record official organisations and engagements.)

But for every man who fought there were even more women — the uncounted volunteers, doing what the armies of those days weren't equipped to do: tending the wounded, often with the shells exploding around them; driving ambulances or even moving troops on trucks or carts; feeding the men — often starving because the army couldn't supply food while they were travelling, or only gave rations like the hard biscuits that the men of those days with crumbling or false teeth couldn't eat. These women faced danger and hardship, too.

Even the women who stayed at home helped to clothe and feed the men: they knitted socks and balaclavas, made and washed bandages, and starved themselves to send food parcels and 'comforts' for the men.

And when the war was over the survivors of this extraordinary army of women went on to fight other battles: for schools and libraries and hospitals for all; for the right to vote; for so many other things you and I take for granted today.

They are the forgotten army. This book is for them.

This book is also the first one where I have thought, I don't know if I should keep writing this. I don't know if anyone should read it.

This is a grim book. It is based on letters and diaries that make even grimmer reading. Much of the time, reading and writing, I was in tears, hearing the voices of so long ago.

Finally, I kept writing.

War is perhaps humanity's craziest invention. But it is also in war — in any adversity — that humans sometimes show their greatest courage, loyalty and love. It is important, I think, to understand the difference between glorifying war and celebrating the triumphs of the human spirit amid the battles.

And I do believe there are times when you need to fight. I don't think any war has ever achieved what it was started for. But I can think of many wars where it was necessary to join a fight that someone else began, to defend a country or a cause, to protect people that others were persecuting, to establish law so there could be peace. Australia and New Zealand's armed forces today are mostly 'peace keepers' in the truest sense. Yet often, too, war is the first resort, not the last, the decisions made by politicians who have no idea of what their orders mean.

It is easy to blame politicians. But we are the ones who elect them; the ones who make the ultimate decisions.

There is another reason I wrote this book. The men and women who lived through World War I are gone. But the words they wrote down survive, and those are the words I've used to write this book.

Sometimes it is almost as though I hear a whisper from the past, calling, 'Remember me'.

We need to know the past to understand today. We need to listen to the past to learn that things can change — and that we can change them. We need to hear those voices, no matter how terrible their stories — perhaps especially when the stories are so hard to bear.

TRUTH AND FICTION

This is not a true book, but it is made of true things.

There was a war, and there were men and women who fought and died, and many who did their best to ease the pain. Every episode and character in this book is based on the words of those who were there, taken from their letters, diaries, the oral history collected years later. I have taken the stories and woven a piece of fiction from the facts.

But because these things *did* happen I've avoided using real place names; to do so would be to rob the memories of those brave girls and women who really were there. I have even avoided naming the battalions and the battles — the 'pushes' in this book — though any reader can look at the dates and probably work out which they were. So all the places and people in the book are imaginary, but the things that happened are real. 'The Duchess', for example, is based on the Duchess of Sutherland (mentioned on page 23), that indomitable lady who crossed to France and Belgium as soon as war was declared to open an ambulance service. Midge's, Anne's and Ethel's stories are based on the tale of four schoolgirls who really did open a canteen in France. And Dolores is based on a dog called

Marta, who wasn't there, but I suspect was pretty much like a few of the much-loved dogs who were.

This book is a tribute, not a history.

THE ROSES OF NO-MAN'S-LAND

World War I was a stupid war — probably one of the most stupid wars that humankind has fought. It was run, on both sides, by mostly incompetent men who had their jobs because they had been born into the class that officers and politicians came from. In many cases they had only minimal, if any, training for the roles they played and no idea of strategy or tactics. (There were, of course, many exceptions to this too, including the brilliant strategies late in the war of General Monash, and the almost unbelievable 'secret' evacuation of Gallipoli.)

These days we think of war as something fought by professionals. But when World War I broke out, the armies on both sides had few doctors or nurses, no dentists or other health professionals, and nowhere near enough people to feed, clothe, transport and care for the soldiers.

From 1914 to 1918 about 65 million men marched to war. Over 8 million never returned; more than half of the men were wounded.

At the same time, tens of thousands of women left their homes and families and journeyed to the battlefields. Many were there officially, as army nurses or with the Red Cross.

But an even greater number had no official role at all. Some were patriots, some adventurers, some felt the need to nurse and cosset; others were simply desperate to 'do their bit' after their husbands, fathers, brothers, sons had marched away into the most terrible battles the world has known.

The men — mostly — are remembered. In many cases, the women are not. Often, too, they had a worse war than many of the men.

World War I was unlike any war fought before or since. It was a weird war, especially on what was known as 'the Western front'. Two armies dug trenches facing each other in a long line across France, Belgium and Flanders, with a small stretch of no-man's-land and barbed wire between them. And for the best part of four years these armies hardly moved at all.

There were times when the men were ordered to advance, when tens of thousands of lives were lost over a couple of days just to win a hill or a few kilometres of ground. But mostly they just sat there, in the mud and smell of death, firing at anyone silly enough to put their head above the trenches, sending in mortars or bombing with planes, or trying to burn each others' lungs and skin with canisters of poisonous gas.

Men didn't spend all their time 'at the front', though there were some horror stretches of months, especially for the Anzacs, who were often regarded by British commanders as expendable 'cannon fodder'. Mostly they stayed there for days or weeks, then were given a break 'behind the lines', and put to building roads, or performing forced marches, even playing football. It was horribly grim, but it wasn't a constant four years of fighting.

The women often had no break at all.

I first caught a glimpse of this extraordinary group of women when I was reading, of all things, a cookbook — *The Alice B. Toklas Cook Book* — by the friend and partner of the writer Gertrude Stein. Miss Toklas recorded memorable meals and recipes during their life in France, including those during World War I as she and Gertrude Stein drove army officers, the wounded and supplies around France and Belgium in their car, which they'd nicknamed Aunt Maud.

How did two women, neither with any official training, come to be driving around the battlefields? And taking their job so much for granted that Miss Toklas didn't even feel the need to explain how they got to be there?

As I kept researching, reading the newly published (and often self-published) diaries and letters of people who were there, I found more women doing similarly fantastic things; an extraordinary number. At first I thought there were dozens — then hundreds — then thousands. I finally realised that if you counted all those women knitting uniforms, cooking and packing food parcels, making bandages and other medical supplies, then perhaps there were millions.

These days the armed services supply the uniforms, the rations, the transport of their units. But in World War I most supply chains seem to have been run by volunteers. The 'official' units were recorded in war histories. The unofficial efforts — by far the larger, at least until America came into the war with all its resources — were mostly unrecorded.

But echoes remain in letters and diaries, and as the often very private people who did those amazing things have died, their descendants are publishing the private records of those times — an extraordinary collection of voices from the past that often gives a very different picture of the war from that of the history books.

WHO WERE THEY?

The women who actually went to the Western front to help the men were mostly English, but they came from America, Australia and New Zealand as well. They simply took themselves and, in many cases, their cars or trucks for ambulances, as well as occasionally their dogs, horses, evening dresses, maids and chauffeurs, over to France. Many set up canteens. Others drove ambulances, or assisted medical officers and nurses. Often wealthy or influential women (like Lady Dudley, the estranged wife of a former Australian Governor-General) gathered together whole medical teams and sailed off to help the wounded. Some of these groups were later gathered into the official net of the army or the Red Cross. Others continued to operate independently. And there were countless other women and girls who just turned up, hoping to help.

It took months of training to become an official nursing assistant — a member of a VAD (Voluntary Aid

Detachment established by the Red Cross and the Order of St John) — and you had to be twenty-three years old to be accepted for overseas service. But if you got to France independently, conditions were so desperate that anyone, no matter how young or untrained, could be useful.

Theirs is still a mostly untold story. We remember the soldiers, we remember the official nurses. But these volunteer girls and women were as much 'the roses of no-man's-land' as those in the army's records.

The nurses, VADs, ambulance drivers, canteen workers and volunteer letter-writers near the battlefields worked under horrific conditions. Nurses and other health workers faced an unending line of maimed and wounded, with no relief at all. Even their one day off a month was rarely given. Leave was almost unknown except in special circumstances. Many women worked for four years of war with almost no break.

It was heartbreaking work in those days before antibiotics, effective painkillers and other drugs. There was so little they could do for the men — but they kept on trying.

Some were wounded, like Australian Sister Rachel Pratt, hit in the lung by a piece of shrapnel while working at No 1 Casualty Clearing Station near Bailleul. (Despite her wound and the advancing enemy, Nurse Pratt stayed working at her post. She was promoted to Sister the next day, and awarded the Military Medal for gallantry under fire, usually reserved for men in those days.)

Others died young, like Matron Mary Mackenzie Findlay from Kilmore, Victoria, worn out by the work, the heartbreak, the poor food, the cold. The women worked in coats and scarves, and there were no stoves to keep their patients warm or even to melt the ice for water to wash with or to drink.

Most women suffered severe infections, especially to their hands, from the suppurating wounds they tended, and in later years would recognise a fellow war volunteer by the scars on their hands, red and shiny and so thick it was difficult to sew or knit or even hold a teacup without dropping it. The women, too, caught the diseases of the trenches: typhus, dysentery, measles, mumps and influenza.

FROM TEA PARTIES TO HEROISM

It is hard for many of us to understand these days how limited most women's lives were before World War I. Few worked for wages; those who did were mostly servants in other people's homes, starting about age twelve, or even younger. Girls from richer homes were expected to stay at home till they married.

Schools for girls
Few girls had more than a rudimentary education, and those who did go to university were usually not granted degrees. Even up until the 1960's — and certainly back when this story is set — many girls' schools concentrated on teaching girls 'deportment' skills like how to sit 'like a

lady' (i.e. with your knees together and back straight); how to write a polite letter in elegant handwriting; and cooking, sewing and mothercraft. Wealthier schools might focus on how to direct one's servants to do the cooking, sewing and mothercraft properly, as well as some embroidery to keep one occupied.

Girls were also taught French, art, music, enough literature, history and geography to conduct an interesting conversation at dinner, and enough maths to supervise the household accounts. But as they weren't expected to go to university, or have a profession, most schools just taught girls the basics.

Many schools, however, did give a lot more private tutoring to any girl who had a lot of talent or did really want to go to university, even if she couldn't get a degree. Some parents also paid for private tutors if their daughters were passionately interested in things like science or wanted to learn ancient Greek. Others were horrified — they were afraid that no man would marry their daughter if he thought she was more intelligent than he was, or was a 'bluestocking', the word used for any girl who was more interested in books and learning than marriage and looking after a family. And in those days, when there were so few careers for women, most parents knew that the only real security for their daughters was in making a man think she'd be a suitable wife.

Women had only recently won the right to vote, first in New Zealand and then Australia; in England, women were still regarded as unable to take on the responsibility of electing governments. Women were regarded as too fragile to be doctors or even bus conductors, too childlike and illogical for business or for any role outside home and family, and too emotional to be reliable under pressure.

But suddenly there were these organised armies of women doing a multitude of tasks, overcoming the most extraordinary obstacles.

Most of the women who served as volunteers overseas were from the middle or upper classes — as they received no wages they needed family money to survive. Some were servants, and their employers supported them. In at least one case a small country town collected enough money to send a volunteer nurse overseas. The women were daughters, with fathers or brothers in the army; mothers, widows, sisters. Many knew each other from school. Others soon became a close-knit group, with nicknames and their own slang.

Many never married. They were a generation that lost its men, with so many killed by war or disease. But by the time the war ended they were also a body of extraordinarily capable, experienced and probably very stroppy women — who were almost unstoppable.

It is impossible to look at the social changes born of the 1920s and '30s without wondering if they would ever have happened without these independent women, no longer content to remain dutiful, housebound daughters and wives, who fought for the right to vote, for contraception, degrees for women, access to both general and higher public education, hospital reforms and far more social reforms than I can list here. The war was their university and their training ground. So many things we take for granted now, we owe to them.

The Red Cross nurse of the song was truly 'a rose in no-man's-land'. But there were so many other roses. And each one of them deserves to be remembered and celebrated.

WORKING ON THE HOME FRONT

Women dedicated their lives to 'the cause' at home as well.

The armies on both sides of the conflict were ill equipped — there simply weren't enough clothes or food, much less medicines, stretchers or bandages, for the troops. In a large part, they were fed and clothed by their families and volunteers back home.

In Australia and New Zealand women knitted socks and balaclavas, rolled bandages, made biscuits to sell for 'comforts' for the men. Each state had a division of the Australian Comforts Fund. In 1916, for example, when the army was short of socks, 80,000 pairs were knitted in a couple of months.

Many women knitted a pair of socks a day, and that in a time when wool first had to be rolled into balls before you even started knitting. Few women throughout the war ever had idle hands — they sewed, they knitted, they crocheted, even when standing in line at the fruit and vegetable shop. They also provided 20,000 tommy cookers (small cans packed with sand and petrol for cooking in the trenches). The Tanned Sheepskin Committee made

110,734 sheepskin vests. Women and girls from 150 schools in the Babies Knit Society made baby clothes for refugees and the orphaned children of soldiers and sailors.

Other committees sent tins of preserved fruit and vegetables, Bovril, condensed milk and toffees, as well as soap, pencils, notebooks, chocolates, ginger, shirts, caps, mufflers, air cushions and fruit cakes. Wives, mothers, sisters went hungry to send their men a fruit cake, long baked biscuits like 'Anzacs' (called 'soldier's biscuits' back then) or a boiled suet pudding — something that would last until it reached the battlefields. Letter after letter I have read talks so much about food. In those days of few dentists — and only for the rich — the majority of men in the army had poor teeth, or false teeth. The only way to eat the 'biscuits' of the trenches was to soak them in dirty water — and risk dysentery too. You relied on your women folk at home to make your cakes, pack them, send them, feed you, as well as knit your socks and underwear . . .

It would take a whole book to list the extraordinary number of women's committees, too, both large and small, that made, collected or bought quantities of supplies that would be regarded as impossible these days.

THE WOUNDED IN WORLD WAR I

Theoretically, the wounded or sick were carried from the battlefield to the regimental aid post. This was, if not in the middle of the fighting, at least on the edge of it. Often two wounded men might support each other, or a friend risk his own life to carry a mate to safety.

The men's wounds were dressed as best they could be at the aid post — bandages put over the bleeding areas, or limbs tied to keep the flesh together. The wounded man was then carried by stretcher (if there were enough) to a field dressing station, where he was given an anti-tetanus injection.

If he survived, hopefully there would be an ambulance to take him to the casualty clearing station, perhaps fifteen kilometres from the battlefield — though all too often 'the battlefield' shifted so that the casualty clearing stations were hit by shells or bombs. Often, too, there weren't enough ambulances. Wounded or blinded men walked kilometres for help, supporting or guiding each other.

Clearing stations were mostly tents, or, like the hospitals, they were set up in commandeered schools, railway waiting rooms, convents, breweries, chateaux and farmhouses.

At the clearing station the men were 'stabilised' — emergency operations performed, wounds sewn up and dressings applied. The men were kept there till they were well enough to be sent by ambulance or hospital train to a base hospital — or until they died. Men with minor wounds might also be kept at the casualty station and sometimes given light work as orderlies till they were ready to go back to their units.

If the nearby base hospitals were full — as they often were — the wounded were shipped hundreds of kilometres to another hospital or even over to England. The men were kept in hospital till they were either well enough to go back to their unit, or to go to speciality hospitals in England for rehabilitation — for false legs or arms, a long convalescence, treatment for badly gassed lungs or burns, or the rudimentary plastic surgery of those days if their faces had been destroyed.

These days we know that any horrible experience — not just war — can cause deep trauma, and physical as well as mental symptoms. But in those days many doctors — and most military men — thought that any failure to cope with the horrors of war was cowardice or 'lack of moral fibre'. They also couldn't understand how some men could cope with an experience, while others couldn't.

But the British Government also didn't want the expense of paying post-war pensions if they could avoid it, so they tried very hard to stop any recognition that men could be mentally injured by the war.

'Shell shock' is a broad term covering many different conditions. Sometimes men might be cold and speechless — literally in shock. Others might seem all right but a sudden noise could send them screaming or cowering away. Some men became violent; some retreated into their own private worlds — the many different symptoms of and variations on shell shock (or Post Traumatic Stress Disorder) are too complex to cover here.

It is probably true to say though that no man — or woman — came out of World War I unscathed. Most men refused to talk about the war at all: some became alcoholics; others had nightmares or attacks of sudden terror all their lives. It was doubly hard for them to cope when the families they had come back to had no idea of the horrors they'd experienced. Many, too, didn't understand that the ringing in their ears was the physiological result of the years of loud noises.

Instead they were afraid they were hallucinating, and still hearing the ring of falling bombs from the war they thought they'd left behind.

I find it amazing that so many people did manage to recover from their experiences, and lead happy and fulfilled lives.

There were never enough clearing stations, hospitals or trained staff to look after the wounded at the best of times; and when there was a 'push' — that is, when the men were ordered out across the barbed-wire entanglements between them and the enemy — tens of thousands of wounded would sweep through the clearing stations (as well as railway stations and hospitals), totally overwhelming the staff and facilities. Stretchers would be piled three high on the beds, and wounded men staggered from bed to bed trying to help their comrades.

It was hell on earth. And in this chaos, anyone with two hands and a willing spirit was indispensable, no matter how little training they had received.

A SHORT HISTORY OF
WORLD WAR I

World War I was called the Great War; and in the beginning it was called the Great Adventure too. People ran cheering through the streets, cheering with excitement, when, on 4 August 1914, Britain declared war on its long-term rival Germany after Germany invaded Belgium.

As part of the British Empire, Australia and New Zealand were also at war, which meant joining Britain's other allies, France and the Russian Empire, against the Central Powers (Germany and Austria-Hungary) and the Ottoman Empire when they too declared war on 29 October 1914.

This was the chance to 'fight for the Mother Country', to show the world what 'colonials' were made of. And for men and boys who had never been further than the next town, many of whom had never even seen a photograph from Europe, it was a chance to see the world.

All were volunteers. Many would never come home.

World War I cost Australia and New Zealand more men than any other war. There were fewer than 5 million people in Australia at the declaration of war, but 300,000 men enlisted. Of those, 60,000 Australian men were killed. And 150,000 to 200,000 more were wounded, gassed or suffered shell shock and other mental problems. New Zealand sent 103,000 troops from a population of just over 1 million — 42 per cent of men of military age. There were 16,697 New Zealanders killed and 41,317 wounded. Australia and New Zealand had the highest casualty and death rates per capita of all countries involved in the war. They were superb soldiers, placed in impossible situations by British commanders. (Even Australia's then Prime Minister, Billy Hughes, felt he could promise that the last drop of Australian blood would be spilt to save 'the Mother Country' — England.)

The Anzacs went first to Egypt for training and to secure the Suez Canal (though some New Zealanders and Australians — like Douglas in the book — travelled to England to enlist, and were then sent directly to Flanders to fight). They were then sent to Gallipoli, where, despite valiant fighting, tactical mistakes by the British commanders meant the campaign was a failure. About 505,000 soldiers from both sides were killed and 262,000 wounded.

The Allied forces eventually evacuated Gallipoli in December and early January of 1916. This was the most successful — even brilliant — Allied operation of the campaign. The full evacuation was achieved quickly, secrecy was maintained and there were almost no casualties.

After Gallipoli the Anzacs were sent to France, beginning in March 1916, while the mounted division that had served as additional infantry at Gallipoli stayed in the Middle East.

By now the war had become bogged down. Both armies were stuck in trenches in the mud that stretched across Belgium and north-east France from the English Channel to the Swiss border, facing each other over a barren stretch of no-man's-land while they tried to push each other back metre by metre.

Both sides advanced a bit at times and retreated at other times. Men would sneak out to cut the tangled barbed wire that was supposed to stop anyone advancing, and then creep forward only to be driven back. But basically things stayed pretty much stuck all through 1916 and 1917.

Rats infested the trenches and feasted on dead bodies and sometimes on the flesh of the living. Men knocked unconscious by explosions drowned in the mud. Poisonous gas seeped through the trenches, killing many and rotting the lungs of survivors. The men lived with the constant stink of rotting corpses lying abandoned in the no-man's-land between the armies' grimly held positions. There was no way to retrieve them without more men dying.

It was a nightmare and both sides suffered appalling losses. Finally, in 1917, the USA joined the war. American troops began to arrive in the middle of that year, although not in significant numbers until twelve months later.

In March 1918 the German army launched a massive offensive in an attempt to break through and win before the Americans could arrive.

To begin with it worked. They advanced 64 kilometres past where the 1916 Somme battles had taken place. But between April and November the Allies began to combine infantry, artillery, tanks and aircraft more effectively. American troops and equipment revitalised the Allied forces and their medical organisation meant that at last many of the volunteers could rest. Finally, too, men like Australia's General Monash were bringing the idea of strategy to the war, using intelligence — both personal and military — instead of just the bodies of the men.

Germany surrendered on 11 November 1918.

At last the guns fell silent on the European battlefields. Germany was forced to accept crippling 'reparation' debts that would lead to poverty, bitterness, political instability and, ultimately, the rise of Hitler, hatred and yet another war. But that was still to come.

Now Australians and New Zealanders rejoiced. Church bells rang out; people sang 'Rule Britannia', 'God Save the King', 'Pack Up Your Troubles' and 'Keep the Home Fires Burning' in the streets. Unplanned processions crowded the city streets, with banners and flags hanging from the buildings.

The war was over.

NOTES

Anzacs: ANZAC stands for Australian and New Zealand Army Corps. In 1917, the word Anzac meant someone who had fought at Gallipoli. It later came to mean any Australian or New Zealander who fought or served in World War I.

Anzac Biscuits: These weren't made by the Anzacs at Anzac Cove at Gallipoli. They were made by women at home during World War I and sold to raise money for 'comforts' for soldiers — soap, books and sweets to be posted to the men serving overseas. They were also a good way to get nutrition to a beloved soldier far away — the hard biscuits keep for weeks or months, and the oats make them sustaining as well as sweet.

This recipe is one my grandmother Mrs Thelma Edwards wrote down towards the end of the war in the green notebook where she kept her recipes. They are very good. (My grandmother hated knitting — she said that she had been forced to do far too much of it as a girl and woman during two world wars.)

Soldiers' Biscuits

1 tablespoon golden syrup

2 tablespoons very hot water

1 teaspoon bicarbonate of soda

half a cup of butter

1 cup plain flour

2 cups rolled oats

half a cup of sugar

Melt the butter, sugar and golden syrup in a saucepan. Take off the heat. Add the water and bicarbonate of soda and let it froth up. Add flour and oats, mix quickly. Place small spoonfuls on a greased tray and bake in a slow oven (approximately 125°C) for about 10–15 minutes or till pale brown. Take off the tray carefully. They'll get crisp as they cool.

Store in a sealed container as soon as they are cool. They'll keep fresh for weeks but, like all biscuits, taste best in the first few days after they are made.

Anzac Day: Australians and New Zealanders commemorate Anzac Day on 25 April every year — the date of the landing of Australian and New Zealand troops at Gallipoli. At first, only veterans of the battle went to the dawn services, 'standing to' before two minutes of silence, broken by the sound of a lone bugler playing the Last Post. In later years, there were marches in towns and cities.

Now, the day has grown, both in numbers and significance. Now it commemorates all those who fight or suffer in war, and the bravery and dedication of those who make the 'ultimate sacrifice' — their lives.

Anzac Tiles: These are what soldiers really did eat at Gallipoli, and in the trenches in France and Belgium. They were high in protein, very tough, and pretty horrible.

2 cups flour (sour, add weevils)

2 tablespoons sugar (add ants)

2 tablespoons powdered milk (rancid)

Mix well. Add water, dust and a few flies and maybe some shrapnel (flying debris from an exploding shell). Mix till it makes a dryish dough. Pat out small pieces till they are thin and flattish (the sweat adds to the taste). Prick with a fork or small stick so there are about 25 tiny holes. Bake either on a greased tray in a slow oven or over the campfire on a pannikin (a tin dish that holds your meal). When hard and a bit burnt around the edges they're ready. If your teeth can't chew them dip in whatever water you can find to soften them into mush, and hope you don't get dysentery.

Batman: Army servant. Even when the army was desperately short of men, all officers had servants to polish their boots, make their tea and beds, and generally look after them.

Billy Hughes: The Australian Prime Minister who tried unsuccessfully to pass a law conscripting men to go and fight in France to replace the tens of thousands already killed.

Breaker: A man who tamed horses so they could be ridden or used to pull carriages.

Carpe diem: Latin for 'Seize the day'. It is a quote from the ancient Roman writer Horace.

Coke and coal: Coal is fossilised wood dug from the ground; coke is made from wood that has been burned slowly and with very little air, to remove most of the moisture. As these fuels were relatively light and burned well for a long time they were often used on 'braziers', small portable fireplaces.

Diggers: The men of the Australian gold rushes had called themselves 'diggers'. Now, as they dug the trenches of Gallipoli and the Western Front, the name was used again — and stuck. 'Digger' now refers to any Australian soldier. During World War II an Aussie might call a fellow soldier 'Dig' — 'Hey, Dig, how 'bout a hand over here . . .'

Influenza: The influenza pandemic (a widespread epidemic) of 1918–19 killed more people than World War I, or any other previous plague: somewhere between 20 and 100 million people worldwide.

Where did it come from? No one knew. It was an entirely new strain of flu, and no one had any immunity to it. Some people thought it might be German biological warfare. Others thought that the smoke of the bombs and the mustard gas used in the trenches might have created a new disease.

Scientists now think that the 1918 flu probably spread from birds to humans — a H1N1 type Influenza A virus: a genetic rearrangement of human and bird flu viruses.

Despite its nickname of the Spanish Flu, the new flu certainly didn't come from Spain. (It probably started in China, then spread to Japan, then Europe, then America, Australia, Southeast Asia, the Pacific and Africa.) But as Spain wasn't fighting in the war there wasn't any censorship there, so the Spanish newspapers were the first ones to report the large number of deaths. And the name 'Spanish flu' stuck.

The war helped the flu to spread. The soldiers were exhausted, hungry, and living in foul, crowded and appalling conditions where flu could easily spread. And then they started streaming back to their far-flung homes — and took the virus with them on the trains and steamships. In the two years that the flu pandemic afflicted the world, a fifth of its population was infected. Around 25 million people died in the first six months.

It was a terrifying disease. It struck quickly. People might have a bit of a temperature in the morning, feel unwell by lunch, and drop dead in the afternoon. It mostly hit young, healthy people too; not children or older people (the usual victims of infectious diseases) but people between twenty and forty years old who should have been in the prime of their lives. Victims turned blue as they drowned in their own fluids and haemorrhaged blood from their noses and ears.

Kiwis: It is possible that the Australians in World War I were the first to refer to their New Zealand comrades as Kiwis after New Zealand's symbolic kiwi bird. Given that the other nicknames the Australian soldiers gave to just about every other nationality (including their allies) were highly insulting, the choice shows the comradeship and affection between the two nations.

Linen scraping: In those days bandages were reused. Women made bandages by cutting up linen sheets, tablecloths and other lengths of material, then scraping off any threads or lint so they'd be smooth and not stick to the wounds. 'Bandage rolling' took a lot of time — after the bloody bandages were washed they had to be scraped free of lint again, ironed (the high temperature would have helped clean them) then rolled up and sent back to hospitals and casualty centres.

Mirabile dictu: This is also Latin, roughly translated as 'Wonderful!' or 'Wonderful to say'.

Peach seeds: There was an appeal for peach and apricot kernels to be collected for use in gas masks, though I don't know how they were used, or if they ever were. Both contain cyanide, so may have really been wanted to try to produce poisonous gas.

Rubber gloves: These were only issued to nursing sisters and doctors. If you scratched yourself you had to soak your hands in disinfectant, but there was rarely time to follow this procedure.

Snigger: A man who 'snigged' (pulled) logs out of the bush, with a horse and chains.

Tablet: A fudge-like Scottish sweet of rich toffee with added milk, cream and butter.

A White Man: In those days most (white) English speakers in Australia, New Zealand, the UK and the USA, as well as English colonies, used the phrase 'a white man' to mean any good reliable person. Most people who used it probably didn't even realise how racist it might sound — they may not even have been racist themselves, just as we usually don't think of the literal meanings of the clichés we use today.

'THE SKYE BOAT SONG'

There are two versions of this song.

One version was published by Sir Harold Boulton in 1884. He may have simply written down an old sea shanty, or he may have changed it and added some of his own words. The tune was written down by Annie MacLeod in the 1870s, based on a Gaelic rowing song, 'Cuachag nan Craobh' ('The Cuckoo in the Grove').

It is about Charles Edward Stuart, the Young Pretender, son of King James II. James had been forced off the British throne in the 'bloodless revolution' amidst fears that he was going to make England Roman Catholic again. His son tried to regain the throne, but was defeated on Culloden Moor in 1746. Aided by Flora MacDonald, Bonnie Prince Charlie escaped to the island of Skye. He was later taken by a French vessel to Morlaix on the coast of Brittany.

The other song sometimes sung as 'The Skye Boat Song', and the one quoted in this book, often uses the same tune and was written by Robert Louis Stevenson (1850–94). It was published in *Songs of Travel* (Chatto & Windus, London, 1896).

Acknowledgements

It's become a cliché for writers to say 'This book couldn't have been written without the help of many people' — probably because it is so often true.

This was a difficult book to write. At times I wondered if I could keep going; partly because of the book's subject matter, but also because despite many visits to New Zealand I was unsure if I could capture the home world of the heroine — a place it is impossible to visit as it existed almost a hundred years ago. If it hadn't been for the superb research material given to me by Liz Kemp and Dr Dot Neutze I doubt I'd have had the confidence to finish this book. Liz was the first person to read the manuscript, too, and as always her brilliant insight gave me a fresh vision so I could start the process of rewriting, rewriting, rewriting.

Much gratitude also to Nicola O'Shea, whose insightful editing makes a book the best it can be.

I'd also like to thank Hugh Grogan for his advice on military protocol, though any mistakes are mine, not his, and many thanks, as always, to Natalie Winter for the magic she adds to the books, and to Kate O'Donnell for the hours of labour, love and discipline she gives to the text.

And, as always, more thanks than I can express to my husband, Bryan Sullivan, who watched and helped as I cried over this book; to my dear friends Angela Marshall, who takes my tatty scribbles and turns them into text, Noël Pratt, who listens ever patiently when I rattle on, obsessed, and Helen Geier, who stood beside me last Anzac Day; and to the ever-wonderful Lisa Berryman, without whom so many of my books would never have been started, or even have begun to echo the themes in my mind.

Jackie French is a full-time writer who lives in rural New South Wales. Jackie writes fiction and non-fiction for children and adults, and has columns in the print media. Jackie is regarded as one of Australia's most popular children's authors. She writes across all genres — from picture books, humour and history to science fiction. Her books have won the following awards (and won and been shortlisted for many others too):

Hitler's Daughter
- CBC Younger Readers' Award winner, 2000
- UK National Literacy Association WOW! Award winner, 2001
- Shortlisted in the Fiction for Older Readers category, YABBA awards 2007
- US Library Association Notable Book
- Koala Awards 2007, Roll of Honour

In Your Blood
- ACT Book of the Year, 2002

Diary of a Wombat (illustrated by Bruce Whatley)
- Nielsen BookData/Australian Booksellers Association Book of the Year, 2002 (the only picture book ever to win this award)
- (USA) Benjamin Franklin Award
- (USA) Lemmee Award
- (USA) Favourite Picture Book of the Year, Cuffie Awards, 2003
- (USA) Funniest Book in the Cuffie Awards (tied with *Diary of a Worm*), 2003
- Cool Award, for Best Picture Book, voted by the kids of the ACT, 2003
- Young Australian Readers' Award winner, 2003
- KOALA Award for Best Picture Book winner, 2003

- (USA) KIND Award winner, 2004
- Shortlisted for the Bilby Awards, 2007
- Northern Territory KROC Award for Favourite Book of 2007

To the Moon and Back (co-written with Bryan Sullivan, Jackie's husband)
- CBC Eve Pownall Award for Information Books winner, 2005

They Came on Viking Ships
- Shortlisted: (UK) Essex Book Award; winner to be announced in 2008
- Winner: West Australian Young Readers' Book Awards (WAYBRA) (Younger Readers), 2007
- Shortlisted: NSW Premier's History Awards (Young People's History Prize), 2006

Macbeth and Son
- Shortlisted: CBC Awards, 2007

The Goat Who Sailed the World
- Notable Book: CBC Awards (Younger Readers), 2007

Josephine Wants To Dance (illustrated by Bruce Whatley)
- Australian Booksellers' Book of the Year, Younger Readers, 2007.
- Notable Book: CBC Awards (Early Childhood), 2007
- Notable Book: CBC Awards (Picture Book of the Year), 2007

Visit Jackie's website

www.jackiefrench.com

or

www.harpercollins.com.au/jackiefrench

to subscribe to her monthly newsletter

Other Titles by Jackie French

Wacky Families Series

1. My Dog the Dinosaur • 2. My Mum the Pirate • 3. My Dad the Dragon
4. My Uncle Gus the Garden Gnome • 5. My Uncle Wal the Werewolf
6. My Gran the Gorilla • 7. My Auntie Chook the Vampire Chicken
8. My Pa the Polar Bear

Phredde Series

1. A Phaery Named Phredde • 2. Phredde and a Frog Named Bruce
3. Phredde and the Zombie Librarian • 4. Phredde and the Temple of Gloom
5. Phredde and the Leopard-Skin Librarian • 6. Phredde and the Purple Pyramid
7. Phredde and the Vampire Footy Team • 8. Phredde and the Ghostly Underpants

Outlands Trilogy

In the Blood • Blood Moon • Flesh and Blood

Historical

Somewhere Around the Corner • Dancing with Ben Hall • Soldier on the Hill
Daughter of the Regiment • Hitler's Daughter • Lady Dance • The White Ship
How the Finnegans Saved the Ship • Valley of Gold • Tom Appleby, Convict Boy
They Came on Viking Ships • Macbeth and Son • The Goat who Sailed the World
The Dog who Loved a Queen • The Camel who Crossed Australia (August 2008)

Fiction

Rain Stones • Walking the Boundaries • The Secret Beach • Summerland
Beyond the Boundaries • A Wombat Named Bosco • The Book of Unicorns
The Warrior – The Story of a Wombat • Tajore Arkle • Missing You, Love Sara
Dark Wind Blowing • Ride the Wild Wind: The Golden Pony and Other Stories

Non-fiction

Seasons of Content • How the Aliens from Alpha Centauri Invaded
My Maths Class and Turned Me into a Writer
How to Guzzle Your Garden • The Book of Challenges
Stamp, Stomp, Whomp • The Fascinating History of Your Lunch
Big Burps, Bare Bums and Other Bad-Mannered Blunders
To the Moon and Back • Rocket Your Child into Reading
The Secret World of Wombats
The Wonderful World of Wallabies and Kangaroos (July 2008)

Picture Books

Diary of a Wombat • Pete the Sheep • Josephine Wants to Dance
The Shaggy Gully times